By Dick Wolf

THE EXECUTION
THE INTERCEPT

DICK WOLF

A JEREMY FISK NOVEL

THE EXECUTION

HARPER

An Imprint of HarperCollinsPublishers

This book is a work of fiction. References to real people, events, establishments, organizations, or locales are intended only to provide a sense of authenticity, and are used fictitiously. All other characters, and all incidents and dialogue, are drawn from the author's imagination and are not to be construed as real.

HARPER

An Imprint of HarperCollins*Publishers*
195 Broadway
New York, New York 10007

Copyright © 2014 by Dick Wolf
ISBN 978-0-06-206850-7

First Harper premium printing: August 2014
First William Morrow paperback special printing: January 2014
First William Morrow paperback international printing: January 2014
First William Morrow hardcover printing: January 2014

Printed in the United States of America

Visit Harper paperbacks on the World Wide Web at
www.harpercollins.com

10 9 8 7 6 5 4 3 2 1

Dedicated to the NYPD,
the greatest police force in the world.

PROLOGUE

January 9
Upstate New York
Half a mile from the Canadian border,
    somewhere west of Lake Champlain

The explosive noise of the guns had set off a chain reaction, sheets of wet snow dropping from the limbs of the pine trees surrounding Jeremy Fisk. Even after the gunfire stopped, Fisk could hear limbs snapping, snow thudding to earth, a circular cataract expanding, fading away from him like ripples in a frigid pond.

And then the endless forest . . . went silent.

My God, thought Fisk. They're all dead.

Ten minutes earlier

The Swedes were late. Maybe they weren't even coming.

Detective Jeremy Fisk of the NYPD Intelligence Division hated upstate New York. Hated the whole idea of it. Even though he had lived all over the world during his childhood, he had spent most of his adult life in New York City and had the passion of the convert for his adopted home. And as a confirmed New Yorker, he despised upstate on principle. Upstate was hillbillies and trailer parks and suicidal deer that plunged heedlessly into the headlights of your car, forcing you to swerve into the nearest ditch. Upstate was country living. Upstate was wilderness.

People who didn't live in New York thought the entire state was paved from one end to the other. Far from it. In fact, the northern part of the state was as rural as Indiana or Kentucky. And right here, where Fisk and the feds were sitting, there weren't even hillbillies or trailer parks or deranged deer. Nothing but trees. Trees and snow. Trees and snow and four citified cops waiting to arrest a couple of Swedes sneaking over the border from Canada.

Fisk sat in the backseat of the unmarked Jeep, snow sifting down in heavy waves like shoals of tiny gray fish. The dirt road, now six inches deep in snow, was one of dozens of logging paths, unofficial border crossings that wormed back and forth like scars through the seemingly endless forest between the Saint Lawrence and Lake Champlain.

"They're not gonna show, Fisk." The driver of the car was an ICE agent by the name of Ralph Carver. "I guarantee you, those Swedish sons of bitches are sitting in a nice warm room at some Best Western in Montreal watching cable porn."

A DEA agent, Ari Schaefer, sat to Carver's right. FBI assistant Special Agent in Charge Mary Rose Palestrina sat in the backseat with Fisk, an empty Thermos and Fisk's holstered Glock between them. It was the usual federal alphabet soup of agencies who didn't like or trust each other—the perfect recipe for a law enforcement disaster.

"That's assuming these jokers aren't just a figment of Fisk's imagination," the DEA agent, Schaefer, added.

The feds didn't believe that the NYPD was capable of scooping them on a solid international terrorism lead, so they'd been baiting him relentlessly for four hours. Thus far he'd managed to resist the urge to tell them to kiss off. It was *his* source, *his* information—his *case* if you got right down to it—but the mandate across law enforcement agencies was to cooperate, to share, if only to show the media and informed citizens that fighting terror was a team sport. It was Fisk's show, it was Intel's interdiction, but still ASAC Palestrina acted like she was running the show. They tried to treat Fisk like a guest at his own party.

"I mean, look at this crap," Carver said. "What kind of idiot would go out on a day like this?" He was running the wipers nonstop, the heater blowing full blast. They could see okay out the front window, but the side windows were starting to get choked with snow, obscuring their view of the road down which the Swedes would be approaching. The car was pulled off the shoulder slantwise, so their best view of the road was from the side windows.

"Goddammit," said the DEA guy. "I have no visual. Whose turn is it?"

"Mine," said Fisk. It wasn't, but he was tired of being cooped up in the car. He suspected it was the egos clouding up the windows as much as their breath. Carver handed him the fragile pink plastic windshield scraper that was their only defense against the heavy white blanket, and Fisk pushed open the door and climbed outside.

The door closed and the silence was a balm. He stood still, exhaling a plume of thick carbon dioxide, refreshed by the cold. The temperature was hovering just below freezing. Heavy, wet snow had formed a crust of ice over every surface of the car, and Fisk began hacking away at the windows.

Fisk was starting to worry. Two suspects were supposed to be making the run across the border from Canada into the States—Swedish Muslim militants smuggling radioactive isotopes for an explosive they planned to detonate in New York City sometime in the next three weeks. If anybody had told him six months ago that there was such a thing as a Swedish Muslim militant, he would have laughed.

But nobody was laughing now, not after Magnus Jenssen had come within an eyelash of blowing up President Obama at Ground Zero last year. Fisk himself had personally stopped the bomber. Now two more members of the same cell in Sweden, undeterred by their comrade's lack of success—and, in fact, motivated by his capture and pending trial—were on their way into the States carrying about half a gram of a highly toxic, highly radioactive isotope of the element polonium-210.

Half a gram didn't sound like much. But one ten-thousandth of a gram was enough to kill a human being.

The original plan for the takedown had included six members of the FBI's elite Hostage Rescue Team tactical unit, an Intel drone, a Border Patrol helicopter, and a team of ICE agents. But the HRT unit's van had encountered one of the aforementioned suicidal deer on the way up north, causing the driver to swerve and the van to slide off the road, where it overturned, putting one of the team members in the hospital with a dislocated shoulder and ending any chance of the HRT team participating in the bust. The helicopter full of ICE agents had to abort due to the miserable visibility, and the drone was grounded, according to the civilian contractor, "due to suboptimal control surface functionality," which was jargon for "remote control airplanes can't fly in snow."

So now it was down to the four people in the Jeep.

On the positive front, the DEA guy had showed them the trunk guns he had requisitioned for the takedown: an AR-15 and a Remington 870 tricked out with so many lasers and flashlights and optical gizmos that it looked like something out of a science fiction movie. If things really went south, he'd said magnanimously, Fisk could grab the shotgun. "The AR's mine, though, bro," he'd added. "Nobody touches my AR. She's my sweetness." He'd picked up the carbine and dry-humped it comically. "Aren't you, baby? Aren't you? Huh? Yeah, talk to Daddy, you sweet little bitch."

This was the quality of agent they had dispatched to the Canadian border with Fisk.

After a minute of chopping away at the snow, the cheap pink snow scraper snapped in half, slicing Fisk's little finger. Fisk cursed and threw the broken scraper on the ground, then stared at the pieces, breathing hard. He would have traded half the gizmos in the trunk for one long-handled ice scraper.

For a moment Fisk vibrated with frustration. The extraordinary silence enveloped him, and he invited it in, hoping for some calming, some perspective. He stood motionless and just listened.

No motor noises coming from the direction of Canada. No voices. No nothing.

It occurred to him that he had never been anywhere quite this silent. Not once in his life. It wasn't just the remoteness of the place. It was the snow itself. It acted like the acoustical baffling in a recording studio, sucking up every scrap of sound in the universe. For a cosmopolitan guy like Fisk, it felt more than a little eerie. It felt like that part in a movie when the sound track drops out . . . when you know something big is about to happen.

But there was something about it that was beautiful, too. The sun was going down and the entire landscape had faded into a curtain of soft gray: a blanket of cold, clean fleece. He could see only a short distance in any direction. It was difficult to even judge just how far he could see. Fifteen yards? Thirty? He'd heard of whiteout blizzards where you couldn't see a car length in front of yourself. So this wasn't that bad.

But still.

It was no kind of day, he reflected, to be taking down bad guys.

Bank robbers love snowy days. Fisk remembered from his days as a rank-and-file NYPD cop, every snowstorm meant at least a half-dozen note jobs. Because the perp could walk into the bank wearing a ski mask or ski goggles without drawing undue attention, and once the alarm was hit the police response time was easily four times the norm. He remembered fondly the brilliant spray of orange against a pure white canvas of fallen snow in Murray Hill, from a dye pack that exploded: bank crime deterrence as public art.

The windows were still coated with icy snow. Fisk dug the broken pink stub of the plastic scraper back out of the snow. The end of the scraper had broken off into a knife-sharp point. It had sliced his finger pretty nicely, cutting right through his leather glove. Fat drops of blood fell one by one into the virgin snow. He made a fist to allow his ruined glove to soak up the blood, and stood there, absorbed by the silence.

He realized that he didn't really want to get back in the car. A bunch of alpha personalities trying to top the others with stories of how tough they were, what great cops they were, how they'd been the best guy on their football team in high school, the toughest guy in their platoon in the army. Blah blah blah blah blah. That stuff got real old, real fast. And the FBI agent, Mary Rose, the fastest sprinter at Fordham and the top shooter in her class at Quantico: she was the worst one of all.

Fisk checked his watch. Theoretically the pair of Swedes should have been here more than half an hour ago. Maybe they just weren't coming. Waiting out the storm. Like reasonable people.

As he stood there stamping his feet in the cold, he felt pressure against his bladder. Another good reason to kill a few more minutes outside the car. He cocked his head and listened. No car engines, no sinister Volvo full of terrorists crunching down the road . . .

For a moment he considered the effect of warm urine on the ice-crusted windows. Kill two birds with one stone. He decided he wasn't that stir crazy yet. He hadn't cleared the windows on the other side of the car, but with the wipers going, they could still see out the front of the Jeep. And it would only take him a minute.

As he walked out into the snow, he was surprised at what a struggle it was to move. He felt ridiculous and awkward, high-kneeing his way through the drifts. But it was better than trying to piss in a

Poland Spring bottle with Special Agent in Charge Mary Rose Palestrina sitting next to him bragging about her marksmanship.

The walking was slow, the snow forming around each deep footstep, gripping his boot. The high-stepping felt ridiculous, and he made a pledge to no longer make fun of people who wear snowshoes. The trees stood brown and black just beyond the curtain of snow falling in front of him. He looked back once, the silver Jeep barely visible. He might have had trouble finding his way back if not for the stark red dots of blood he had left in the snow like a bread-crumb trail.

He reached the first trees and, after laying the broken ice scraper on the surface of the snowfall, made quick work of his belt and zipper. Afterward, zipping up, he felt better, determined to shake off the stasis of the stakeout and power through this job to the next. He looked at his finger, the cut starting to clot in the cold, and was stooping to retrieve the broken ice scraper when the gunshots ripped through the silence.

Fisk instinctively reached for his Glock. Of course it wasn't there. It was tucked away in the backseat of the silver Jeep some fifty yards away.

He felt a blinding surge of emotion—anger and self-recrimination and fear. Then more shots followed—a terrifying number of them, a fusillade of automatic weapons, burst after burst in efficient succession. The shooting was accompanied by metallic thuds and the sound of shattering glass.

He had just started to run back when the sudden cascade of snow fell upon him, descending from the treetops, knocking more snow loose as it plunged to the ground with a hiss and a wet, inevitable thud. Fisk was half buried, and then more limbs cracked above and a second load of snow dropped, a chain reaction spreading all around him.

He dug himself out with his gloved hands. The top layer was loose, but the bottom was already compressed, and he chopped at it with the scraper, almost losing a boot as he pulled out his left leg. He picked up a jagged pine branch near him and charged out of the tree cover—into white blindness.

He knew he was looking in the right direction, but no silver Jeep. No noise either, nothing over his own rapid breaths: no gunshots, no screaming.

How many had he heard? Thirty? Forty? Fewer than ten seconds in duration, but the intensity had been shattering.

He was moving forward. Stumbling through the deep snow, assuming the worst.

It was an ambush. Had to be. Somehow the Swedes had caught the feds flat-footed, comparing war stories instead of watching for trouble.

He looked for his own footprints, already smoothing over under fresh snowfall. He saw a drop of blood, from his own finger, and knew he was headed in the right direction.

Then another controlled burst of gunfire. Fisk stopped and froze, listening. The sound was so crisp and near, everything seeming dislocated, eaten up quickly by the swirling snow.

Were those thumps behind him? Another small clump of snow dropped from the trees. He looked back at the dim black trunks. Then back in front of him.

Two figures. Barely visible. Slashes of color—black and brown—moving in the whiteness. Maybe a scarf, a cap . . . a weapon.

They were shooting at him now. They had seen his footprints leading away. They were following his blood trail. Their first burst had missed, two rounds thudding in the tree trunks behind him.

Fisk turned fast. He was vulnerable out in the open. Only distance would obscure him. He tossed the branch and tore back toward the trees, waiting for the next burst of gunfire.

It came just as he bladed himself behind the first tree. He looked back, unable to see them for the moment. Focus, dammit! He hadn't heard a car motor, or the crunching of tires. The only thing that made sense was that they had left their vehicle somewhere and come on foot.

The silence was excruciating. Because it told him that, regarding the feds, the fight was over. If they were still alive, he'd hear something, yelling, *anything*.

The three people he had just been sitting in the car with, swapping boasts and drinking coffee—Ari Schaefer, Ralph Carver, and Mary Rose Palestrina—they were all dead. Of this much he was certain.

He had three brother law enforcement officers down.

And with this realization, his momentary confusion and self-disgust evaporated, replaced by a wave of cold, hard anger.

He glanced down at his hand. He was still clutching the sharp, broken stub of pink ice scraper. It wasn't exactly a Glock 17. But it was something.

A burst of nausea. That's how quickly the adrenaline surged. These two guys—if there were only two—were out to finish the job now.

Voices. Singsong, at least to Fisk's ears. Fisk spoke Arabic like a native, fluent Spanish, high school French, a little German, a little Thai, some Bahasa Indonesia. His father had been a diplomat; Fisk had traveled a lot as a kid and had a natural ear for languages.

But he didn't speak Swedish. He couldn't tell what they were saying.

One man's voice, low and terse. Another responding. They sounded near, almost on the other side of the tree . . . but it was a trick of the snow. They couldn't see Fisk if he couldn't see them.

They sounded like soldiers to him: calm, self-possessed. He could tell from the sound of the ambush that these two Swedes had military training, as opposed to being amateur goofballs who'd taken up jihad because they were bored with their jobs in IT.

His phone was in the car, too, charging. But it didn't matter. Zero cellular service here in the ass end of nowhere. Mary Rose had a satellite phone, didn't she? He needed that phone as much as he needed a handgun.

He saw the colors reappear, vague against the white. Under even sparse tree cover, their visibility would improve dramatically. Fisk tightened his grip on the broken plastic window scraper and took off running through the trees. The snow cover was more shallow here, around a foot deep. He expected gun reports at his back yet heard none.

He felt something expanding inside him, something he had experienced a half-dozen times before in his life but had never been able to put a word to. The threat of imminent death has a way of uniquely focusing the mind.

After the episode with Magnus Jenssen, the NYPD had mandated that he attend counseling sessions. Not only because he had been in a violent confrontation—what the department called a "major incident"—but because his partner and girlfriend had been murdered. In a case like that, counseling was mandated.

Fisk had talked to the counselor about the episode, about racing through the tunnel to stop Jenssen, who was strapped with several kilograms of C-4 explosive, a trigger hidden inside a cast wrapped around his left arm.

"You know, Detective Fisk," the counselor had said, "there are a lot of people who might say what you did was crazy. How would you respond to that?"

"I was just doing my duty, Doc," he said.

Dr. Rebecca Flaherty was a redhead, not the brassy orange kind, but a darker, autumn red. She was very attractive, and Fisk thought that was part of her power, sitting there like an ideal, someone beyond reproach. She tilted her head and looked at him. "Well, that's obviously bullshit," she said. "Are you contemptuous of the process or of me?"

Fisk's eyes widened. She had him.

"Now tell me how you really felt?" she asked.

Fisk closed his eyes. Part of his resistance to this process was having to go back there at all, even for answers. "It felt amazing."

She held her expression in check, but there was no way she absorbed that without the mental equivalent of a deep breath. "Care to elaborate?"

"You ask me how I felt, and you insist on the truth. It felt amazing. It was the right thing to do. No equivocation. No choice, really. I had to do it. To go all out. All or nothing. And something else."

A tiny smile licked at the corner of her mouth. "Go on."

"I thought I was going to win. Check that. I knew I was going to win."

"Knew this how?"

That, he had no answer for. "I just did. I suppose . . . what's the alternative? If I lose, I'll never know it. I'd be obliterated. So no recriminations. No 'Aw, shucks.' Either I'd succeed, or nothing. Look at it this way. What if I did fail? What if I got blown up along with a lot of innocents and some glass and steel? And this is my little dream-state afterlife." He shrugged. "Same result."

"And same pain," she said.

Fisk nodded. Dr. Flaherty was good indeed, and he was willing to open up now. "A lot of pain. She is gone. Were she to walk in the door right now, then I'd know I was dead. Or dreaming."

"And would you prefer that?"

"Not that I have a choice . . . but sometimes. Absolutely sometimes."

Dr. Flaherty shifted in her chair. She was wearing a business suit with pants. The chair made no noise as she moved in it. "Mightn't I be her, were this some sort of afterlife episode?"

"Very likely," said Fisk. "But if you're going to ask me to speak to you as though you were my dead girlfriend . . ."

Dr. Flaherty was already waving that off. "No, no. Just trying to draw a line between fantasy and reality."

"I know the reality," said Fisk. "All too well. The bottom line is that when I ran toward Jenssen, I felt pure. That's the best way to put it. Clean. Pure. That sprint through the tunnel? At the time, it was pure hell. But now looking back, I think it was the best feeling I'd ever experienced. Following the worst feeling I'd ever experienced."

Dr. Flaherty brushed back her hair, which had fallen over one eye. "And how do you feel now? On that register, from what you describe as a peak experience to the lowest moment perhaps of your life."

"Now?" said Fisk. "Right now?"

"Generally. These days."

Fisk crossed his arms. The air conditioner hummed, raising little bumps of gooseflesh on his arms. He held the counselor's gaze because it seemed important to do so. This process was akin to a polygraph, except instead of a lie detector, he was sitting with a truth detector.

He was stumped.

She said, "You're trying to cook up the answer that gets you back to work the fastest."

He shrugged. "Maybe."

"This is not a place to censor yourself. Everything we say is completely—"

"Confidential, right." Did she believe that? "Something is going in my permanent file, something that could affect the rest of my career. I like my career. I don't want any liabilities."

"Such as?"

"Such as getting a lift out of putting myself in harm's way. I'm not blind to how that can sound. Like I've lost it. Like I might go *looking* for those kinds of moments again. Chasing that 'peak experience,' as you so aptly termed it."

She nodded. Was she interested in his concern now? "What would you like to have in your file?"

"It's not what I want, it's what they need. 'I felt frightened. But I thought I had a shot at taking down a very bad man. I just wanted to do my job and save lives.' Unquote. Like the experience humbled me, but I'm better for it somehow."

"That's not the truth?"

"I honestly think it's too early to tell. But I don't want to feed any half-baked revelations to that douche bag desk jockey captain in Human Resources down at One Police Plaza. Because that guy has never truly laid out for one."

"Laid out?" Dr. Flaherty smiled coolly, leaning back in her caramel-leather-upholstered chair. "Interesting terminology, Detective. Because the literature says there are two kinds of people who react the way you did in the face of extreme danger. Top-performing athletes. And sociopaths."

Fisk made an interested noise and crossed his legs. "I had a pretty good jump shot back in high school," he said. "Just never got the NBA height, or the NBA legs."

"So if you're not an elite athlete . . . ?"

"I'm an elite cop," said Fisk. "Or trying to be. Look, I think what this all boils down to is, can this detective before you do the job he did before the traumatic thing happened. In layman's terms, there it is."

She waited to see what he was going to come up with next, either dig a deeper hole or climb out and brush off his hands.

Fisk said, "I think the people of New York City will be better off with me inside the department than outside of it."

isk emerged from the trees, having traced a wide arc through them. Two killers on his trail, probably armed with AK-47s and who knew what other guns. Fisk had a sharp piece of plastic.

He was out of the tree cover and back into the maelstrom of snow. He was circling back toward the Jeep. At least, that was his hope. Had the snow let up a bit? He thought it had. Good for his visibility, but worse for him because now he was more visible, too.

Where was the road? Every facet of topography was smoothed over by the snow. They had been turning the Jeep's engine on every twenty minutes or so for a few minutes of interior heat, but now he didn't even have that sound to aim for.

Then he saw the snow craters. Faint, filling up quickly with freshly fallen snow, but there was a twin pattern, he could see it now. Faint skateboard-sized impressions: huge footprints.

That was why he had not heard the sound of the Swedes approaching.

They were on snowshoes.

He tried to match their stride, sweating through his North Face parka, but moving with renewed energy now that he felt he was on the right track.

He checked behind him. Still no sign, but he knew they were there.

A broad hump appeared up ahead. Fisk paused before the snow-buried Jeep, steam from his huffed breath obscuring his view. Then he went at the windows with his forearm, clearing it in a broad swipe.

Holes in the cracked glass. The driver's door open.

He checked the pulses of his comrades, because that was protocol, though it was clear there was no need. All had been sprayed with gunfire and dispatched with bursts to the head, execution style. The dash was cracked, the radio shattered, the smell of cordite hanging in the car. They had been ambushed at close range. Fisk suspected that not one of the agents' sidearms had even cleared their holsters.

Stuffing was blown out of the backseat, such that Fisk wasn't certain his Glock was gone until he searched. But it was gone. So was the satellite phone.

Fisk circled to the rear hatch, which had been left open. The ATF agent's long guns were gone, no AR, no 870. Maybe they had hurled them away into the deep snow. Perhaps if he hunted around in the woods long enough he might find them. But he had no time.

Desperate, Fisk ran around to the front again. He felt under the dash. Sometimes cops screwed holsters to the firewall to hold a backup gun. But there was nothing there—no spare under the seat, no snubbie in the glove compartment.

Nothing.

Think. What did he have? *The scraper.*

What else?

Footprints.

Fisk looked around. He tried to remember the road in from I-87. There were more trees in the opposite direction, he was certain.

He looked at the dead agents one last time. He needed to make a noise. The anguish that came out of him was real.

"NO!"

No echo. His voice expanded into the snow, which quickly blanketed it like everything else.

But the Swedes must have heard it.

Fisk tightened his grip on the ice scraper and took off away from the Jeep, at an angle from the trees, away from the circle of footprints. These had to be easy to follow. He had to make certain that the Swedes didn't give up on him and head back to their transpo rendezvous. They were moving faster than he was, thanks to their snowshoes. They were closing the gap. He let the images of the dead feds chase him into the snow, along with the Swedes.

One burst of gunfire shook him. He felt no displacement of the air around him, so the rounds never came anywhere close, but he didn't want them shooting at him yet. He pushed himself as hard as he could, adopting a gallop-style gait that got his legs into and out of the snow as quickly as possible. And he never looked back. Gunfire would tell him if he was in range or not.

A roadside line of trees emerged out of the snowy curtain, a forward column of soldiers awaiting him. Fisk almost fell into the first black trunk, coughing into his sleeve so the sound would not carry. He pulled off his coat, and steam lifted from his soaked henley.

He stumbled several feet into the woods and found a low branch. The dark blue of his parka would stand out starkly from the snow. He hung it gently from a splinter on the branch.

Fisk hurried about ten yards away and dove head-first into the ground cover. He used his empty hand to push more snow over his blue jeans and his green shirt, covering his knit cap as best he could.

The snow started to soak through his clothes immediately. In about one minute, his extreme body heat was gone, the sudden temperature change making him lightheaded. He lay as still as he could, slowing his breathing. Surprise was his only chance.

And then, suddenly, there they were. Vague colors moving through the snow curtain. Twin gray-black shapes. He heard the soft *crunch*, *crunch*, *crunch* of the snow beneath their flat shoes.

Then a voice of warning.

And burst after burst of gunfire.

Fisk could not help but flinch. His parka danced on the branch.

And then, just as he'd hoped, the snow plummeted down from on high once again. It landed hard on him and all around, falling with the force and weight of dozens of heavy down comforters. His view was blocked and his hearing muffled. He had not expected quite that much snow.

He hoped the parka was also buried.

His scraper hand was near, and he picked away at the snow before it hardened, creating first some air-space around his head, then carefully reaching out, trying to poke open a hole to see through.

He stopped and listened. A soft mutter of whispered conversation. A disagreement between the two men, perhaps. Who would go first, or who would take point.

Impossible to tell. Fisk felt the snow weighing on his legs and back. He rolled a bit back and forth so as to create a buffer of space, and so he didn't get packed in there beyond escape.

Again, he went still. He heard faintly the soft shushing noise of someone sliding through the snow as quietly as they could. He cleared more space in front of him and the snow above it settled into the void—and then his hand was free.

He pulled it back immediately. He could see. Not well, but well enough to watch the two Swedes advance. They were already at the area where they presumed him to be buried and dead.

One was near the mound. He was exploring it with his boot, the muzzle of his AK-47 aimed and ready.

The other one was the flank. He was shockingly near, just a couple of yards away, his back to Fisk.

Fisk pushed up out of the snow. It seemed to take forever in his head, speed at war with silence, and the crunching of the parting snow roared in his ears like artillery explosions.

He was on the near Swede as the man turned. Fisk buried the dagger edge of the broken scraper in the side of the man's neck, just above the shoulder. He pulled out the blade fast, uncorking a spray of blood, and went for the Swede's rifle.

Fisk twisted it from the falling man's grip. The

Swede had let out a strange cry, and his partner—spooked—fired a burst into the mound, thinking it the source of the threat.

Fisk barked at him. The man froze. Fisk had one boot on the Swede bleeding out below him.

Fisk barked again. Fisk spoke fluent Arabic—his mother was a Lebanese Christian—but the only language available to him at this moment was his native tongue. What he said, he wasn't even certain. But the other Swede heard the murderous rage that translates fluently across language barriers.

He had hunted terrorists long enough to know that the chances of this guy winding up unarmed and spread-eagled with his hands clasped behind his head were slim verging on none. And on the one hand, that was fine. Fisk was ready to light this guy up for what he'd done.

On the other hand, nobody had any intel on where the bomb was supposed to be detonated, or by whom.

The guy was waiting. Maybe praying. Fisk barked at him again, and the Swede wheeled around.

Fisk opened up, firing on the man's hands as he swung the AK around. He shredded the man's forearms and saw sparks play off the chromium-plated chamber.

The rifle popped out of his hands, sinking muzzle down into the bloody snow.

The man stood staring at his arms and hands, howling in pain.

Below Fisk, his partner's strength was fading, the arterial flow slowing to a dull pulse. He had pulled off his balaclava, exposing a short, strawberry blond beard, rimed with ice. The man's blood was warm against Fisk's pant leg.

Fisk felt him check out beneath his boot, relaxing into a lifeless heap.

"*La ilaha illa Allah, Mohammadun rasulu Allah.*" It was the other Swede. His howling had turned to praying. He was trying to chant his pain away.

Fisk rushed up to him and chopped him on the back of his head with the butt of the AK, just enough to put him down.

He cut open the man's coat with the blade. In the inside pocket, Fisk found a small, stainless steel vial, carefully machined, about the dimensions of a small bottle of aspirin.

Fisk squeezed the vial in his fist. No sense of victory. No sense of achievement.

He pocketed the vial and tossed the ruined coat aside. No coats for anybody now. He pulled the Swede up by the collar of his thick sweater, and with him began the long march back to Champlain.

BOOK ONE

July 23
Nuevo Laredo, Mexico
2.7 miles from the U.S. border

amon's uncle stopped what he was doing. Ramon followed the man's eyes—dark beneath his New York Yankees baseball cap—to a spray of bright red hibiscus flowers in the bushes next to the Palacio Municipal.

A tiny bird, hovering in the air. Brilliant feathers glinting in the pallid light of dawn. It darted back near Ramon for an instant, close enough that Ramon could hear the sound of its tiny wings thrumming, just barely audible over the sound of the men screaming.

"See it hover," said Ramon's uncle, marveling at the bird. He was a small, compact man, with an expression of earnest concentration on his face. He was one of those men, Ramon noted, who took up very little space. The Zetas around the plaza, the ones now pulling naked corpses out of a stake-bed GMC and throwing them onto the ground, were generally loud, bullying men. Not Ramon's uncle.

He noticed things like birds. They were beautiful to him, or at least, in his world, rare. But they also came as signs. Omens. And Ramon's uncle paid great attention to them.

Not all of the bodies were corpses: not yet. Several of the people lying in the back of the truck were still alive, howling piteously now, begging for their lives, but mainly making a lot of noise.

Twenty armed Zetas occupied the square in front of the long white colonnaded government building that lined the west side of the Plaza de Something-or-Other. (Ramon's uncle had told him the name of the town square, but Ramon had already forgotten it.) The government building had rounded arches running along the entire front, such that it looked like a cheap stucco version of a Roman aqueduct. Most of his uncle's men were lounging around smoking, their AR-15s hanging from their necks on black nylon slings. Some wore bandannas over their faces, others balaclavas. But not all of them. They didn't seem overly concerned about being caught. And the masks were sweaty in the early morning heat.

One of the Zetas, a fat, powerfully built man with a blue Tecate T-shirt stretched over his pendulous gut, was cutting the heads off of the bodies. The fat man used a strange tool for the beheadings, a sort of spade-shaped blade attached to a heavy, rough-hewn piece of wood about three inches thick and six feet long. The tool was crude and appeared to have been handmade, perhaps by a blacksmith. But the cutting edge was very sharp. The fat man used the tool much like a post-hole digger. He straddled the bodies, one foot on either side of their chest, lifting the heavy tool up in the air with the blade pointing down. Then he would drive it straight down with a heavy *thunk* on the necks of the dead and the not-yet-dead, severing their heads with one stroke. With each cut he muttered curses under his breath—*coño chinga puta madre pendejo*, an unconnected string of obscenities—the way a man might curse his work while digging a well in stony ground.

Then another Zeta grabbed the head by its hair and tossed it back onto the truck bed, where it thudded and bounced like an American football before settling still.

"Won't someone hear all the screaming?" Ramon said to his uncle. The desperate howls of the three or four live prisoners were starting to wear on Ramon's nerves. He was sweating and feeling a little like he might throw up, and he did not want his uncle to know.

His uncle seemed to read Ramon's distress in the way that he shrugged. "Take some water if you want." The hummingbird zipped overhead again, returning to the red hibiscus flowers. "You are among friends here in Nuevo Laredo. And we have work that must be completed." He turned away from the grisly work being done behind the truck, briefly more interested in the flight and habits of the hummingbird. "*Selasphorus rufus*. The rufous hummingbird. The only bird capable of hovering. So still, and yet so alive with movement."

Ramon thought: This is why you identify with them, Uncle.

"They only feed in the earliest morning and the latest afternoon," his uncle said, continuing. "Feeding and hovering takes so much effort, you see, that they must spend most of their time resting."

Another *thunk* behind them. Ramon tried to listen to his uncle, he wanted to learn . . . but it was impossible to concentrate while the fat man was be-heading bodies. Ramon's eyes cheated back to the fat man; specifically, his blade. Ramon wanted to look at hummingbirds instead, but he could not.

Who were these dead and near-dead people? And why desecrate their bodies with such workmanlike efficiency? His uncle had not said, and so Ramon did not ask. Some had been burned or beaten. Some had had their eyes gouged out. Some were already missing their feet and hands. After the fat man cleaved the heads from the bodies, two other Zetas would drag the headless corpses by their feet over near the front door of the Palacio Municipal, where they laid them in a shoulder-to-shoulder line.

At one point Ramon's uncle looked over and called irritably to them, "Please! Neatly! Have some pride in your work."

"*Sí, patrón!*" the men said, bobbing their heads nervously. Country boys, with the habit of obeisance to authority. And yet Ramon's uncle was not their boss. But none would cross him.

The fat man had finished with the dead. Now he was dragging one of the live men off the truck. The prisoner was very hairy, and he screamed and squirmed continuously . . . until, as he fell from the truck, the back of his head bounced off the pavement with a sharp *crack*. It was an awful sound, but then for a moment the plaza went blessedly quiet. Ramon heard only the whir of the hovering bird. It sounded ominous now, and horrible, like the sound of some machine-beetle designed by American military scientists, ready to drill its beak into Ramon's body and feed.

The stunned man who lay on the ground stirred, then moaned. His hands and feet were bound with heavy black zip ties. The fat Zeta dragged him over to the work area. *Chunk!* went the spadelike tool. The man's body went limp as his head flopped off.

Blood gushed out for a moment, then ceased. The dead man's eyes stared unblinkingly at the sky.

This work was easier on the dead.

In the distance, Ramon heard a thin whine. For a moment he thought it was another hummingbird, perhaps a flock of them.

But then he realized it was a siren. First one, then another, then another.

His uncle heard it, too. He glanced at his watch—it was an elegant and thin timepiece, to which his uncle had given a fancy foreign name, "Patek Philippe"—and scowled. "The lesson here, Ramon? Never trust a policeman. They were supposed to wait until seven thirty sharp. You see what time it is?" He held out the watch on his thin brown wrist. "Seven oh nine." He shook his head in disgust. "Incompetence."

"We should go then," said Ramon, trying not to sound too eager.

Ramon's uncle neither agreed nor disagreed, turning instead to watch the fat man decapitate another prisoner. One more to go.

Ramon's uncle called to the fat man. "Bring that last one over here, Carlito."

Ramon shuddered. He wished the sirens would speed up.

The executioner dragged the final prisoner over to Ramon's uncle, dropping his legs there. Up close, Carlito was even more powerful in appearance. Even with a custom tool, it took strength to chop off men's heads.

Ramon's uncle nodded toward the spadelike tool. He said, "Give the blade to my nephew, Carlito. The time has come for him to see what this business is all about."

Ramon's uncle's life had always seemed romantic and exciting. His estate, his fine things, his commanding attitude. Just being in his presence was seductive.

But now that he had seen his uncle's work up close, Ramon felt sickened. His uncle, he knew, was not paid by the head. The job was already completed. This was more of a flourish. And Ramon had seen quite enough already, thank you.

But before Ramon could think of an honorable way to protest, the fat man shoved the tool into his hand. Extremely heavy, the wooden handle smooth and worn from having seen so much use. Its crude fan-shaped blade dripped blood onto the ground.

"I made this tool with my own hands," Ramon's uncle said. "Mesquite wood. Very tough. And the blade was hand-forged from steel from an excavator tooth. A Caterpillar 321, if I'm not mistaken. American steel, the highest quality."

Ramon held in his hand the weapon that had beheaded dozens of men. "What is it called?" asked Ramon, stalling desperately.

Ramon's uncle eyed him, shaking his head. "It has no name."

The last prisoner rolled from side to side on the ground, his flex-cuffed hands covering his crotch. He was a thin, hairless young man, not many years older than Ramon himself. He had pure Indian features. And all Ramon could think, looking at him, was: Why do you not scream?

The prisoner just stared up at Ramon, his eyes dark and frightened . . . and yet he did not break Ramon's gaze.

Ramon's uncle motioned with his hand, a precise downward motion. "Let the weight of the thing do the work. Half of the job is just lifting it up and dropping it."

Ramon said, "What is the other half?"

"The muscle this task requires is not mere body strength. You must commit to the act. You must drive the blade down and make sure it finds its mark. The thing knows its job. If you do it carefully, and decisively, the thing will do its job kindly. Otherwise . . ."

"Otherwise?" asked Ramon.

"Otherwise you will bungle the job, and try again. Do not take many hacks where one is sufficient."

The sirens were getting louder. Ramon knew he did not have much time. He also knew he did not want to do this. And he knew that his uncle knew.

"Now is your time," said his uncle, the brim of his ball cap shading his penetrating eyes. "This tool is a special object. It will find you out. It will do the command not of your grip, but of your will. Of your commitment."

The tiny hummingbird flew between them, zipping right, then darting away, heading in an upward arc toward a long row of palm trees on the far side of the plaza.

Ramon's uncle said, "Do you see? Even our little friend knows. It is time to go."

Then his uncle turned, made a circle in the air with his hands, and began walking away. Suddenly the Zetas around the plaza weren't lounging anymore. Everyone stood and began sprinting for their trucks: two armored Humvees, an Escalade, and a Ford pickup with a heavy tube frame welded to the back, on which was mounted a belt-fed machine gun.

The fat man, however, stayed with Ramon. He stared at him with black, expressionless eyes. "Come on, you little *pendejo*. Get it over with. Your uncle is not someone you want to disappoint."

Ramon looked into the face of the decapitator. He saw pleasure there. "Leave me."

"You can't do it."

"Leave me now," Ramon said. "I'll *do* it. And then I will tell my uncle how you doubted me."

The fat man shrugged, but didn't give up on taunting Ramon with his eyes. He walked back to the big GMC and started closing the gate to the bed, obstructing Ramon's view of the litter of heads lying there.

What had become of his world? Ramon felt his entire body trembling. His armpits and face were slick with sweat, even though the sun was barely higher than the buildings at the edge of the square.

He was aware of the eyes of the man at his feet, looking up at him. Ramon did not look down.

He had to do it. He *had* to. If he didn't kill this man, his uncle would never respect him.

Or worse.

Let the weight of the thing do the work. That's what his uncle said. Whether he was referring to the weight of the object or the psychological measure of the act, it was all the same. If Ramon could just let the weight of the thing do the work, he would not have to get involved at all.

His hands would be clean. And it would be done with.

"You don't have to," came the voice.

Not Ramon's own voice. The young man's beneath him.

"No one will care if you don't."

"Shut up!" said Ramon, kicking his bare shoulder.

The sirens grew closer. Ramon felt eyes on him, real or imagined. The eyes of his uncle, the eyes of the dead, the eyes of the fat, taunting Carlito . . . and the eyes of the young man at his feet.

In that single moment, Ramon could see his entire life ahead of him. Why had he ever wanted this? He had not been forced into it. He had sought it. His older brother was a simple farmer like their father. His younger brother was going to the military school in Mexico City.

There was no need for this, he realized. There never had been.

"This is insane," said the young man on the ground. "You see that, can't you?"

Yes. Maybe it was. But perhaps it came to this: Who would Ramon rather be in this insane situation, the man at his feet, or the man wielding the blade?

It was too late to stop this. Ramon moved toward

the young man. The man tried to roll away, but Ramon got his feet down on either side of his chest, straddling him. He did not want to look at the man's face, but there was no doing the job without it.

The young man was looking up at him. Not at the blade: at Ramon.

Ramon raised the blade all at once. He lifted the spadelike tool high into the air—and smashed it downward. But as the tool plunged toward the ground, Ramon realized he'd done exactly what his uncle had warned him not to: he had tried to muscle the blade into the man, instead of simply letting the tool do the work.

His hands and arms attempted to do what his heart could not.

And so he missed—the blade twisting slightly in its descent, whacking the man in the upper shoulder. It opened up a gaping, smile-shaped gash just above his clavicle.

But it was no killing blow. Ramon saw white flashes of bone in the moments before the wound filled with blood.

The young man grunted like he'd been punched. His eyes went white and teary, his eyelids fluttering, his mouth grimacing.

Ramon looked around. He thought he saw his uncle on the running board of the Escalade, a ball cap shading his face, obscuring his expression. But it was another man. This man gave Ramon a simple wave. A summons. A hurry-up gesture.

From that distance, it must have looked like a killing blow. The young man lay still.

Ramon checked for the fat man, Carlito, but he

was loading his own bulk into the driver's seat of the truck.

But he could not step away without being sure that his uncle . . .

There he was. His uncle was up at the front door of the Palacio Municipal, kneeling over one of the beheaded corpses. He was writing something on the body's bare back.

No—a writing gesture, but not with a pen. A knife. Cutting swiftly yet delicately.

For a moment Ramon wondered vaguely what he was doing. But the sirens were loud now, and almost upon them. Ramon knew that, whatever he was going to do, it had to be done *now*.

On the ground beneath him, the young man gritted his teeth as though biting down on his pain.

Ramon quickly leaned down. "Don't scream," he said.

Then he began to run toward the knot of Humvees.

Juan de Jesus Ramos Diaz, the chief of police of Nuevo Laredo, considered himself to be *uno hombre moderno*—a modern man. He had graduated from the Instituto Tecnologico with a *licenciado* in business administration, where he had written his honors thesis on "The Use of Decision Trees in Managerial Problem Solving."

There were a great many interesting tools at the disposal of the modern managerial executive. Decision trees, game theory, statistical analysis. Whatever. The point was that one had to remove emotion from the process and make decisions that were rational and sensible, that encapsulated all environmental and human factors within a matrix of clean, pure logic.

Chief Ramos's predecessor, Chief Cardenas, had been a romantic, a man who made decisions based on emotion. And yet to make decisions based on one's desires, while at the same time lacking true passion: that is a recipe for mediocrity.

"We are cops, Juan. Cops make decisions with their balls."

And then he would helpfully grab his own through his uniform pants and give them an overly generous squeeze, in case Ramos forgot where men's balls were located.

Before being named chief, Ramos's predecessor had thundered about winning back the town from the Zetas—the notorious criminal cartel that controlled Nuevo Laredo—making speeches about the great evils of crime and drugs, the plague of corruption, the necessity for facing down the thugs, and so on and so forth. It was all very inspiring, if one had never heard such platitudes before. Without a doubt, Chief Cardenas imagined himself a man of very big *cojones*, a noble man, a man of firm moral courage.

Six and one half hours after Cardenas was sworn in as police chief of Nuevo Laredo, three vehicles pulled up next to the Ford F-150 in which the noble and courageous man was riding and blew the living shit out of him. The best estimate was that over 140 rounds were shot into his car, with at least 39 of them entering Chief Cardenas's body.

Cardenas had left four kids and a wife, no pension, eighteen thousand pesos in the bank. His shredded balls were buried with him.

Chief Ramos was not going to make the same mistake. It was a simple matter of reason, of management science, based on fact and information and analysis. The Zetas were here for the duration. They were an established force and an accepted evil. And *uno hombre moderno* simply made his peace with that and integrated the fact of it into his strategic plan.

"How many bodies?" said the chief, with one boot on the stone step.

Detective Inspector Luis Delgado had seen a lot of horrible things over the past few years, but after walking the plaza, even he looked a little green around the gills. "Twenty-two, *jefe*." Delgado then flipped open his notebook. "We thought there were twenty-three, but we have a survivor."

Chief Ramos's mouth went dry. "*Puta madre*." He blew out a long breath and adjusted his sunglasses. "Where?"

Delgado pointed to the far end of the colonnade, well away from the line of corpses.

An anomaly amid such a carefully arranged scene of horror. This was not good.

"Is he going to make it?"

Delgado hiked up his pants and scanned the plaza once again before looking back at Ramos and shrugging. "Do we want him to?"

"What kind of stupid question is that?" snapped Ramos.

Delgado shrugged again. There had been more than 250 murders in Nuevo Laredo over the past three years. The Zetas had been in a fierce war with the Gulf Cartel for much of that time. And now that the Zetas had all but declared victory, wiping out the Gulf Cartel, the Sinaloa Cartel was getting involved, too. Nuevo Laredo, a sleepy little city of about 350,000 people, had the highest murder rate of any town on the entire North American continent, sixty times greater than the murder rate in New York City. In a place like this, a homicide cop had better get good at shrugging. There was little else he *could* do. Sure, the *policía* solved the occasional domestic killing, the occasional bloody dust-up between a couple of drunks in a bar, even one murder for hire involving a hot-blooded farmer's wife. But there had not been a single gang-related murder placed in the "solved" column since Chief Ramos took over. And this was no accident. Not solving that many murders took a surprising amount of work.

Unless the Zetas *wanted* the murder solved, of course. It happened occasionally. Maybe this was one of those.

Chief Ramos had not looked closely at the bodies. That was what management was all about. These things you delegated.

"Where are the heads?" Chief Ramos said.

Another shrug. "Not present."

"Do we know who any of these people are? The corpses?"

Delgado fired up a Marlboro and surveyed the plaza again before he finally spoke. "Sometimes I think about quitting and just walking across the river, you know? I got a cousin lives up in Texas. Manages the sporting goods department at a Walmart up in New Braunfels. You remember Helio Diaz? He was a couple classes ahead of us in high school?"

The chief of police shook his head. The name rang a bell, but it was hard to say.

"Well, anyway, nicest guy in the world. Helio went over the Rio Grande back in the eighties, got his citizenship, makes about the same money as you and me. Forty-hour week, health and dental. This with very few decapitations. Never has to worry about this lunacy, this . . . sickness."

Delgado waved his cigarette at the plaza. The sun was still low in the sky, the blue lights of the police trucks bouncing manically into the shadows at the corners of the square. The corpses lay in their row, unmoved. Flies clouded the air above them. Cops stood near their vehicles, shaking more hot sauce onto their Subway sandwiches, waiting for orders.

Chief Ramos knew that they didn't have enough space at the morgue for all these bodies, so once again he was going to have to figure out some kind of temporary solution. Maybe he could rent a refrigerator truck. He'd read that they did that in New Orleans during the hurricane, when their morgue was inundated with water. Perhaps he could draw on the discretionary fund, which still had forty-one thousand pesos left over after paying for the Police Athletic League expenses, night soccer to keep troubled youth off the streets.

These were the kinds of details that Chief Ramos enjoyed working with. Thinking outside the box.

But unfortunately, right now refrigerator trucks weren't his main problem. His main problem was this survivor. Any way he looked at it, this didn't make sense. Survivors talked, and the Zetas were notoriously reliable in never leaving any loose ends. The Zetas had been formed by a group of twenty or thirty Mexican Special Forces soldiers hired as enforcers for the Gulf Cartel twenty years ago. Eventually they'd gotten too big for their britches and split from the Gulf Cartel, forming their own sect. Their hallmarks were that they were disciplined, well trained, heavily armed, and ruthless well past the point of sadism.

In other words, their decision trees were to be admired as pitiless models of efficiency.

If the survivor talked, it would create problems for them; more important than that, it would create problems for Chief Ramos. The chief considered the matter from several angles, but the truth was there was only one rational solution. And he did not need a decision tree or a statistical analysis to be able to see it.

"Bring the survivor over there to that truck," the chief said. "Take great care. I will interrogate him personally."

Delgado looked at the chief for a minute, then sighed and tossed his cigarette butt on the ground. He seemed very sad. "I'll have one of my guys take care of him if you want. You shouldn't have to do this yourself."

"Just bring him to the damn truck!"

Chief Ramos wheeled around and walked over to the pickup truck. It was the curse of responsibility. Delegation was all good and well, but sometimes you had to sink your own hands into the dirty soil. That was the challenge of leadership: when to do . . . and when to tell. Now it was time to do. Time to lead by example.

After a minute a couple of uniforms arrived at the truck where the chief stood. The bloody, naked young man had been moved to the bed of the truck.

"Leave us while the boy and I talk," said the chief.

The young man was in bad shape. A large, blood-soaked towel covered his right shoulder.

"Let me have a look at you, son," he said. He lifted the sodden towel and saw that the young man's shoulder was a bloody mess. The bone might have been cracked. Chief Ramos laid the towel back on his wound. "You're losing a lot of blood."

The young man stared up at him. He had already been through a lot. He wanted to get this over with. "Just make it quick, would you?" he said.

The chief considered it. The kid had no gang tattoos. He had the hooked nose and high cheekbones of an Indian from Central America or southern Mexico, descendants of the Maya. Sometimes the Zetas would kill immigrants from El Salvador or Honduras, just to make a point about how bloodthirsty they were. The message to their enemies was: *If we would do this to a man who has done nothing to us, imagine what we would do to you.* Poor kid, he probably paid a coyote his entire life savings to take him up into America. He was headed north to the good life. And this was what he got for his money.

So it was a fair request to make it fast. And indeed, the solution was simple and effective. It was the sort of act one usually delegates to a subordinate, but some tasks needed to be dealt with directly.

So why did he feel sick to his stomach? Chief Ramos undid the snap on the holster of his .45 automatic pistol, as though this act might chase the nausea away. He hated the Zetas, hated the bastards for painting him into a corner, for forcing him to react. Hated them for putting him in a position where a monstrous crime like this was the one logical move he had.

The young man before him was dying. Not there yet, but on his way. An ambulance had been called, of course. He might make it to the hospital. He might linger long enough to talk.

The kindest thing was to get it over with quickly.

But Chief Ramos never pulled his sidearm. He still had his hand on the gun when a convoy of black SUVs and white pickup trucks burst into the plaza. Within seconds, they had screeched to a halt, and black-clad members of the Policía Federal—the elite national police—leaped from the trucks. As always, they wore the full ninja: black masks over their faces, Kevlar helmets, M4s and G36s on single-point tactical slings, bulletproof vests over their chests—the good kind, like the American military wore, the ones with the ceramic plates in them.

Chief Ramos felt rooted to the spot. He snapped his holster and stood ready to greet them.

The last car, a black Suburban, pulled up ten feet from where he stood, tires smoking as it skidded to a stop. The rear door opened. A black-clad figure emerged.

She wore the standard uniform of the PF, but she was not masked, nor did she sport a helmet. She wore a comandante's insignia on her shoulder. Her glossy black hair swung back, revealing startlingly pale skin, a broad mouth, and wide green eyes. She was even more beautiful in person than she was on TV.

Puta carajo. It was Cecilia Garza. They called her the Ice Queen.

The famously incorruptible crime fighter looked at Chief Ramos, then at his holster. Had she seen him resnap it over the butt of his .45? Perhaps it was the way he stood over the bloody prisoner, still bound hand and foot with flex cuffs.

Without a moment's hesitation, she drew her sidearm and pointed it at Ramos's face. "Step back!" she shouted. "Don't even think about it."

Chief Ramos glared ferociously at her. "Who do you think you are talking to?"

Still, he stepped back. It was the way she held her weapon. She made him feel like this was no idle threat. His bluster was a ruse, for she had done him a great favor by arriving when she did. The Ice Queen had relieved him of the terrible responsibility that had dropped in his lap.

"I know exactly who you are, Chief Ramos," she said. "Now get your goddamn men and their goddamn sandwiches the hell off of my crime scene! Where is this man's ambulance?"

"On its way, Comandante."

She looked at him, judging what he said to her to be the truth, and lowering her weapon. "It better have the right address."

Chief Ramos smiled and nodded. Because what else could he do? A sane man yields to superior force. It was the only rational thing.

Comandante Cecilia Garza sent two men with the ambulance. She did not want the witness to get into any "accidents" on the way. Nuevo Laredo was a Zeta town from top to bottom. There was no knowing who might be working for them—paramedics, cops, nurses. It could be anybody.

Garza avoided the headless corpses for now. Not because of squeamishness, though she certainly had no eagerness to see a bunch of mutilated dead people. But her first priority was to see if there was any recoverable evidence in the plaza.

She checked in first with the head of her forensics team, Sergeant Herrera, who was clad in a white moon suit and white booties. "Anything yet?" she said.

Herrera shook his head. "Not much. This is the main public square of the town, so we've got a lot of residual cigarette butts and drink cans and things of that nature. We might get lucky and get some DNA off a smoldering cigar butt or the like. But there's no brass I can find, nor blood spatter consistent with gunshot wounds. I believe these men were killed somewhere else and brought here already dead."

He walked over to the edge of the plaza where a

large pool of coagulated blood had attracted a cloud
of hungry flies. "Except right here. Some of them
were murdered right here. Dead corpses don't bleed
like this. We should be able to figure out from looking at them which ones they were."

Garza nodded. "Anything else?"

"You see this?" Herrera pointed at the pavement
with his booty toe. There were a series of strange
divots in the pavement. "Just like the other ones.
Same mark from the same blade. It's him."

Garza nodded. She knew these scars in the pavement. They all did. She had seen them in concrete,
in soil, in wooden floors. She counted them twice.
"Twenty-two," she said.

"And twenty-nine corpses, yes," said Herrera.
"As before, whoever does the head chopping seems
to enjoy his work very much. He is good at what he
does."

"Except for the guy in the ambulance," Garza
said. "He missed bad on that one."

Sergeant Herrera agreed. He saw her glance at
her watch. "Are we keeping you from something?"

Garza said with a smile, "Nothing, no."

Herrera said, "You are going to Mexico City?"

Garza squinted at him through the strong sunlight. "You heard?"

He nodded. "They said you might become head
of the Presidential Guard."

That rumor was easy to shoot down. "The president must choose someone from the army, for political purposes."

Cecilia Garza was indeed due in Mexico City in
less than twenty-four hours, for a meeting with her

old teacher from UDLA law school, also known as "the Harvard of Mexico." Garza's budding legal career had not worked out quite as she had planned or hoped, and she had turned from practicing law to enforcing the law soon afterward.

Her teacher's fortunes had also changed. Just a few weeks ago, he had been elected president of Mexico. President-Elect Umberto Vargas was pressing her to join his personal protection detail, the EMP, Estado Mayor Presidencial. Though technically an army unit, it included fifty or so Policía Federal officers in its ranks. As far as Garza was concerned, the request was an honor but nothing more, and she planned to continue in her present capacity. But when the president calls and requests one's service, one does as the president wants.

"He is single," said Herrera. "You would make a fine first lady."

Garza actually laughed, a rarity for her. "Yes," she said, "that is the job for me."

Vargas was a charming man—he was a politician, after all—but on top of being twenty years her senior, she had never felt any romantic impulse from him whatsoever. She realized, though, that tongues would wag. Dealing with that on the job would be the least of her problems.

One of Herrera's white-suited forensic techs was methodically photographing the bodies. A pair of PF officers stood at each end of the row of bodies, scanning the empty plaza. The other man near them was Garza's second in command, a big tough man named Major Alonso MacClesh. MacClesh was a common name in Mexico, thanks to long-ago

Scottish immigrants—though, with his dark hair, high cheekbones, and black eyes, MacClesh looked as if he came from 100 percent Indian stock.

"Any witnesses?" she said. "Apart from the guy in the ambulance, I mean."

MacClesh shook his head. He was smoking a cigar, the smoke trailing away from him in the warm evening wind. Garza had not trusted MacClesh at first. He was a hard man to read. He had been slotted to command the elite unit until Garza had been promoted over his head. If she had been in his shoes, Garza would have been pissed, so she trod gently around the man. But if MacClesh resented her, he never showed it. In fact, he never showed much of anything. His reputation, like his performance file, was stainless. Garza trusted him implicitly. But this was Mexico, the home of corruption, and you never knew anything for sure.

"Do we know who they are?" Garza said.

MacClesh pointed to a heavily tattooed torso—the arms and legs of which had also been cut off. "Tats say he's Sinaloa. Probably a high-level guy. A lieutenant from Monterrey went missing last week. Ten to one that's him. Alfredo Luis Jimenez. They call him Cinnamon." He pointed at another legless, armless, headless corpse. "Probably Ronaldo Gutierrez, Jimenez's bodyguard. Based on the tats on the next guy, probably also in Jimenez's set." He pointed down to the end of the row. "Four or five guys down there have tats consistent with the federal prison in Michoacán." Michoacán was on the west coast of Mexico, where the Sinaloa Cartel was strongest.

Most Mexican prisoners went to prison near where they were arrested.

"You're saying these victims were probably from two separate snatches?"

"At least." MacClesh puffed on the cigar. "Some of them, though, I don't think had anything to do with gangs. Probably just random people they killed to pump up the body count. When tomorrow's news says, 'Zetas kill twenty-two members of Sinaloa Cartel,' it makes the Zetas look strong and the Sinaloas look weak. The Gulf Cartel's falling apart right now, so you got a lot of low-level players making up their minds whether they want to jump toward Sinaloa or the Zetas. This is the Zetas saying, 'You want to play in this part of the world, you better sign on with our team.'"

MacClesh stubbed his cigar out on the sole of his boot, then slid it in his pocket. He didn't want to drop his cigar butt on a crime scene. Garza liked that. Most Mexican cops—even in the elite PF units—had a contempt for physical evidence. And given how useless physical evidence generally was in the corrupt Mexican courts, she could hardly blame them. The PF went to a great deal of trouble to accumulate evidence . . . and it rarely proved the slightest value. Herrera and his men were trained by the Americans. They did their best. But it was mostly pissing in the wind.

"You know what this means, right?" he said.

Garza nodded, plucking her bottle of water from the loop on her belt and taking a swig. "The Sinaloas will retaliate soon."

For a moment their eyes met. They said nothing. But she couldn't help thinking she knew what they shared—the feeling that they were in a hopeless battle, that as long as Americans kept buying black market drugs, this madness would not cease. And there was a corollary to that recognition—the thought that maybe the battle wasn't worth fighting, that it would be easier to look the other way, to stop fighting this uphill struggle.

During Garza's college years, her mother and sister were kidnapped and held for ransom. The ransom was paid, but they were never returned. Suddenly the dry academic grind of writing contracts and filing real estate deeds had seemed to her an absurd waste of time. Despite the fervent opposition of her wealthy father, she joined the PF, naively determined to find her mother and sister's killers. While she soon realized that the task was probably hopeless, she also realized that she had inadvertently found her calling. She had a natural talent for police work. But along the way she lost a marriage to a sweet young lawyer, became estranged from her father, and lost a lot of her old friends . . . and still found herself a social outsider in the lower-middle-class boys' club of the PF.

Sometimes she wondered: What is the point?

MacClesh looked down expressionlessly at the dead. Finally he crossed himself. "I don't mind when these animals kill each other. But this . . ." He shook his head. For a moment his face showed a rare expression of emotion: a mixture of sadness and disgust. "Who could possibly think this madness was a good idea? What kind of mind dreams up an abomination like this?"

Garza agreed. "I ask myself, if this is the face they want to show publicly . . . what then is their private face?"

MacClesh nodded. "Uglier still." His face hardened, as though he had let more of his emotions show than he wanted to. "Well, I better get to work."

"Thank you, Major," Garza said.

MacClesh turned and looked at her with curious expectancy. "For what?"

"For reminding me why we do this."

He looked at her without expression for a moment, then nodded bitterly. "Animals belong in cages. I don't see why people find this so hard to understand."

He walked away from her then, barking at his men as he moved toward the other side of the plaza.

Garza took a deep breath, tugging a pair of blue latex gloves from her belt and pulling them on her hands. Now came the hard work. She had a theory about this crime scene. The divots out of the pavement: that was something she had seen many times before. But there was one thing she hadn't found yet . . .

She began walking up and down the row of bodies. She had been comandante of Unit 9 for about a year, but she knew that many of the men still didn't quite believe in her. Not only had she been promoted from outside the unit, but she was the only female member in the history of Unit 9. Any sign of weakness and they would pounce. This she carried with her everywhere. So she had to be tough all the time, even when toughness was not needed.

She knew what they said about her, that she was a bitch, that she was cold and unfeeling, that she only cared about her career, that she was ruthless. . . . They called her the "Ice Queen." The list of her supposed character failings was a long one. But she knew, too, that they respected her. These men, most of them, were like MacClesh: men with a simple and instinctive sense of morality, men who respected strength and courage.

But to keep that respect, she could never show weakness. Never.

She waved her blue-gloved hand at the two nearest PF officers. "Roll them over," she said.

"Pardon, Comandante?"

"On their stomachs, *cabrones*!" She made her tone as cold and impatient as she could muster. "Roll these corpses over on their stomachs. Don't make me say it again."

She was perhaps overcompensating for letting down her guard a bit with MacClesh. She was imprisoned in her role, not unlike a telenovela character actor doomed to repeat the same leer, the same squint, the same grimace in performance after performance. But there was no going back. Not now. Too many bridges had been burned.

This character Garza had forged out of necessity had become who she was now.

The men were halfway down the row of bodies when she saw what she'd been looking for. It was the body of the man MacClesh had fingered as a Sinaloa lieutenant from Monterrey.

Carved into his upper back was a small design, beginning just below his heavily tattooed neck.

The design so brutally carved into the fleshy canvas of this dead man was a hummingbird. To Garza's experienced eye, this little collection of lines was a signature, carved by a confident hand.

Garza would never have admitted it to anyone in Unit 9, but she had studied art once and had even considered becoming a painter before taking up law at her father's insistence—and before the kidnapping of her mother and sister. The man who carved this little design had what artists call a "good fist"—confidence, joie de vivre, purity of line. Something that could not be taught, something you were born with, a certain ruthless clarity of mind.

Garza felt a stab of envy. She had come to the realization that while she had an eye and a light touch for portraits, she simply had no talent to be a true artist. And so going into law seemed like a reasonable change of course.

But this son of a bitch . . . the *animal* who did this . . . he was an artist. A natural.

Why would God throw away such talent on a thug? It made no sense to her.

And for that, she hated this man even more.

She had been on the trail of this animal for a long time. And she was getting closer. She reached down and laid her hand on the decapitated man's back. She could feel his presence. She felt certain it would be a long time before she got this close again. For the moment, at least, she had a living witness.

"I'm done with this one," Garza said to the men who were still supporting the headless, handless corpse.

There must have been something cold in her

eyes, something frightening or even monstrous. Because out of the corner of her eye, Garza saw one of the officers exchange a glance with the other officer, then make the sign of the cross.

She shouted across the square to her driver, Sergeant Chavez, who stood silently by her big black Suburban.

"Start the car, Chavez," she shouted.

Ninety seconds later, they were barreling down Avenue Vicente Guerrero, heading toward the hospital.

When she arrived at the hospital, Cecilia Garza found a number of local police milling around in the lobby. There were more of them up in the wing where the injured witness was situated.

She had sent two PF officers with the witness, for protection, and was glad she did when, as she was approaching the nursing station, she spotted the chief of the Nuevo Laredo police, Juan Ramos. He was a neatly dressed man who could have passed for an American businessman: light skinned, clean-shaven, with sandy razor-cut hair. Unlike most Mexican police commanders, who favored starched uniforms with lots of gold braid, Chief Ramos wore a dark suit, a white shirt, and a necktie. The only sign he was a cop was the bulge under his coat where he kept his pistol. She had seen it earlier in his holster, a .45-caliber 1911 auto, all black, no pearl handle, nothing showy about it. A businesslike weapon.

"Comandante," he said, "I am afraid we got off on the wrong foot."

She glared at him. For a moment she considered ignoring him altogether. "We might have gotten along better if I hadn't gotten there in time to find you contemplating executing a wounded prisoner."

Ramos frowned thoughtfully. "I hear what you are saying," he said. "I understand what you think you saw. But I can assure you, we have strict protocols when securing and arresting *narcotraficantes*. I could show you our training manual. It is very specific."

Garza studied his face. Ramos looked most sincere. She suspected that by this point he might well have convinced himself that what he was saying was true. The worst kind of liars, she had found, were the ones who could convince themselves of their own falsehoods.

"I do not have time to argue the point," she said.

He sighed, playing the Mr. Sincerity thing to the hilt. "Look, you and I both know what a difficult situation we are in here. Everyone in this town feels it, myself especially. I'm sure you breeze in from Mexico City with your team of incorruptibles and you look at me and think, 'Well, there's another scumbag in the Zetas' front pocket.' Am I right?"

She stared stonily at him and didn't reply.

"But I do my best. We all do. I take no money from them, ever, and do my best to offer security to the people of Nuevo Laredo. Sometimes I get up in the morning and hate myself for not being able to do more. But my best is all I have to offer here." He lowered his voice and leaned toward her. "I want to help you. God knows these monsters are a plague on this city. Nothing would relieve me more than to be rid of them."

"Come right to the point, Chief. I have very little time."

"The witness is still alive. I know you're here to

interview him. Just let me sit in with you. Perhaps I can add something to his information. Or, if you like, I won't speak." He took off his coat, folded it neatly on the counter of the admissions desk, then took off his gun and handed it butt first toward Sergeant Chavez, who stood next to Garza. Then the chief held up his hands. "Harmless as a baby, see?"

"And, of course, you would like to know what information this dying man might share."

"The crime did occur in my jurisdiction, Comandante."

Garza frowned. Still, Chief Ramos was a source of potential communication with the Zetas. If she did learn something, it might be fruitful to let them know she was onto them.

He continued, "There are things I know. Connections I can make. Just let me help you."

Garza shrugged, as though the point didn't matter to her. "All right, Chief. But you will remain silent. Not one word. If you speak, I'll arrest you on federal charges of witness intimidation. Understood?"

The chief made like he was locking his lips, then tossing away the key.

"Lead on, O Comandante," he said.

THE WITNESS LAY ON THE BED, pale and looking weak. His upper chest and shoulder were now covered with a thick gauze bandage. Tubes connected him to the monitors. He had received two blood transfusions, but it would not be enough. Nor was surgery an option. He had lain out in the plaza too long.

The young farmhand looked up at Garza. His faraway eyes sparked to something, perhaps her appearance. Her beauty was a useful tool. And this young man had been on his way to America: perhaps he was a born dreamer.

"What is your name?" she said.

"Manuel," he whispered. "Manuel Pastor."

"Where are you from, Manuel?"

"El Salvador." His breathing was slow and labored and he winced each time he drew in air.

"They have given you medicine for the pain?" she said.

The young man—barely more than a boy—nodded. She studied his eyes. He appeared coherent enough for questioning.

"Do you know why these people did this to you?" she said.

The boy shook his head. "I paid a coyote to take me to the United States. We were in a truck. The truck stopped. Then some men burst in, dragged us out. I was hit on the head. Next thing I know, I'm lying on a pile of dead bodies in the back of this open truck. I tried to get out, but . . ." He raised his left hand, showing where the zip ties had left their mark on his wrist.

"Who ran the coyotes? Were they Sinaloa?"

The boy shrugged. "I don't know nothing about that. I just paid a man."

"So you don't work for the Zetas or the Sinaloas?"

The boy looked at her without any apparent comprehension. If the boy was faking, he was doing a hell of a job of it.

A nurse tried to enter, but Garza asked for another minute. Once they gave this man morphine, his intelligence would be lost, perhaps forever.

She leaned closer to the young man. "More medication is on the way, but I have just a few more important questions. Can you respond?"

He blinked his assent, rather than nodding.

"Thank you, Manuel. So you were in the back of this truck. Then you arrived at the plaza. What happened next?"

"There were two others . . . also alive. They were both with me all the way from El Salvador. I don't know their names or nothing . . ." His eyes clouded. "Then they dragged everybody off the truck. There was a fat man. I did not know what the sound was at first. I thought it was a machine. But no. This man was chopping heads off."

"With what? A machete?"

He frowned. "I don't know. I never seen nothing like it. It was like . . . one of those things you dig holes with. For fence posts. Except there was just this one big heavy blade on the bottom." He pantomimed lifting something in the air with his left arm, but didn't get it very high before wincing in pain.

"Any other information you can give me? I want to catch these men. Who was in charge? Did you see the man in charge, Manuel? Was it this fat man?"

The young man's eyes were full of tears now. He shook his head.

"You saw the man in charge," said Garza, pushing.

"Dark eyes."

"Was he tall? Short?"

"Baseball. A hat."

"A baseball cap? But he was Mexican. Yes?"

"There was another. A boy."

"A boy?"

Manuel pointed to his wound.

"A boy did this? A teenager?"

"The one in charge . . . he made him do it."

Garza nodded. Manuel was fading fast. "Is that why he failed? With the tool?"

Manuel blinked several times, loosening the tears in his eyes. It meant yes.

Garza had seen enough. She turned back to Chief Ramos. "Get the nurse."

Garza looked back at Manuel, leaning even closer. She wanted Manuel to feel her presence here at the end. "Anything else you can tell me? Anything else you want to say?"

"They . . . they call him something. The man in the cap. Chupa . . ."

Garza could have finished the word for him, but she wanted to hear it herself. She leaned even closer, the name coming on Manuel's foul breath.

"Chuparosa."

Garza heard stirring behind her. Despite her order, Chief Ramos had not left the room yet.

Garza said, "You're certain?"

"Chuparosa . . ." said Manuel, closing his eyes, his head sinking further back into the pillow.

Chief Ramos said, "I will get the nurse." He left the room quickly, and Garza could hear him shouting, "Nurse! Nurse!"

Alone for a moment, Garza laid her hand atop Manuel's hot forehead. She stroked his hair until the nurse entered.

"Thank you," Garza whispered into Manuel's ear. She stood, watching the nurse's ministrations for a few moments, said a little prayer for the young man from El Salvador, then opened the door and stepped out into the hallway.

Chief Ramos was nowhere to be seen. Apparently the health crisis was too much for him to bear.

GARZA WALKED THE HALL of the hospital, thinking about Manuel's ride in that truck.

All those men. Beheaded and set in the town plaza. It was an obscenity, and yet one the Mexican people were tragically growing used to. And like all obscenities, the more times it was used, the more it lost some of its power to shock and offend. How would they top this? What was the next disgraceful step?

And how could she head it off?

Down a stairwell, she strode out the rear entrance of the hospital. She did not go to her vehicle, continuing on to a blue panel truck parked at the back of the lot, its side emblazoned with a logo that read CERVEZA DOS EQUIS.

The rear door opened as she reached it. She stepped inside, and it closed.

Two technicians sat on opposite sides of the truck, facing matching computer screens. The cargo space was crammed full of modern communications gear, much of it provided to the PF by United States Immigrations and Customs Enforcement.

"You get it?" she said.

By way of reply, the technician pressed the play button on the screen. A voice came out of a pair of speakers. She immediately recognized it as that of the police chief of Nuevo Laredo, Juan Ramos.

"The witness knew nothing." Ramos's voice was flattened by the poor cell phone reception. "Your man failed to finish the job in the plaza. That is dangerous."

"That is being addressed." To Garza's ears, the voice was soft, calm, almost pleasant. "But of course he knew nothing. Did you think anything would have been discussed in his presence? He was in the back of a truck."

Ramos said, "No, I thought you would want assurance . . . and that is what I am calling to offer you."

"And where are you calling from?"

"I am still at the hospital—"

There was a beep. Interruption of signal.

Ramos said, "Hello? Hello?"

The line was dead. The technician turned off the playback.

"The call went to a cell phone, Comandante," the tech said. "Probably a burner. But we traced it to the cell tower. Telmex tower T-421." He pulled up a map, zoomed in on a tiny village. "Nacimiento de los Negros. That is where the other phone's signal was captured."

As she had for Manuel, Garza said a brief prayer for Chief Ramos. He would need it.

In the three long years she had been tracking this killer, this was the first time she had heard his voice.

The Hummingbird. The assassin they called Chuparosa.

She checked her watch. She had so little time before her flight, and yet she was finally so close.

She pulled out her phone and called Chavez. "We're rolling. Right now."

Midblock on Broome Street off the Bowery, Fisk turned in to the door under a black canopy with white cursive lettering that read PENCE.

This had been one of their places. His and Gersten's. He liked the mix of upscale club and old-school downtown gin joint, with brass rails and banquettes with cracked leather upholstery. She had liked the fact that there was not one television screen on its walls; Gersten believed that sports bars should be sports bars, but that a real bar should be free of distractions. It was also a cop place, for those in the know, as well as a neighborhood spot, with a good flow of regulars that kept things steady and fresh.

As he walked in now, a sign reading UNDER NEW MANAGEMENT! was tacked to the unmanned hostess's podium. Instead of the regulars and low-rent boozers, the place was filled with lawyers in suits and hipsters in thickly framed eyeglasses. The daily specials were chalked on a blackboard in pastel lettering: veggie sliders, broccoli rabe pot stickers, chicken and gorgonzola panini bites. The barmaid, when he made it to the sticky brass rail, wore a tank top tied up under her breasts, showing off the tattoo of the sun around her taut, bejeweled navel.

"What's funny?" she asked him, in greeting.

Fisk was smiling but he wasn't laughing. He was thinking about how much Gersten would have hated this, how she would have grabbed his hand and led him out of there.

But through the filter of reminiscence, he could see enough of the old in the new. The scarred oak bar, the spidery crack in the corner of the mirror.

"Jack, neat," he ordered.

The barmaid slid a cocktail napkin down on the bar in front of him, leaning over a bit so he could get a good shot of cleavage with his drink. "We have a beer back special, five dollars."

"Just a water," Fisk said. "But make the Jack a double."

"Bad day?" she said breezily, wiping the bar clean around his napkin. "Or good day?"

"Long day," he said.

She went off to pour his drink, and he looked around for an empty table. The barmaid might as well have worn a sign reading, "Will Flirt for Tips." Fisk had zero interest right now. He spotted an empty high-top and retreated to it as soon as his drink came, sitting facing the door.

The first sip of Old No. 7 hit his throat with a warm hello. The end of the day had officially been reached. And what a day it had been.

The terror trial of Magnus Jenssen had ended as it must: with a guilty verdict. Jenssen had all but admitted his guilt from the beginning, but pled not guilty just to gum up the courts and roll the dice and maybe luck into some sort of acquittal on procedural grounds. It didn't happen. Neither did the trial afford Jenssen much of an opportunity to air his anti-American screed.

Fisk had avoided the trial altogether. The government's case was so exceptionally strong that Fisk's testimony was not needed. Gersten's murder was included in the charges, yet Jenssen was spared the death penalty due to a pretrial agreement with prosecutors in which his cooperation—he divulged his methods and detailed the participation of his accomplices—was taken into consideration.

Today was the sentencing. Fisk had been invited to make a victim's statement and declined. Gersten's mother went full Staten Island Grieving Cop's Mother on him: it had been a rough several months for Mrs. Gersten, and as much as Krina might have wanted him to get close to her, the woman's finger-wagging left him cold. She had slumped, nearly lifeless herself, as the bailiffs finally removed her from the courtroom.

He had sat in the back of the courtroom looking at the back of Magnus Jenssen's blond head. Jenssen never once turned to look behind him, so Fisk had not seen his blue eyes. Fisk had expected him to turn. Not wanted it, or needed it, but expected it. And now that it hadn't happened, he felt a tug of disappointment. He had managed to give Jenssen very little emotional consideration, reserving all his thought for Gersten.

They had come here a few times before they ever became a couple, with that feeling hanging in the air between them, a pregnant feeling of anticipation and longing as their attraction gathered steam. She would sit at the bar, and Fisk would stand next to her, talking close, she swinging her leg into his, little bumps of camaraderie and flirtation; spying is not the "great game," flirting is. Gersten never wore perfume, but he still had a bottle of the shampoo she kept at his place, and for a while he uncapped it every morning, never to use it, only to inhale the scent. Now it stood in the wire basket that hung from his showerhead along with his own Head & Shoulders and his razor, his focal point every morning and every postworkout shower.

Would he and Gersten have married? Had kids? Moved to Staten Island (if she'd had her way) or Brooklyn (if he'd had his)? What color would the door to their house have been? Or would it all have come crashing down in time, the way of most relationships? He wasn't an easy guy to love.

It was easy to go on loving someone who wasn't there anymore. But he knew this in his bones: she had been The One. It would have taken another cop, and a tough one at that, to put up with him.

He sat facing the door, as most cops do, but his gaze was far away. It had been a long time since anyone had snuck up on him, even without meaning to.

"Hey, whoa. Easy. I come in peace."

Fisk must have looked startled and angry. He recognized the sandy-haired man standing at his table. He looked like he could have been a computer programmer, probably a science fiction buff: pale skinned, plain faced, wincing.

"Dave Link," said Fisk, making him. "Sorry, man. Weird moment."

"Not a problem," said Link. "Good to see you, Fisk."

Link had two identical drinks in his hands. Whiskey, neat. Fisk looked down at his own glass. To his surprise, it was empty.

Link set one down in front of Fisk. "Compliments of the Central Intelligence Agency," he said. "May I?"

Fisk nodded to the empty seat. Link sat, turning the chair so that he was facing half toward the bar, with the back wall at his shoulder. "Thanks," said Fisk, raising the fresh drink from the tabletop to toast him, but not drinking it yet.

"Here's to the light of day," said Link. "And that piece of shit Jenssen never seeing it again."

Now Fisk had to drink. And so he did. "Didn't see you at the sentencing."

Link winced after the first swallow. "Wasn't there. Heard you were."

Fisk nodded.

"It's a tough damn thing, just sitting there. Watching. Especially for guys like us."

Spies like us, thought Fisk. Here was the CIA agent trying to flatter him, to sympathize. But for what reason?

"Great work on those other Swedes up north. Tough outcome, but that's what happens when you poke the hive, huh?"

The surviving would-be terrorist had been born with the name Nils Olaf Bengtson, but had changed it to Khalid Muhammad upon his conversion to

Islam. Bengtson had been a model soldier, serving as a first sergeant in the Rapid Reaction Battalion of the Swedish Army, but became embittered after being turned down for promotion to flag sergeant. After becoming Muhammad, he was thrown out of the Swedish army for refusing to keep his beard trimmed to regulation length. His descent from there was swift, apparently hastened by certain psychological issues.

"It should have gone much cleaner," said Fisk. He knew how people—other Intel cops, especially—looked at him now. Gersten had died, and so had the three agents up near the Canadian border. Good people had gone down around him. Cops are, like baseball players and gamblers, some of the most superstitious people out there.

No one said this to his face, of course. But he was a cop, too: he knew. Though a pure odds player might go the other way, thinking all Fisk's bad luck had run its course, instead everyone felt he had the mark on him. He was radioactive now.

"And all the shit you had to go through," Link said. "No witnesses, all that. Reconstructing it. That had to wear you down."

Fisk took another drink. "Little bit."

"Gotta stick to your story. I don't mean it that way. I just mean you gotta tell that same story fifty goddamn times before anyone believes you."

The CIA agent saw that he had misplayed that. Fisk's body language was telling him to fuck off.

"Hey," said Link. "That came out wrong. Look, I got into it myself once. A little dust-up in Fallujah. Took down an insurgent and one of our own translators who flipped on me. Entrenching tool. Saving my own life cost me two months of inquests, affidavits, all that muck. No time for the act of it, the killing, to get digested. That shit sticks to your soul."

Fisk nodded like maybe Link should change the subject now. The barmaid breezed by, eyes wide in a *Want another?* expression. Fisk needed to slow down. He ordered a Peroni. Link asked for two.

"On me," he said, as she went away. "I guess with tits like that she doesn't have to be friendly." Link trying to worm his way back into Fisk's good graces. Fisk wanted to ask him to what he owed this honor, but instead chose to watch Link work for whatever he wanted.

"Bottom line is, you took another major threat off the street. With the added bonus of putting the fear of God in people. Fifty bucks says everybody in this place knows what a smoky bomb is."

A dirty bomb is a radiological weapon that disperses radioactive material via conventional explosives. The explosive blast would cause moderate short-range lethal damage, and the blast wave carrying radioactive material would sicken a wide radius of innocent persons. At least, that was the theory: in fact, no such device had ever been used as a terror weapon. Two attempts at radiological terror had been made, both in Chechnya, both involving cesium-containing bombs, but neither of which was ever detonated.

"Dirty" isotopes emit penetrating gamma rays, which are difficult to shield and handle safely. A so-called smoky bomb uses alpha radiation instead, produced by the radioactive decay of certain isotopes, such as polonium-210. Polonium is unusually common and is used in industries involving static electricity control and ionizing air. Alpha radiation is easily shielded and therefore easier to handle safely. A thin layer of aluminum foil is enough to safeguard its handling. Polonium must be eaten or inhaled to cause harm.

The Swedes had hit upon a way to finely divide and pulverize the polonium into particulate matter for explosive dispersal. The bomb, if detonated, could have killed hundreds. A few breaths were all that was necessary to sicken a victim, perhaps fatally. And the long-term psychological damage to a region such as Manhattan—Times Square was allegedly the Swedes' intended ground zero—would have been sociologically crippling.

Most first responders, including those in and around New York City, carried only gamma radiation detectors, suitable for dirty bomb fallout, but unable to detect alphas. Pending federal legislation aimed to remedy that.

Fisk looked around at the drinkers filling Pence, people filing in after work, singles, couples. A few breaths of smoky radioactive debris. Ten seconds. An ugly death or a lifetime of illness.

"And how you faring?" asked Link, after the barmaid left their drinks. He had handed her a credit card this time, and she frowned, now needing to make an extra trip back to the table, and tucked the card into her cleavage for safekeeping.

"Good," said Fisk. "Medically cleared."

The Swedes had apparently overestimated just how "safe" it was to handle polonium. Fisk had taken the stainless steel container, which was apparently somehow not airtight. About an hour after seeing his prisoner booked into custody, Fisk began throwing up. He had tremors and some localized burns on his hand and hip. His long-term diagnosis was uncertain, depending on the amount of cellular and genetic damage he had suffered. His relatively quick recovery boded well, according to the doctors, but ultimately only time would tell.

Bengtson/Muhammad had not been so lucky. After losing three fingers to frostbite, he started hemorrhaging a few weeks after his arrest due to radiological poisoning and suffered a disabling stroke. He was currently on life support, and his trial had been postponed indefinitely.

Fisk held out his hand. Fairly steady. The tremors had continued long after the exposure, and his therapist, Dr. Flaherty, helped him see that the lingering effects were at least partly psychological. He had come back to Intel two months before but hadn't yet been returned to full duty, working special projects and generally riding a desk until he was cleared psychologically.

But some days—even in the late-summer heat—Fisk still found himself shivering.

"Thank you," said Link to the barmaid, who winked and hustled away to the next customer. Link held his credit card to his nose for a moment before returning it to his wallet. "Ambrosia," he said, with a sigh. Then he ribbed Fisk with his elbow. "Kidding. Sweat and maybe moisturizer. I've never been jealous of a credit card before."

Fisk drank the top inch or more of his Peroni,

the Italian beer a nice change of pace after the Jack Daniel's. "This is the longest sales pitch in history," he said to Link.

Link shook his head, drinking his own beer, unoffended. "Not a pitch at all. Just an offer. And this isn't just me, this is a bunch of guys, we think we can pull this off. We like your style, Fisk. We know you've been through hell. We're doing this for you."

Fisk was skeptical. "Who do I have to kill?" he said.

Link laughed, nodding. "Kill another swig of that beer, and I'll tell you."

Fisk did as he was told.

"Jenssen moves to Florence, Colorado, in two days. He'll be in the supermax there, total isolation, a deep, dark hole from which he will never emerge. Nor will anyone except maybe his lawyer be able to reach him."

"And?"

"Tomorrow night, there's a window of time. Maybe as much as an hour. We can put you together with him. One on one."

Fisk felt icy needles enter his chest—even as he was trying to figure out this guy's game.

Link added hastily, "I'm not talking anything physical. You want to kick his ass, you're shit out of luck. Can't make that happen. But we can do this. The marshals are on board. Jenssen would have no warning."

Fisk snuck a look at his hands. No shaking.

Link said, "'Closure' is such a bullshit word. You're never gonna get that. This guy took your lady. Even if you did take him out—fantasy talk here—as good as that might feel in the moment, it gets you nothing. But sitting before him, eye to eye . . . with no pretenses. No cameras. No judge to play to. Nowhere for him to hide. Sit with him as you sit here with me."

Fisk was shaking his head.

"Don't say no yet."

"No," said Fisk. "You just said, it gets me nothing. Nothing."

"I think what it gets you is up to you."

Fisk put his hand around his cold glass of beer, but did not drink from it. "And? What's it get you?"

"So suspicious," said Link, taking a drink. "I'm being up front about wanting to do this for you. Will we be listening? You can assume we will." Link gave a cursory glance around the immediate area for eavesdroppers. "Jenssen is a very disciplined guy. But he's also a braggart. Big ego. And it was kind of *mano a mano* between you two. You kicked his Swedish ass. Took him apart like a chest of drawers from Ikea. So, sure, Jenssen could be off his game here, knowing the future he's facing. His last chance to bark and be heard. Maybe he's holding something big back? Maybe it slips? Maybe it's a name, or some little detail? Maybe it's nothing. Maybe we do you this solid for exactly the reason I'm giving you. Because you earned it." Link knocked once on the table. "Catharsis, man."

Fisk just wanted to finish his beer and get out of there now. "No," he said. "Appreciate the offer."

Fisk walked ten blocks with his phone in his hand. He had Dr. Flaherty's number, or at least her answering service. She had told him many times to call if ever he needed counseling, and he had never taken her up on it, never even come close. This didn't feel like a crisis necessarily, but at least something he should raise with her.

Did I do the right thing?

But hitting Send, connecting that call, was a line he was loath to cross. And why did he need her to tell him what was right and what was not? And she wouldn't decide that for him anyway, she would insist that he answer his own question, which was what he was doing right now.

What would you hope to gain from sitting with Jenssen?

So the therapy had indeed been a success: Dr. Flaherty had taken up residence inside his own head.

So had the booze. What was he really doing here? He was calling her to tell her what he had done. He was calling to say, I am fine. I did the right thing.

He was calling for her approval. He was acting for the therapist in his head. He was doing what he thought she would want him to do, what he thought would please her.

Fisk stopped in the middle of crossing the street.

What would please Krina Gersten?

Hers was the only voice he needed to satisfy.

The voice Jenssen had silenced.

The car horns came into his consciousness only gradually. Drivers yelling at him to get out of the way, calling him a drunk.

He was not drunk. He reached the curb and looked at his hand, the one holding the phone.

The phone screen was still and readable.

His hand was not trembling. His mind was clear.

He knew what he was going to do.

He dug into his pocket for Link's card, cleared Dr. Flaherty's number, and started dialing.

Nacimiento de los Negros meant *Birthplace of Darkness*. "One hell of a name for a village," said MacClesh.

The little town was situated several miles off State Road 20, a loop of empty highway circling around a desolate upwelling of mountains that had no name on Cecilia Garza's map. It was a road that led, in essence, to nowhere—the country dry, stony, empty.

"You're too poetic," said Cecilia Garza, seated next to him. "The village was founded by a group of escaped slaves from the United States. They came here about one hundred and fifty years ago. The people here still consider themselves to be black."

Four Policía Federal vehicles pulled into the center of the town, stopping in a cloud of dust. Everyone piled out. The center of town—such as it was—consisted of a few open-air stores, a stucco church, and several acres of packed, weedy dirt surrounding a statue of the Virgin. The pedestal on which the Virgin stood was badly cracked and canted forward a little, so that even the Virgin looked as though she were preparing to break into a run.

Two dozen people in the streets surrounding the square all stopped. Men wearing cowboy hats and boots, women carrying string bags full of dried beans and rice and meat wrapped in bleeding butcher's paper. They all stared apprehensively. But unlike the Virgin, they showed no impulse to flee.

Garza watched MacClesh walk around the square, his thumbs in his belt. He sized up each of the citizens, then approached perhaps the oldest man, hatless, his skin darkened by the sun. He had a weather-beaten face, curly hair, and what at first looked like a sizable facial tumor but was in fact a large plug of chewing tobacco lodged inside his left cheek.

MacClesh looked at the old man. "Those are some very fine boots, señor."

The old man looked down at them as though he didn't realize he had them on.

MacClesh said, "I am ashamed to compare them to my own."

MacClesh showed him his—and the old man flinched, as though he thought he was about to be kicked.

MacClesh smiled at the old man. He stepped closer to him—almost close enough to touch his forehead with the brim of his hat.

"You know why we're here," said MacClesh.

The old man spit tobacco juice on the ground between the toes of his fine boots, but did not answer.

MacClesh smiled again, then stepped back. This left enough room between them for another of Garza's men to step up and punch the old man in the stomach.

It wasn't a hard punch, out of respect for the

man's age. But it was more than enough to double him over.

The old man dropped to his knees, bending forward until his forehead touched the dusty ground.

Garza preferred to let her men operate without her direct instructions. She did not like to be the mother hen. Nor did she care for their predilection toward casual violence. But it was a part of the macho culture of the PF, and Garza had to be judicious about interfering with it. So when she stepped in here, she did so not with the appearance of ending the violence, but of capitalizing on it.

"Pick him up," she said.

Two men grabbed him, one at each armpit, and hoisted him to his feet. His face was empty, though he was gasping for breath. The lump in his cheek was gone. A string of amber saliva stretched across his dark chin, in contrast to the powdery oval of white dust on his forehead.

The brown plug of tobacco lay in the dirt. Next to it, a device that had fallen out of the old man's pocket. It was a cell phone.

"His phone, please," said Garza.

Garza stood before the man. She did not smile, she did not play the "good cop." She did not indulge any of her femininity. She was not soft. This was about finding and stopping a violent murderer.

One of her men placed the old man's phone into Garza's hand.

"There are no secrets in this world, señor," she said to the old man.

The old man's eyes, damp from the force of the punch, looked off toward the Virgin.

"There are satellites in the sky, airplanes with cameras, helicopters, radar. Even these . . ." She waggled the man's cell phone in the air in front of his face. She brushed off the whitish dust. It was the latest model, immaculate, much nicer than the phone she carried. "We track the radio waves that come out of them. You, me, Major MacClesh—all of us—we have American machines that tell our exact locations right down to the millimeter."

The old man looked mutely at the phone as though he had never seen one before.

"Please take no offense when I say this," Garza said. "But your town . . . it is a miserable shithole."

The old man grunted. He agreed with her.

"And yet, look!" She pointed to the one modern feature of the village, just visible past the steeple of the church: a huge galvanized steel tower that loomed over the town. "Your village has its very own cell tower. And a simple farmer such as yourself has the very latest phone in his pocket. And those trucks parked over there by those stores? Very nice trucks. Even my men can't afford such nice trucks."

The old man shifted from one boot to the other, looked sadly at his plug of tobacco staining the ground in front of him.

"What do you grow on your farm?" Garza inquired. "These phones? Those boots?" She stepped back, taking in the old man's boots, smiling brightly. "Here we are in the very birthplace of darkness, at the ass end of the earth. And a simple farmer—and I mean no disrespect—but a simple farmer walks the town wearing beautiful new boots." Garza made a long, slow sweep of the town with her arm. "Señor, I see no factories here. I see no mines. I see no groves of fruit trees. In fact, I must tell you, the fields as we were driving into this town . . . they did not seem well tended. Not at all."

The old man wiped at the saliva on his chin, trying to clear it off but instead smearing it more deeply into the hard lines etched in his face. If Garza hadn't known better, she might have thought the tobacco juice was blood.

Garza sighed. "We can play this game as long as you like, señor," she said. "I can talk about this and that, this and that, this and that. And you can stand there pretending you don't hear me. But in the end I'll get what I came here for. We both know that. Don't we, señor? Nod if you understand me."

The old man sighed, tremulously.

"Please. Señor. Do me this simple courtesy. A nod. Or else my men . . ."

The old man nodded. Almost imperceptibly.

"Yes," said Garza, "the good times are about to come to an end for this town. You know his name, señor. I'm certain you know where he lives."

The old man had stopped looking at his feet. Now he was looking intently at her.

"I can't," he said.

"But you must," she said, moving closer—so close that she could smell the tobacco on his breath. "All you have to do is whisper it."

Still no response.

"My men can go over there and take all those trucks. Major MacClesh can make a phone call and we can bring a bulldozer and knock over every house in the village. Even the church."

That made the old man's eyes twitch.

"The beautiful Virgin. We can box her up and carry her away. Perhaps to a town where they care enough for her to put her on a decent pedestal, even if they cannot afford phones, boots, and trucks."

She leaned her head toward him. His lower lip was trembling and his eyes were wet as though he were about to break down and cry. "Please, Doña Garza! Don't make me say it."

Secretly, she was pleased that her reputation had reached all the way to this miserable and desolate place. But she didn't let her face show it.

The Suburban bounced along the rutted dirt track. It was a dry, barren country, the high desert of northern Mexico. Every rock, every blanched sage plant and twisted mesquite tree, every dusty scrap of ground seemed to have been punished by the sun, cooked into submission. The thermometer on the dash of the Suburban said it was 114 degrees Fahrenheit. This was a place where human beings were not meant to live.

Even a killer like Chuparosa.

She was close, very close. According to the old man from the village, Chuparosa kept a hacienda tucked away in the mountains, an opulent mansion situated in a remote canyon. He claimed that Chuparosa had been born in Nacimiento de los Negros, and so this had been his refuge ever since, here in this place where no one ever came.

Unlike most Mexican gangsters, Chuparosa had never been arrested, never spent time in prison, never been fingerprinted or put in a lineup, never even had his mug shot taken. As far as law enforcement was considered, he was a ghost. There were people in the Interior Ministry's Centro de Investigación y Seguridad Nacional (Center of National Security and Investigation, the interior Mexican intelligence agency), who thought Garza was a fool. They believed that Chuparosa was a shadow criminal, a horror story created by one cartel to intimidate another.

But Garza had followed his trail—the strange divots in the ground, the headless corpses, the hummingbirds carved in a fencepost, spray-painted on a door, carved into skin. She had always known he was real. The reason was that she had seen the very same hand in each of the tiny hummingbird portraits. In truth, she had felt jealousy the first time she had seen the economy, the grace in every line, the thing that her own labored art had attempted yet never achieved.

Now she had a real name: Soto. Chuparosa had grown up under the thumb of a domineering uncle with the same last name, an exceptionally cruel man, a drinker. The uncle's memory was so damaged by years of bad mescal, he had called the boy by a host of first names—Jorge, Juan, Jose—none of which ever stuck. And so the boy's actual first name was lost to history.

Soto had been a quiet boy, said the old man, with only one interest: baseball. It was his uncle's interest as well, and so the man would hit grounders to the boy for hours after work, until the uncle passed out. He would beat the boy's shoulders black and blue if he failed to charge a ball with sufficient vigor.

At ten, Soto dropped out of school to assist his uncle in the fields. Allegedly, he had played several years as a shortstop in the Mexican baseball league, a couple of years at Tabasco, a season at Quintana Roo. She would have to confirm this.

At some point, evidently, his baseball career gave way to a career with *los hombres malos*. By Garza's back-of-the-envelope tabulation, Chuparosa was personally responsible for at least two hundred murders.

MacClesh alerted her that they were close. The Suburban slowed down at the crest of a hill.

Commanding the heights over a small, dry valley was a high compound, a fortress, ringed by an ancient wall. The wall predated anything Chuparosa could have constructed, perhaps by a century. It was the remnant of some kind of old fortification— maybe even from the time of the war with the United States back in 1848.

The high guard tower that loomed over the arched entrance of the fort appeared to be unmanned.

Garza stepped out of the vehicle with MacClesh. She raised a pair of binoculars.

"What do you think?" she asked.

"I don't like it," said MacClesh. "They probably got snipers on the walls. I think we need to wait on air support."

She stood very still, watching for any movement through her glasses. Did Chuparosa know they were coming?

"No," she said. "That's a three-hour wait, minimum." They had left officers back at the town center to make certain that no one tried to warn the town's number-one benefactor. But the news would only hold for so long. And Garza had little time left before she had to return to Mexico City. She never wanted to move in haste. But here she felt she had no choice.

"We have to go in on foot," Garza said.

MacClesh surveyed the area with his own binoculars. "Maybe if we circle around the back side of the mountain to the east . . . we could scale whatever rocky inferno lies out of view back there, then cross over to that promontory that has a higher sight line over this fortress."

Garza saw the same thing through the shimmering heat, and agreed with his assessment. "We'll have clear lines of fire right down into the compound. But . . ."

MacClesh lowered his glasses. "Yes?"

"It's a hundred and fourteen degrees. Black clothes, helmets, ballistic vests . . . we'll be carrying men back down the hill because they can't walk any farther."

"I agree, Comandante."

Garza went on. "I can think of two reasons for the apparent stillness of the compound. One, he is unaware of our approach. Or two—"

"He is avidly aware of our approach."

"I want to ride in directly," said Garza.

MacClesh nodded, but he was thinking, she could see that.

"I will go to the promontory alone," he said. "We cannot go in blind."

Garza was too anxious. She knew this without MacClesh having to tell her. He was right.

"We will both go," she said.

IN A WAY, the chauvinism of the men in her unit provoked her into being so tough. They had created her reputation as much as she had.

MacClesh was huffing by the end of it. The climb was more treacherous than it had appeared. It wasn't a cliff, exactly . . . but it was close. The rock was so hot from the sun that Garza felt her soles—good boots, American made—softening. She had no gloves, and her fingers were blistering on the blazing rock.

It was too much time to think. Chuparosa was anything but careless. Perhaps he had—by giving the mayor of Nuevo Laredo a phone number that led straight to Nacimiento de los Negros—been hoping to provoke a fight? Was this to be an ambush? Was his goal to destroy the famous Unit 9 in order to further demonstrate his power to the world?

Eventually they made it, crouching behind a jagged line of rock that constituted the ridge at the summit of the small mountain. Garza drained the last of the water from the bladder of her CamelBak, while MacClesh took out his binoculars.

They were roughly two hundred yards away—close enough for a trained sniper to pick them off if exposed. And the Zetas, with their military background, were full of men who knew how to use a gun.

MacClesh slowly scanned the compound from behind the rock. When he turned back to Garza, his dark, craggy features showed nothing.

Garza looked. The old fort was about two hundred yards wide and maybe half as long. In the center were the foundations of some ruined building. Next to them stood a huge house of tasteful modern design, with expansive glass windows, broad decks, and patios. Surrounding the house was a small patch of lushly planted earth, featuring beautifully maintained bushes, fruit trees, and beds of flowers. A huge pool lay behind the house next to several plain adobe outbuildings.

"My god," she said, amazed at the existence of his oasis in the desert. Such beauty required water to be trucked in every day—probably from at least fifty miles away. The expense in water alone must have been enormous. Every bush and every plant in the garden was in full flower. Hothouse plants, she supposed, trucked in and replanted, then pulled up and discarded as soon as the flowers began to fade. How many gardeners did it take to keep it like this? Ten? Fifteen?

But there was no evidence of gardeners—or anyone else, for that matter—in the compound.

Then she began to see them. Dark lumps scattered here and there.

"Madre de Dios," she said.

"Indeed," MacClesh said. "Shall we go down, Comandante?"

"Right away."

THE RUN TO THE small dirt track that circled the fort took less than half a minute.

The gate was closed and locked. It was constructed of two-centimeter steel plate. A ribbon of Semtex made short work of it, blowing a jagged-edged rectangular hole out of the gate.

Before the dust settled, and as the hollow boom was reverberating back and forth between the sheer sides of the valley, the line of men entered the compound.

"Clear right!"

"Clear left!"

"Cover!"

"Moving!"

The men gradually hopscotched across the dry ground, covering each other as they moved from one position of cover to another. Garza waited at the gate with MacClesh.

The silence was deafening. It was over in a minute or two. There was no gunfire, no opposition.

After what Garza had seen through MacClesh's binoculars, none was expected.

Her radio crackled finally. "All clear, Comandante."

Garza stepped through the hole in the gate and strode across the open ground toward her men, who stood in a ring around the house.

As she neared them, she heard a soft buzzing sound. For a moment it puzzled her. But then she recognized it.

Flies.

There were more than twenty bodies on the ground, scattered seemingly randomly around the property. They had all been shot in the back of the head.

And they weren't gangsters. None of them had tattoos, and none of them appeared to carry guns.

Three were women wearing maid's uniforms. Several carried gardening tools on their belts.

One was a boy no more than eleven or twelve years old.

It was immediately clear that somebody had killed all the people who worked for Chuparosa.

The blood spatter pattern told Garza that none had been moved. Blood and brain matter were splashed in front of each of them. They had died where they lay.

The most striking thing was that all the blood spatter radiated out from the villa at the center of the compound. The dead lay all around the building, 360 degrees.

This told her that they had not been shot by intruders. Indeed, the gates had been locked.

These people had been murdered by someone inside the house.

MacClesh came out of the house. "There's brass on all of the patios," he said, holding up a bottle-necked brass bullet casing. "Military rounds. Four shooters armed with SCAR-Hs."

Garza knew that these rifles that had been proposed as a replacement for the American M4 carbine used by the U.S. Army. They were much desired among the criminal element in Mexico, but still very hard to get hold of, very expensive. Even the U.S. Army didn't have many of them yet.

"Four shooters?" she said. "How do you know?"

"Because they are dead also. Someone executed them, too. There was one shooter lying on each corner of the house. SCARs lying on the decks next to them. Expensive weapons, left behind. We'll know all the details once we run all the ballistics."

Garza looked up at the sky. None of this made sense. But instinctively she knew that, whatever terrible and puzzling thing had happened here, Chuparosa would not be among the dead.

He had done this. Ordered the shooters to wipe

out his people—his cooks, gardeners, maids—and then executed the shooters.

"When do you think these people were shot, Major?"

"All the blood's dried out in the sun. Flies have had time to gather. Five, six hours, maybe?"

This confirmed what Garza suspected. She got on her radio immediately. "I want everyone to exercise extreme caution. There may be booby traps here."

She felt a pang of anger. She had truly thought she had a shot at finding Chuparosa today.

A call from the main house broke into her thoughts. "Major! Comandante! I think you need to see this!"

THE INTERIOR OF CHUPAROSA'S house was startlingly beautiful.

Most of the gangsters' houses Cecilia Garza had seen were expensively acquitted, but sad and seedy. Especially the few larger mansions she'd been inside, owned by cartel higher-ups, which were without exception gauche and hideous—full of huge mirrors, gold furniture, self-portraits, expensive nudes, and paintings of tigers and Ferraris.

But this place had an austere beauty. It was immediately clear that someone had collected every item in the house with care. And with an artistic eye. Which made it all the more bewildering that they had—apparently—left it all behind.

Had she chased out Chuparosa? Or had flight been his plan all along?

The decorative theme was Mexican. A small

Toltec carving here, a Mayan mask there. But there was the strong sense of a very particular personality here, unlike some houses of the newly rich, which felt as though they'd been bought by the yard from a bad interior decorator.

In a large vase on the long, spare kitchen table stood a single orchid blossom.

Leaning against it was a small, folded card on heavy stock. On the face was written "Comandante Garza."

"Shit," she said.

The inside of the card was blank.

MacClesh made certain his men went first, in the event Chuparosa had any surprises in store for her. Garza followed the PF officers up the stairs and down a long hallway lined with what must have been family photographs. She felt something unusual from them: protectiveness. It went beyond their jobs. They construed the card as a threat, and for the first time she felt a true concern for her well-being from her men.

"In here," the officer said, pointing to a set of double doors leading into the master bedroom.

She walked inside. The bedroom was large, without seeming silly or pretentious. A giant canvas covered the far wall, and while Garza did not recognize the artist, she indeed recognized its quality.

"Here," the officer said.

On the floor near the bed lay a boy of maybe fourteen or fifteen. Barely even old enough to shave, curled into the fetal position.

He had been shot execution style in the back of

the head. His blood had splashed across the neatly folded covers of the bed before he fell.

MacClesh went around to look at the boy's face. "We passed a photo of this young man, hanging on the wall. He must be related to Chuparosa." The major cleared his throat. He had a grandson near this age. "Who do you think did this?" he asked Garza. "Who could be this angry at Chuparosa?"

Garza shook her head, surprised by MacClesh's shortsightedness. "Major, this is him. He did this. Chuparosa."

MacClesh looked at the boy once again. Now he understood. "Because of the survivor. This boy failed him."

"The man murdered his own blood. Probably right as they were getting ready to leave."

MacClesh was shaking his head. Not in disagreement. In disgust.

Garza said, "He was sanitizing his trail, Major. Erasing his past. What for? That is the question."

MacClesh shook his head again—though this time, he was angry. "What kind of madman . . . ?"

"An artist," Garza said.

MacClesh's eyes narrowed, blazing with anger at her. "You cannot be serious."

"Sometimes an artist has to wipe the slate clean before he can move on to a new period, a new style, a new . . ." She ran out of words for a moment, thinking back to her own artistic crisis when she'd been in college. She had wrestled for several years over whether to be an artist—and not a very good one—or to pursue law, something she found dry and uninteresting. From the vantage point of her present existence, it seemed like a foolish little adolescent crisis now. But at the time, she had been racked with turmoil.

Only the abduction of her sister and her mother had brought clarity—had indeed chosen her path for her.

"Once you exhaust the seam," she told MacClesh, "you have to move on."

Major MacClesh stared at her without comprehension, his eyes still ablaze with rage. Not at her: at Chuparosa. "You speak of him with respect," he said. "I cannot. These were his own people, Comandante! Not his enemies. His people! His blood." MacClesh got hold of himself then, moving to the door. "When we find him, Comandante, he will not stand trial. I promise you that."

Garza had never seen MacClesh so embittered. She said nothing, allowing his threat to hover in the air like the flies. He turned and walked out of the room, his shoulders tight.

"Comandante, over here."

Garza walked over to a drawing desk by an open window. The sketches, if there were any, had been taken. All that remained among the charcoal pencils was a single piece of paper.

It took Garza a moment to figure out what she was looking at. Once she did, she carried it out of the bedroom and through the house, looking for MacClesh.

She found him outside, standing near a pear tree that stood at the edge of the lush greenery of Chuparosa's garden. The sun was an orange ball now, just starting to hide behind the dry black teeth of the mountains.

The pear tree was alive with rapidly darting shapes, glinting in the last orange light of the desert sun. Hummingbirds.

She showed him what they had found. It was a printout of an article from *Reforma*, the big newspaper in Mexico City. A story about President-Elect Umberto Vargas.

Drawn in red over the accompanying photograph was a small design: a picture of a hummingbird, scrawled across the president-elect's face.

By Chuparosa's own fingertip, no doubt. Using the blood of his own nephew.

"He's going after Vargas," said Garza.

The highest-security wing of the Metropolitan Correctional Center of New York is on the tenth floor of the Foley Square building, just across from the federal courthouse.

Ten South, as it is known, has been home to many notorious criminals with New York ties. Mafia bosses such as John Gotti have called it home. Infamous Ponzi-schemer Bernard Madoff traded in his seven-million-dollar East Side penthouse for a tenth-floor bunk there. Bloodthirsty terrorists such as Sheik Omar Abdel Rahman and 1993 World Trade Center bomber Ramzi Yousef resided in Ten South while awaiting their trials.

Ten South's windows are blacked out, but the lights shine inside twenty-four hours each day. There is no interaction between guards and prisoners, and meals—the law mandates that prisoners be fed twenty-five hundred calories each day, for which the state budget allocates $2.45 per prisoner—are served through a narrow slit in a stainless steel door.

Fisk entered the building through an underground tunnel from the courthouse. He moved slowly from secure area to secure area, and in the midst of his rise to the tenth floor he realized why: security cameras had to be turned off at every stop along the way. He had left his mobile phone at home, where he had been picked up by Dave Link. There would be no electronic record of his visit with Magnus Jenssen.

"You bring anything for me?" asked Link, as they waited to enter Ten South. He was referring to the small cardboard box in Fisk's hand, folded similarly to a carton of takeout Chinese food.

Fisk did not answer. He wore his best suit, a dark, three-button Canali; he had given his appearance perhaps too much thought. He wanted to make a lasting impression on Jenssen. Because of the physical restrictions imposed upon him, he wanted to maximize this visit's psychological impact.

"I can trust you, right?" said Link. "I mean, something like an open-hand slap isn't going to matter, but no marks, no bruises, no nothing. In other words, there won't be any telephone books in the interrogation room."

Fisk nodded.

"We'll be watching and listening. Don't make us come in there."

Fisk nodded again. This felt like a prefight talk between a trainer and a boxer.

Link continued, "This is not a regular interrogation room. There is no window or mirror. In case you're curious, we're in the crown molding running around the top of the walls. It's molded to the wallboard so that prisoners can't pry it off and stab you to death with it. It's all prefab with access holes for installing sensors, microphones, cameras, the usual. All that is going to be erased after you're through. No, you don't get a copy."

Link was smiling. Fisk was not.

Link said again, "Fisk, you're worrying me here. I'm not making a mistake doing this, am I?"

"It's fine," said Fisk, his voice distant even to himself. "No worries. Let's get this over with."

THE HEAVY METAL TABLE was bolted to the far wall. Two chairs were set on either side of it.

One chair was empty. The other one held a man, hooded and shackled.

The white hood turned as the door lock clicked behind Fisk. The prisoner was listening.

Fisk stared at him. Waiting for Jenssen to speak.

He did not.

Jenssen wore an orange jumpsuit and plastic flip-flops. His ankles were shackled tight to the legs of his chair. His wrists were shackled together, but at Fisk's request his arms remained in front of him, chained to the chair back behind him. Just long enough to reach onto the table, though his empty hands rested in his lap now.

Fisk walked toward his chair. The hooded head tracked him until Fisk was opposite Jenssen, the hood facing forward.

Fisk placed the carton in the exact center of the table, equidistant to both of them. He pulled out his chair and sat.

He did not remove the hood at first. He let Jenssen bake in silence.

He watched the little patch of hood get sucked in

and out on Jenssen's foul breath. He wanted to hit him so hard. He wanted to shatter teeth.

Link wouldn't be able to get inside fast enough to stop that.

After some amount of time—one minute or ten, because everything had slowed down for Fisk—he reached across and slowly pulled the hood from the prisoner's head.

The blond hair was short, as he had seen it in court. So was the beard Jenssen wore now. He wore a white knit skullcap. His face had lost the health it once had: Jenssen was a marathon runner and fitness buff. Now he had to make do with sixty minutes a day outside his eight-by-eight cell in an "exercise" room that was entirely empty and nicknamed "the rat cage."

But his blue eyes still burned bright. Brighter now as he recognized the man across from him.

Jenssen brought up his shackled hands to rub his blond beard. He smiled, and Fisk briefly entertained a fantasy of grabbing Jenssen across the table and strangling him to death with his own handcuffs.

"Jeremy Fisk," said Jenssen.

The smile held, trying to come off as superior, but behind it was concern, even worry. Fisk could see that. Jenssen was utterly vulnerable here.

So Fisk just looked at him. Jenssen stared back for a while, then bailed out on the staring contest as though it were beneath him. But he was nervous. Fisk watched his throat work as he swallowed saliva three times in quick succession.

Jenssen looked at the carton in the center of the table. He was surprised and intrigued, wary.

"You brought me some dinner," said Jenssen.

It was supposed to come off as bravado, but when Fisk did not respond, the words hung in the air like a foul odor.

"I was disappointed that they could find no role for you in that courtroom farce," Jenssen said. His Swedish accent was recognizable, but like most educated Scandinavians, his English was better than that of a great many Americans.

Fisk was regretting coming here. He thought about standing and walking out now, and leaving it at that. Putting the hood back on Jenssen and walking away from him forever was a very attractive option. His one goal was to allow Jenssen no satisfaction whatsoever.

But he was here, and he stayed. He let his eyes drop once to the carton.

Jenssen said, "Ah. A prop. Bravo. I'm supposed to inquire about it? Fixate on it somehow? We're to go back and forth about it? And then you'll never reveal what is inside. And that is supposed to haunt me for the rest of my days."

Fisk reached out and unfolded the top of the carton. He peeled back the flaps and lifted out the small white foil-lined bakery-style bag inside. He opened that and pulled out a cupcake.

He set the cupcake, nestled in its ridged foil baking cup, on the table. The cake was yellow, the frosting mocha.

"Dessert?" said Jenssen. But he was truly mystified. He regarded the cupcake as though it contained a bomb.

Fisk said, "You don't have cupcakes in Sweden?"

Jenssen could not figure out Fisk's game. "No, this we don't have in Sweden." He studied the dessert treat. He could smell the coffee and chocolate scent of the frosting.

Fisk said, "I made this myself."

"For me?" said Jenssen.

Fisk said nothing.

Jenssen sat back a bit, trying to assume control over the conversation. "I presume this little culinary presentation has some didactic purpose?"

"I don't know what that means."

"Don't play stupid. It offends me. Was I caught by a stupid man? I don't think so."

Fisk said nothing.

Jenssen continued, "I read the articles about you. I know you speak five languages. And I killed your girlfriend with my bare hands." Jenssen cocked his head a bit. "You did not come here to bring me sweets as a peace offering. So? By all means. Instruct away. Teach me your pious little lesson."

Fisk shook his head, as though Jenssen had just proved his point. "See, that's the thing. There's no ulterior motive here. No lesson, really. It's just a cupcake. Something for you to contemplate."

Jenssen stared at it. His eyes were shining. He was engaged. "You have poisoned it, and need to trick me into eating it."

Fisk smiled.

"No? You certainly hate me enough."

"Why would I want to release you from the years of deprivation awaiting you in prison?"

"Because of the satisfaction you would receive from the sight of me dying before you."

"That would be your final triumph, wouldn't it?"

"I don't follow you, Detective."

"If I did something to cause your death, and then ended up spending my life in jail for it? I'd really be giving you the last laugh then, wouldn't I?"

Jenssen eyed the cupcake again, this time with undisguised loathing. "You made this thing?" he said. "This glob of unhealthy garbage? In one small package, you have managed to encapsulate everything I hate about your world."

"Dessert?"

"Your compulsion to appeal only to animal appetites. To disgrace your bodies with this filth."

"Lighten up, Jenssen. You're eating healthy in here? It's not going to get any better in the penitentiary. Poor nutrition is just another circle of hell for you."

Fisk reached out, pushing the cupcake toward Jenssen.

"This is the last treat you'll ever be offered. You can eat it, or not. See, I haven't sat around thinking about you. I've been busy."

"So my lawyer told me. But do you think those two crossing the Canadian border are the end of it?"

"Of hatred disguised as a holy war?"

"The ground is crumbling away beneath your feet and you can't even feel the tremors. Your failing is the same as your entire society's. You have no real beliefs. And so you lack will."

Fisk held up one hand. "Don't waste your time with this."

"I know your type," said Jenssen. "Remote. Superior. So you came here to gloat. To visit me in my cage. Knowing you are safe. You have every advantage. You can afford to be magnanimous and patronizing. It makes you feel powerful, doesn't it? Like a winner. Like an American."

Magnus Jenssen would never give Fisk an inch. He was a highly disciplined man going to seed, but he would not crack. Fisk had zero interest in sparring with him, allowing Jenssen to spin out his tired brand of Islamic fundamentalism to justify what he felt in his own rotten little heart.

"The problem," Jenssen continued, "is that I, too, know I am safe. This is why your country is so vulnerable to jihad, because it cannot and will not respond to blood with blood. Thanks to your outdated Constitution and your Byzantine system of justice. What is a jury trial now but a television entertainment show? I do not fear you, Detective. As you yourself said, in wounding, maiming, or even killing me, you would only be harming yourself. I have nothing else to lose. You have everything."

"You are correct and wrong at the same time," said Fisk. "I could certainly kill you right now. With ease. But where is the sport in that? What you see as weakness—my forbearance—is in fact a sign of strength. But you can't know that, because you can only function in terms of revenge, of lashing out, of punishment. I could kill you where you sit right now. Instead I bring you a cupcake."

Jenssen laughed at Fisk.

Fisk nodded to it. "This cupcake is a symbol of your fear, Jenssen. You can trust no one and nothing any longer. You are completely at the mercy of others. Think about what it took for me to get in

here right now. No one else will ever know of this
visit. It is one hundred percent deniable. I want you
to talk about it. Talk all you want. No one will believe you. And yet . . . here I sit. Within a second's
reach of your throat. If I can make this happen, I
can make just about anything work. You can expect
the rest of your days to be a living hell. Knowing
that, anytime I want, I can reach into that hole and
get you. Perhaps you'll come to desire it. To hope
for me to come and end it all for you, to release you
from this curse. Paranoid fear is going to eat away
at you like a cancer. For the very reason you do not
dare to taste even a crumb of this cupcake."

Jenssen sat forward, eyes blazing. "You are wrong,
Fisk. I have a strength. Allah gives me strength
beyond all this." He waved his manacled hands in a
circle, as wide as his chains allowed. "Beyond your
laws, these chains, your reach. Do you know what
the *ummah* is?"

In his excitement, Jenssen had apparently forgotten that Fisk had spent the past five years in
antiterrorism, or that his mother was from Lebanon.

"The body of the faithful," said Fisk.

The surprise of him answering threw Jenssen for
a moment. "The people of the Word. Those who
follow Allah. Inside the body of the faithful, the
people who truly believe in Allah and follow him,
there can be no strife. Inside the *ummah* is the Dar
al Islam—the House of Peace. Outside—where you
live, among the godless and faithless—is the Dar
al Harb. The House of War. I welcome prison as a
retreat from this world. My actions are a reflection,
not of the nature of Allah, but of this world of filth

in which you live. It is the ooze in which you crawl, the slime you eat. I am not these things. I am just a messenger. A holy messenger. Holding a mirror up to you. Showing you your own true face." His eyes shone with self-righteousness. "When the roll is taken at the end of time, it will be clear that you and your girlfriend Gersten were infidels fighting on the side of evil, destruction, perversion, and corruption. And I was fighting on the side of good."

Jenssen realized he had become carried away, and reacted as though Fisk had gotten him to reveal something of himself that he did not wish to be seen. For a moment, the ugliness that was inside Jenssen almost clawed its way out, wearing its usual vestments of religious fervor.

He made his body relax now, and he smiled again.

"So you eat the cupcake, Detective," he said. "You put that shit in you. I am pure."

Fisk's body felt almost as though it was vibrating, like he was running a low-voltage charge through his entire nervous system.

"You see," said Fisk, "in spite of everything you did and tried to do, I have not lost the capacity to enjoy life. Not that that was your goal, only your hope. Yes, to be certain—your life in prison is inestimably preferable to mine. Please keep telling yourself that until you choke on the words. And now I will eat this cupcake in front of you, but I will imagine that it is your heart, condemned to an eternity of fear."

Fisk reached for the small cupcake—and suddenly Jenssen's hands shot out to the length of their chains, seizing the cupcake and mashing it into his mouth.

It was a supremely violent act. Jenssen stared at him, fire eyed, making quick work of the dessert.

Fisk sat back in his chair, watching him.

Jenssen swallowed the cupcake with less bravado than he had when he began eating it. Fisk's manner put him off.

Fisk said, "I thought so."

Jenssen rallied. "You are weak, Detective Fisk. America is weak! Your government, your people . . . You will never prevail. We will consume you."

Fisk waited until he had been quiet for a while. "You've got some frosting right there," he said, touching his own chin.

Jenssen glared at Fisk until uncertainty crept into his gaze. Eventually he reached up and brushed the frosting away roughly.

Fisk reached across the table suddenly—as though to grab Jenssen by the throat.

The terrorist jerked back in his chair.

Fisk's reach stopped at the empty baker's foil cup on the table, crumpling it in his hand, swiping the crumbs into the carton.

"You flinched," said Fisk.

Jenssen trembled, as if about to explode with anger. Fisk's eyes remained unwaveringly on Jenssen's face as he retrieved the cloth hood and pulled it down over Jenssen's head.

He paused a moment, lowering his head to Jenssen's ear.

"Have fun dying in prison," said Fisk.

BOOK TWO

Fisk spent most of his morning in the Midtown North precinct, because one of the diplomats from Ghana had spent most of his night there.

United Nations Week wasn't supposed to be like the navy's Fleet Week, but for some a short week in the capital of the world was like a Las Vegas convention. The man from Ghana had hired a prostitute who visited him at his room in the Millennium Broadway Hotel. The police only became involved when the escort called them, after Mr. Ghana neglected to come up with the entire agreed-upon fee. There was a currency problem as well as a language problem and a bit of a vodka problem, and then apparently a cultural misunderstanding, and Mr. Ghana wound up in a pair of dirty bracelets, necessitating a six-hour sojourn in Midtown North.

The working girl was let go with a warning, but never recompensed the remaining two hundred dollars she was owed.

Fisk caught the guy's ticket after a flurry of phone calls and drove over to pick up Mr. Ghana. Only problem was, Mr. Ghana's shoes had gone missing. They had his belt, his wallet, and his passport, but no loafers. Chasing those down ate up another forty minutes of Fisk's time. The only upside was that, once he got his shoes back, Mr. Ghana was all smiles and very happy to be chauffeured directly to his consulate on East Forty-seventh Street.

Fisk finally returned to Intel headquarters in Brooklyn—a shabby-looking, unmarked, one-story brick building on a block of auto junkyards and warehouses—just in time for a call about a suspicious car parked outside the Chinese consulate over on the West Side. This dustup was solved with two phone calls: as Fisk suspected, it was the host nation's own federal police force, the FBI, clumsily keeping tabs on the Chinese envoy in a gray Dodge Avenger.

"Your guys might want to move farther down the street," said Fisk, on the phone with the FBI field office at Federal Plaza, rubbing it in a little.

In late August, the same week Jenssen's verdict was read, Fisk's boss, Barry Dubin, had called him into his office.

The Intel chief was a bald egghead with an impeccably groomed goatee that hung on his face like a soft silver pennant. Ever since his divorce, Dubin wore his chunky Fordham class ring on his ring finger, which Fisk never understood. Maybe he hadn't been able to give up his habit of twirling something on the fourth finger of his left hand.

The NYPD's Intelligence Division was formed following the New York City terror attack of September 11, 2001. The police commissioner at the time, tired of seeing his hometown serve as the favorite target for terrorists, determined that nobody could take better care of New York City than the men and women of New York's Finest themselves.

Many police forces across the country had bolstered their budgets and departments in the wake of 9/11—from large cities to small towns, law enforcement expenditures rose precipitously throughout the first decade of the twenty-first century—but only one municipal agency created its own mini-CIA. The Counter-Terrorism Bureau of the NYPD was the public side of their efforts. It liaised with the Joint Terrorism Task Force, an amalgam of law enforcement agencies with a mandate to trade information and cooperation.

But the true face of counterterrorism in the NYPD, the Intelligence Division, was little known and rarely seen. For example, while undercover work is a staple of every big-city police department, no other urban law enforcement organization in the nation worked as aggressively to infiltrate potential terror cells as the Intel Division did. Its employees and advisors included various former national and international espionage experts, educated in the tradecraft of information gathering, interdiction, and threat assessment. Intel analyzed intelligence, gathered both by human means and electronically through the five boroughs that comprised New York City, cultivating a broad network of informers—both sympathetic and reluctant.

Recently, however, the Intel Division had seen a backlash, particularly in the press. This, officials knew, was the downside to success. The ten-man Demographics Unit drew fire for keying in on ethnic hot spots for incubating terrorism, including mosques, coffeehouses, and pizza parlors: 262 hot spots in all. They cranked out report after report but never developed a single concrete lead as to any plot. Of course, one uncovered plot would have justified the entire operation, but the difference between zero and one was a big one. Profiling in general had become a dirty word, in no small part due to Fisk's own capture of blond, blue-eyed, Swedish Muslim terrorist Magnus Jenssen.

Surveillance on Muslims continued to be a controversial subject, especially since the perpetrators of recent successful terror incidents—such as the Boston Marathon bombing—were not members of any identifiable cell or larger network of bad actors. Rogue criminals were the hardest to catch.

The most recent blow to Intel's profile had come in the form of several million e-mails passed on to WikiLeaks, many of which discussed or involved secondhand allegations of civil liberties violations committed by the NYPD's secret mini-CIA. This same batch of e-mails also pulled back the lid on continuing tensions between Intel Division and the New York JTTF.

Nothing had been ordered, but the sense among the rank-and-file Intel operatives was that the division's previous mandate—that of locating and neutralizing pockets of domestic militancy before they became fully radicalized terror cells capable of threatening life and limb in New York City—was being drawn back into something less invasive. There was a difference of opinion inside the division, whether this was indeed the product of success and would weaken Intel's abilities, or whether this was a necessary shift in technique, nearly fifteen years after 9/11.

Coincidentally or not, Intel had lost a few key advisors to private-sector jobs recently, as the patriotic urgency that the commissioner had used to strong-arm experts into working more hours for less pay no longer held sway. Whenever asked, Fisk always said that he was paid not to have an opinion on these matters. His job remained the same: stop terrorism.

"How are you feeling?" asked Dubin.

Fisk's least favorite question. One he was asked at least five times each day. It was like asking a cancer survivor, "Still in remission?" Sometimes he thought that people were afraid he might suffer a breakdown in the room with them, and wanted a heads-up so they could be somewhere else when it happened.

"Feeling fine," said Fisk.

"Glad to see you're physically cleared for duty. No aftereffects from the radiological poisoning?"

"None," Fisk lied.

"I'd say you're damned lucky."

"Well, there is the matter of the extra toes. Buying shoes is a real pain in the ass."

Dubin smiled after a moment. "I get it," he said. "No more questions. I'll stop showing any hint of concern for your well-being."

"I appreciate it," said Fisk.

"As to the psych thing, it was a box we had to put a check mark in. Sometimes I think it's more about choice. God knows there are guys on the force who use an after-action inquiry to malinger and call it a vacation. I say good riddance to those guys. Most everybody who wants to stay, stays. I knew you wanted to stay."

Fisk nodded.

Dubin blew out a breath and twirled his class ring. "Still, we're going to continue to ease you back into things."

Fisk sighed. "I'm using my highly trained cop instincts to guess that you're leading up to something you think I'm not going to like."

"Not going to *love*," said Dubin. "It's an assignment. A special project."

This was code for desk duty. Fisk's reaction surprised him. He showed Dubin nothing, but inside his chest he felt the sensation of a tight fist easing open, just a bit. It was relief.

Dubin went on, "We're going to turn back the clock a bit on Intel in the coming weeks. Can you guess why?"

Fisk did not follow him, at first.

"Before 9/11, Intel was primarily an EP unit. Executive protection. Escorting visiting dignitaries around the city and providing them some security, but really the air of importance. These were generally foreign politicians who liked to be handled. Back then Intel was a cushy preretirement assignment, the waiting room before the twenty-year handshake. Taxi drivers with badges."

Fisk got it now. "UN Week."

United Nations Week occurred around the opening of the General Assembly at the United Nations Headquarters in New York. Heads of state, ministers, and other diplomats from the member states, as well as various nongovernmental organizations, arrived in New York for the annual general debate.

"Obviously," said Dubin, "we're not going to be ferrying these tourists around the city. But as you know, a lot of that post-9/11 money dried up during the recession, and every department is being asked to do more with less. We are tasked with security measures and contingency planning."

Fisk crossed his legs. "Spreadsheets," he said, with the force of a filthy invective.

"Some of that. I'm not taking this lightly, though, and neither will you. The grand finale is the president coming to town to address the assembly and sign a narcoterrorism treaty with Mexico. Also known as 'the worst traffic day in New York.' Besides, the president requested you personally."

Fisk barely even shook his head. He could not exactly tell his boss to screw himself. "Enough," he said.

Everybody ribbed him about being President Obama's good buddy after saving his life at the Freedom Tower dedication. Fisk used to play along with it—"we're going to a Nationals game this weekend"—but by now it was so old and tired he couldn't even muster the energy for a flip response.

The president had been perfectly gracious to him, but—as the saying goes—they didn't keep in touch. Fisk had, however, received an autographed photo from President Bush, forty-three, with an inscription Fisk had never been able to make out.

"Anyway," said Dubin, "after that, we can see about getting you back out on the street. Assuming that's what you want, of course."

"I do," said Fisk.

Dubin nodded, pausing, looking as though he wasn't sure he wanted to say what he was going to say next.

"A lot of people thought you were going to jump to the feds after the Freedom Tower save," he said. "Lord knows you've got all the tools. Brainy cop with street instincts. Languages. FBI would love to get their hands on you. CIA, too."

Fisk thought back to his recent meeting with

Dave Link and briefly wondered if there was any connection here.

"You'd be a natural," continued Dubin. "And you could command better than a detective two's salary."

"This sounds like a good time to ask for a raise," said Fisk.

"Denied," said Dubin quickly, with a smile. "Seriously. We're glad you're back. Weird time here, lots of things in flux. Sometimes that creates opportunities, you know?"

For advancement, he meant. Fisk wasn't sure he wanted that either. "Sometimes it eliminates them," said Fisk, referring to the rocky road Intel had been on recently.

Dubin put his hands on his desk and stood. "Let's make this a quiet, incident-free UN Week and go from there."

Fisk's task was mostly administrative. Drunk tanks aside, he was not spending his days standing out at the exit gate at JFK wearing a chauffeur's hat and holding a small whiteboard with some dignitary's name misspelled on it. Security was paramount, and that took a great deal of coordination. But now, as the General Assembly had opened and the week was under way, things were getting hairy. At its worst, his job was akin to herding cats. Cats who drove cars with diplomatic license plates. Cats with their own security service people. Cats with varying fluency in the English language.

Security aside, life in the city had slowed noticeably, especially on the East Side. Fisk wondered what the exact algorithm was, the relation between the number of automobiles with diplomatic plates and the density of New York City traffic.

Diplomats parked anywhere. Loading zones, valet drop-offs, cab stands, but especially out in front of hotels. Gridlock outside the Waldorf had turned Park Avenue into a parking lot north of Grand Central Terminal. Traffic patterns weren't Fisk's concern, but the speed of incident response was, so he had to plan for it.

All in all, he was surprised at how okay he was with the assignment. It was challenging and it allowed him to focus. Alternatively, being off the street full-time kept him away from the places and people he associated with Krina Gersten. She hadn't just been a colleague, she had been his girlfriend, and he was finding it difficult to move back into life at Intel Division full-time. Despite what he had told Dubin, he had been thinking about other opportunities elsewhere. But for him it wasn't about moving up, it was about moving on. Every success had come with a grievous loss of life. It seemed to Fisk like there wasn't much left for him here at Intel.

Fisk had been living under a dark cloud both professionally and personally for the past year. Maybe it was time to go out in search of blue skies elsewhere.

He disliked his lack of direction but felt stuck, rudderless. And if Fisk wasn't decisive, then he wasn't anything at all.

"Fisk!" It was Bluestein, over on the Threat Desk. "Line two."

Fisk picked up. "This is Fisk."

"How ya doin'?" The accent was outer borough and strong, that of a man who probably had not spent more than twenty minutes outside the environs of the city of New York. Fisk heard something that was either distant traffic or a steady wind blowing into the caller's cell phone. "My captain said I should call you."

Fisk rubbed his forehead. The prime minister of Canada lock his keys out of his car? An envoy from Poland get in a fender bender? "Who are you and what can I do for you?"

"Kiser at the One-oh-one. Robbery Homicide."

Fisk picked up a pen. "Rockaway?"

"The Mediterranean of the east. You hear about this thing yet?"

Fisk said, "Just got back to my desk. What thing?"

It was definitely wind, whipping at the phone, making it difficult for Fisk to hear Kiser, whose response sounded like, "The heading thing."

Fisk said, "This sounds like a mistake, Robbery Homicide. I'm on UN Week duty here. You got a diplomatic threat out in Rockaway?"

Kiser said, "Judging by the tattoos, I'd say these bodies definitely aren't diplomats."

Fisk said, "You said 'bodies'?"

Kiser said, "This is maybe a little more serious than you're expecting. Let me give you an address for your GPS and you can come on down to the beach."

Fisk badged his way inside the perimeter, parking in a sand-strewn beach parking lot that was a portrait of the desolation of the end of summer. Mostly empty and silent under an overcast sky. He stood out of his vehicle, and a burst of wind brought gritty particles of sand to his face, as well as a hint of ocean spit. Nothing dies so alone as a summer beach in September.

He crossed the boardwalk into the dunes. Dress shoes walking in sand. He followed a path through the sea grass, at first trying to be careful, taking shallow steps. Then the first spoonful of sand beneath his heel and it was over. Only pride kept him from rolling up his pant cuffs and walking out there barefoot. Another pair of shoes ruined.

"I'm looking for Kiser?" Fisk said at least three times. A Crime Scene Unit photographer finally heading back to his car pointed Fisk down the shore. He saw a dozen or so uniformed cops standing around a temporary fence of white plastic sheeting whipping in the wind and started toward it.

Nothing out on the horizon, no barges, tankers, or pleasure boats. The sky was gray but visibility was good. Fisk shivered and stuck his hands in his pockets, and it was the first climate-related chill he had felt since at least June.

"Kiser?" said Fisk, finally reaching the crime scene.

A slight man in his forties looked up from his notepad. He wore khakis and a pink button-down shirt with a heavy, wrinkled, unzipped all-weather jacket. He had a fringe of dark hair, just enough to clip his yarmulke.

"Fisk?" he said, offering his hand.

Fisk shook. He could not see over the top of the plastic sheeting yet. Most of the cops standing around it were holding the wooden stakes into the sand, keeping the temporary fence from lifting off and tumbling back to the parking lot.

Kiser said, "I know you?" Then, seemingly in reference to Fisk's name: "I thought so."

He stood looking at Fisk a moment, placing him as the guy who got Jenssen. The pause was not one of admiration or respect, but more along the lines of *Why is this guy riding the UN Week desk?*

Fisk, referring to the fence, said, "How bad is it?"

"It's grim. Worse than grim."

Fisk figured it was violent. That was why the plastic sheeting. The *Post* loved making a front-page meal out of murder scenes. Fisk looked up at the dunes. Any one of them could have hidden some punk with a four-hundred-millimeter lens.

"Killed here or dumped?"

"Dumped," said Kiser, with a nod of certainty. "We tried scouting the sand for tire tracks, foot-prints, but this thing happened overnight."

Fisk stepped over to the fence. He was unprepared for what he saw.

"Jesus."

Kiser said, "A baker's dozen. There were seagulls picking at them. Dog walker found them."

The bodies had been decapitated. Thirteen of them, all shoulders, trunks, and limbs. Amazing how incomplete and inhuman a body looks when the head is gone.

Fisk looked back toward the dunes again. "Dumped."

Kiser said, "No cameras on the beach parking lot. You got Kennedy airplanes masking your noise. We're going to have to get plenty lucky to find anybody with eyes on this thing."

Fisk looked back at the bodies. An identification nightmare. Only fingerprints and tattoos. Not so bad if they were felons, but Fisk could already see that they'd be lucky to get ten names out of thirteen.

Kiser said, "Ever work a mass murder before?"

Fisk shook his head.

Kiser said, "This precinct, you know, tends to be more your floaters, your hobos OD-ing under the boardwalk, night swimming accidents, late-night domestics. Things of that nature."

Fisk was still thinking crime scene contamination. "You should string off the most direct path from here back to the dunes."

Kiser followed Fisk's eye line.

"Schlepping bodies is hard work, especially through sand. They parked somewhere up there. As they string, have your guys sift for trash. Things get lost on beaches in the dark. Check the parking lot up there, too. Pay special attention to the edges, because of the wind. You never know."

Kiser nodded. He went off and spoke to another officer, leaving Fisk to look at the dead bodies again.

He could see the seagull bites. A few of them circled overhead now, beach vultures raised on Doritos, half-eaten hot dogs, and trash. They had picked at the edges of the neck wounds, which were otherwise surprisingly flat and neat. Fisk wondered what kind of tool had been used.

Kiser came back. "Thanks for the help. Thought Intel didn't work crime scenes."

"We don't. Almost never, anyway." Intel was about collating information, working sources, going undercover, but rarely working a scene. "But I was a cop before I was an Intel cop."

Kiser was nodding, debating whether or not to say what was on his mind. "I gotta get this outta the way. I saw the *Dateline* on you—"

Fisk tried to stop him. "It wasn't on me."

"On your thing, with the tower, and your girlfriend—"

"I didn't have anything to do with it and I didn't watch it," said Fisk, turning back toward the bodies. He would rather have dealt with corpses than talk about a television "documentary" that apparently made a soap opera out of his and Gersten's love life. All he knew about it was that they had broadcast video of him walking into his mandated therapy meeting, shot from the backseat of a car across the street. Until then, Fisk had never known what it was like to be one of the people he followed for a living.

Kiser realized he had spit in Fisk's coffee here. "Do you want to get inside?"

The plastic sheeting, he meant. Fisk shook his head. He could see plenty from where he was.

Each corpse was naked, male. No wallets to go through, no cell phones to check for messages or unanswered calls, no IDs or credit cards. He noticed that a few were missing one or both hands as well as their heads; others retained their hands, even a few wedding and pinky rings. One of the more heavily tattooed bodies had burn marks around his thighs and genitals. Two others showed bruising inconsistent with lividity or decomposition. They had been, if not tortured, sadistically beaten before they were beheaded.

Kiser said, "Colombians, maybe? Going by the skin, which is a little dark. Spanish in the tattoos. Salvadorans?"

Fisk turned his head sideways to try to read one of the tattoos. Across one pair of shoulders, partially obscured by dried black blood, over the rendering of a scarlet red pistol was the word SINALOA.

"Mexicans," said Fisk. "At least that one is."

Kiser tried to read what Fisk was seeing. "Cartel stuff?"

"That's the idea."

"In Rockaway?" Kiser hooked his fingers into his belt loops. "We don't see too many Mexicans here in the One-oh-one. Puerto Ricans, sure. Over off Mott, some Colombians. Salvadorans, as I said. But not like MS-13-type guys," he said, name-checking a prominent El Salvadoran drug gang. "We get workers. Quiet people. Housekeepers, maintenance workers. Gardeners."

The wind shifted for a moment and Fisk and Kiser got a noseful. "Doubtful they were killed here."

Kiser said, "So maybe somebody mistook all this sand for a landfill. I think if you dump bodies on a beach, you're trying to say something."

"Agreed," said Fisk.

"If you have the space and the tools to decapitate thirteen grown men and get rid of heads, you can certainly get rid of the rest of the body."

Fisk nodded. "This is cartel-level violence." He looked at Kiser. "This is why your captain had you call me."

Kiser nodded. "The T-word."

Fisk winced. "Maybe. They used to call it crime. Now if it hits a certain number on the meter it becomes terrorism. In this case, narcoterrorism."

"You're not interested?"

"You mean Intel?" said Fisk. "Not my call. Depends on what you get. Processing these hunks of meat is going to be a bitch."

"You're telling me."

"I would reach out to OCB. The Organized Crime guys have a good grip on gang stuff, at least stateside in NYC. Maybe you'll get one guy on ink alone, and that ID might beget another, and so on. Word to the wise. Be meticulous. You caught a big fish here, everyone's going to want to get in on it. Every police inspector in all of Queens is going to want to come down here for a look himself, but don't let them. No stomping around your crime scene. This is your realm now. If any i's don't get dotted, it's all on you."

The wind came back on them again. Kiser spun away hard.

"I'm going to go find a nice clean spot in the weeds for a good puke."

"Do it," said Fisk. "You'll feel better."

Fisk returned to Intel, still unsettled by what he had seen. The sight of thirteen beheaded humans, dumped on a beach in Rockaway looking like they had washed ashore from Mexico, had rattled his cage. This was cartel-level violence here in New York City.

It did not take much checking to confirm his assumption that the pervasive and extreme violence of the Mexican drug gangs had not migrated north of the border. If anything, drug-related violence in the United States was trending downward. The overall murder rate in Mexico was more than five times as high as the United States. Fifteen percent of all drug-related murders in Mexico involved torture, including roughly five hundred beheadings in the past year. Fisk found exactly one case of a drug dispute resulting in a beheading in the United States, and that was in 2010.

So why here? And why now? There hadn't been any uptick in turf wars or drug prices that he was aware of. As a strange anomaly, he was intrigued but as the point man for United Nations Week, he was too preoccupied to do anything about it.

FISK COULD NOT IMAGINE a more complicated tangle of law enforcement agencies and conflicting jurisdictions than he was seeing here during United Nations Week.

The United States Secret Service is the designated agency for protecting the president, vice president, and their families, of course. It is also charged with protecting visiting heads of state. This week provided an unusual challenge, obviously. The Secret Service has a uniformed division of roughly thirteen hundred officers—they resemble military cops in their blue uniforms and baseball caps— many of whom had been summoned from Washington, D.C., for the week. Fisk was in contact with their New York agency, but it was more of a courtesy situation involving information sharing and daily briefings.

The State Department's Diplomatic Security Service played a smaller role. Their primary job is to provide bodyguard-level protection for U.S. diplomats overseas, as well as police-level work inside U.S. embassies and consulates. They also protect State Department people and facilities in the United States, as well as visiting political dignitaries unqualified or not warranting full Secret Service protection. DSS special agents tend to be ex-military, and DSS does not have a uniformed division. They provided the protection detail to the U.S. ambassador to the United Nations.

The United Nations Headquarters property itself in Turtle Bay, occupying six city blocks on the site of former slaughterhouses overlooking the

East River, is policed and protected by the UN's own police force. (The UN also has its own fire department and postal service.) The sovereignty of the United Nations is such that New York Police Department personnel may not enter the property without being invited.

The FBI had more of a presence than usual in the Big Apple that week. They were responsible for domestic counterintelligence, and United Nations Week represented a premium opportunity for foreign nationals to enter the country as part of a nation's diplomatic contingent or security detail. It was also the opportunity for some spy gamesmanship, which was probably why the FBI had allowed itself to be made outside the Chinese embassy earlier that day.

Of course, there was the New York Police Department, Fisk's own employer and the largest police force in the country, with more than thirty-four thousand sworn officers. The department represented the outer ring of general security, doing crowd control, bomb sniffing, metal detectors, and pat-downs, as well as the all-important traffic details. But the NYPD had little or no authority inside the inner security ring, including embassy properties, which are considered foreign soil.

Finally, there were the visiting dignitaries' own security teams, who were subject to the laws of New York State but carried concealed weapons and generally enjoyed certain courtesies that occupied a gray zone between local and international laws.

Fisk himself and the Intel Division in general had little or no actual authority in any of these individual security matters. His brief was to over-see general security within New York City and to safeguard against any outstanding terrorist threat to the proceedings as a whole. This was what Intel did on a day-to-day basis throughout the five bor-oughs, except that United Nations Week provided a potentially tempting buffet of hard targets over the course of six days in September. With every other law enforcement agency and guest nation focused on their own areas of concern, Intel's self-appointed assignment was to take in the view from the air and zero in on potential threats.

FISK REALIZED HE WAS long overdue for lunch and did something he routinely promised himself he would never do: he ate a chicken salad sandwich out of the break room vending machine. He ate it standing up, looking at the CNN coverage of the "Rockaway Massacre." He ate it quickly, lest anyone snap his picture and caption it SMART PEOPLE MAKING DUMB FOOD CHOICES.

He saw himself on television, a brief glimpse of him talking to Detective Kiser near the plastic sheeting rippling on the beach, part of a looping video package. As Fisk had suspected, the camera shot was from hundreds of yards away, the zoom shaky. It was followed by footage of officers string-ing off the path back to the parking lot, and then a glimpse of Kiser near the dunes, bent over at the waist, hands on hips, getting sick. Fisk laid his hand on his own stomach, suffering from instant eater's remorse.

Nicole Heming came around the corner. "There

you are," she said. "People here to see you. From the Mexican president's protection detail." She looked at the triangular plastic sandwich carton in his hand. "You're the one who eats those things?"

"Thank you, Nicole," said Fisk, tossing it into the trash and walking out to the waiting area instead of returning to his desk. Intel headquarters wasn't built to host visitors or guests; out through the pass-card door was a bench, a fake ficus tree, and a black rubber mat for snow boots during the messy winter months.

The woman wore a black jacket over a white blouse and gray pants. She had the sleek, raven-black hair common to many Mexicans, but her complexion was so unusually pale that she could have passed for black Irish. The contrast was striking. Fisk might have looked at her a moment too long.

One man with her wore a thin tweed suit but had a military bearing. He was a hard-faced man of sixty or more with a thin silver mustache. He introduced himself as General de Aguilar, Jefatura del Estada Mayor Presidencial. He was the chief of the Presidential Guard, the EMP, a unit of the Mexican army. Fisk remembered his profile from one of many briefings. He was a two-star general who had been handpicked by the recently elected Mexican president to head his security detail.

The man with him looked like a soldier, big shouldered with an athletic bearing. He wore a dark suit with a pin of the Mexican state shield on his lapel, along with the symbol of the Estado Mayor Presidencial, a maroon square featuring five gold stars over the initials EMP. The suit was double-vented, suitable for carrying various types of concealed weapons. Despite the formal attire, a pair of wraparound Oakleys sat atop his head. He was introduced to Fisk as Virgilio, no first name, no rank.

"Cecilia Garza," said the woman, offering her hand. Fisk's first impression was that she wore an icy, supercilious expression, like that of a Latin American aristocrat.

Aguilar said, "Comandante Garza is with the Policía Federal, our federal police force. She is assigned to President Vargas's security for this trip."

"Garza," said Fisk. He had heard of her. "Mexican intelligence, aren't you?"

"Civilian intelligence," she corrected him. "I am attached to the *federales*."

Fisk believed he was looking at his Mexican counterpart. "I know you by your reputation."

"And I you," she said, with no hint of a smile.

"Detective," said Aguilar, "we are here to ask a favor."

Garza said, "There was a mass murder reported earlier. We would like any information the New York Police Department has, and to offer our assistance."

Fisk nodded. He had assumed that their showing up today was no coincidence. "I don't know what to tell you. Thirteen men beheaded, dumped on a beach in Rockaway. I can give you the name of the detective leading the investigation in that precinct. His name is Kiser."

"Can you take us to him?"

"Can I take you . . . ?" Fisk looked out the window at the auto junkyard across the street. The windows were one-way. The sun was getting low in the western sky. "No, I cannot. I can give you an address to put in your GPS, however."

Garza said, "This Kiser will brief us?"

"Well, I didn't say that. That's his call. Though not really. His captain, more like it."

"How far?" asked Aguilar.

"This time of day, Rockaway is a hike."

"A hike," said Garza, puzzling through the idiom. "A long walk. We do not have time. The president— our president—lands in three hours. Can all information be sent to us electronically?"

"Again, that's not my call. Not my decision. You'd have to go through Rockaway for that. Or straight over my head. I assume someone could arrange a briefing for you. Is there a connection to your president's visit?"

"What condition were the bodies in?" she asked, blowing right past his question. "Were they all beheaded?"

"They were all beheaded, some missing hands—"

"Were they all Mexican?"

"I don't know that. It's still early days yet." He recalled the Sinaloa tattoo, but kept that to himself for the moment. Garza's obvious and intense interest intrigued him, but he had other things to do. "Now, I don't mean to be rude, but I've got a meeting with the head of the UN's security service in about forty-five minutes."

"Do you have any identification on them yet?" Garza continued, as though not having heard Fisk's answer. "What about tattoos?"

Fisk looked to the other two men. Clearly Garza

had insisted on this visit. They appeared to be sup-
portive of her questioning, but just along for the
ride. Fisk attributed any anxiety on their parts to
the impending arrival of their boss. "Look. It's an
ongoing investigation, and it's not my place to get
into it. Sorry. You know how it is."

Garza looked away . . . and when she looked back
at Fisk, it was as though a different Cecilia Garza
had taken her place. This one was softer in expression, more solicitous. It was chiefly her eyes. "We
would like very much to help. I believe we could be
of service."

She was smart. She was wily. She was impressive.
Fisk said, "How does this relate to President Vargas's visit?"

Garza offered a generous shrug. "I don't know that
it does. I consider this more a point of national pride."

"Shame is more like it," said Fisk. "I get it now.
It's an embarrassment on the first day of the UN
General Assembly. But I'm sorry, I can't help you. If
this involves a threat to the Mexican president, then
I can at least point you in the right direction or offer
additional assistance."

Garza's gray eyes turned cold again. "I assure
you, Detective, we need no assistance."

Fisk smiled and nodded, including the two men
in his remarks. "Then I'm not sure what we're all
here talking about."

Garza turned to Aguilar and spoke in Spanish.
"This is the man who stopped the presidential assassination at the Freedom Tower. Somehow, he has
been relegated to desk duty here. I don't know what
he did to receive such punishment."

"It's not punishment," said Fisk, in English. His father had been posted to Panama for four years when he was young, and he understood Spanish with the fluency of a native. He could even discern between accents: Panamanian, Castilian, Colombian.

Garza looked a little surprised, but only for a moment. Fisk could see her recalibrating her assessment of him, promising herself not to underestimate him again. For his part, he was a bit stung by her remark. But more than anything he was curious as to her objective here.

He said, "Either this has something to do with your president's arrival, or you are here as a point of national pride. Either way, you refused to admit the problem, or that there is a problem. Which is par for the course, I suppose."

"Par for the . . . ?"

"It's routine. For a country known for its law enforcement . . . shall we say, moral vulnerability."

"Ah," said Garza, nodding as though accepting a challenge. "Corruption. Malfeasance. That is what you think of all *federales*."

"I'm saying admitting the problem is the first step toward curing it."

Garza said, "That sounds like good advice for our noisy neighbor to the north, with their voracious appetite for illegal narcotics."

Fisk nodded once, pulling back emotionally from the exchange. "You came here asking for help, or offering to help? Either way, you won't identify the problem you need help with. This cartel-type violence, the point of it is to do something to get people's attention. You can't look away from thirteen beheaded bodies, you can't bury that at the bottom of the news hour. It's to announce their presence and intimidate their enemies. If you're expecting trouble for your president, I would like to know. Otherwise?" Fisk shrugged. "I'm afraid this is United Nations Week. Not Mexican beheadings week."

Garza looked at him with quiet contempt.

And Fisk wasn't quite sure how or why it happened, but he knew that he had, here, this afternoon, made an enemy for life.

"Thank you so much for your careful attention to this matter," she said.

Fisk shrugged again. "Good day, Comandante. Gentlemen."

The silver Chevrolet Suburban had been transported up to New York ahead of UN Week, along with the Mexican president's black Suburban and the rest of his convoy.

Garza sat in the front passenger seat. Once the reinforced doors closed, the silence inside was profound. Even the running engine was fire-walled off from the passenger cabin.

Aguilar, familiarly known as Jefe, said from behind the wheel, "We approached the wrong policeman. That is clear. We will find someone more sympathetic, and with more authority."

Virgilio, not looking up from his phone in the backseat, said, "Someone with any authority at all."

Garza simmered. She felt the sting of failure, as well as the pain of embarrassment in front of these two men. She had thought she might find a *compadre* in Detective Fisk; on this point, she was quite incorrect.

"Perhaps there is still time to go to Rockaway . . ."

Jefe shook his head, his tanned hands on the steering wheel, pulling out past the automobile yard and a plumbing supply warehouse. "The Aeroméxico 737 lands soon. I must be there at Vargas's arrival, and so must you."

Garza made a fist of her hand. The beheadings, so dramatic in their cruelty: it had to be the work of Chuparosa. He was here in New York City. She only needed proof.

"I'll go," said Virgilio from the backseat.

Garza turned. "You have no credentials to go to this Detective Kiser."

"Not to Rockaway," said Virgilio, popping a square breath freshener into his mouth. "Not to the police. I go to the neighborhoods. Boots on the ground. North Corona. Jackson Heights. I have a cousin who knows some people who might know anyone who could be missing."

"Fine," said Garza, wishing she could go with him. "But very quietly. That is imperative."

"*Sí,* Comandante," said Virgilio, with a smile.

Jefe said, "And now we will turn our full attention to the president's security, no?"

Garza sat back in her seat. "It has been foremost in my mind the entire time."

Back inside, Fisk caught Dubin as his boss was leaving for dinner. He needed to report the meeting.

Fisk said, "Our president and their president are set to sign a cooperative treaty Monday night. Drug interdiction, something like that. Calling it narcoterrorism. So that's something we need to keep an eye on."

Dubin nodded. "Look, maybe they're just embarrassed, looking to cover their ass. Damage control for their new president. Or maybe something is brewing and they're not being as cooperative as they say they are. Maybe it's pushback from these cartels. If so, if they think they can get away with that shit here in New York, they're in for a real surprise."

Fisk said, "I'll dig in a little deeper."

"Only as it relates to diplomacy. You're still on the UN desk." Dubin was powering down his computer. "You have enough to do."

Fisk said, "Narcoterror is a bullshit euphemism, right? Narcotics traffickers, from the lowliest mule to the fattest cartel leader, have zero interest in attacking the political foundations of the United States. They have one interest only, and that is *dinero*."

Dubin stopped him there. "They can be called terrorists if that brings funding to our efforts. Maybe their profits are used to fund some sort of backdoor political action or terror squad. That much illicit money can do a lot of damage."

"Committing horrific acts does not make them terrorists, though. It makes them violent narcotic dealers."

Dubin said, "You're so sure these thirteen headless bodies are a drug hit?"

Fisk shrugged. "What else could it be?"

Dubin grabbed his briefcase. "I don't know. But whatever it takes to give us a smooth ride through next week, that is what we will do." Dubin checked his watch. "Don't you have the dinner with the UN security team tonight?"

"I do," said Fisk.

"Crosstown traffic," said Dubin, himself heading for the door. "Better be on your way."

Back at his desk, Fisk had Nicole call and cancel the meeting with the UN security team. For the past few weeks, he had been doing lots of very long strategy meetings, lots of hand-holding, lots of bureaucratic back and forth that didn't feel anything like police work.

Fisk called up Garza's bio, running her name through Intel's own interior search engine. She was a lawyer who had somehow migrated out of the Ministry of Justice and into actual law enforcement. Vargas, the newly elected Mexican president, had been one of her professors. Fisk watched one video on the LiveLeak video-sharing site, stamped with the Policía Federal seven-starred silver shield, showing Comandante Garza walking around a murder scene wearing a black uniform with a SIG Sauer on her hip. He wondered how she had become attached to the EMP: Was it perhaps at her former professor's special request?

The unfortunate thing was that a person like Garza in Mexico was liable to get blown away eventually. Her two predecessors had both been killed on the job. His respect for her rose, even as he wondered what truly drove her. Especially someone—

and this trait was impossible to overlook—so attractive. In such a male-dominated field as law enforcement, beauty was an impediment to success, because others tended not to take an attractive person quite as seriously as a person of average looks—and even more, because such people are used to being catered to and generally are given special consideration early in life, advantages they come to take for granted. Garza apparently had never fallen into this trap.

Aguilar had a straightforward military career. Vargas, the new president, had no military background, and the choice of Aguilar to be the head of EMP was read as a political rather than a personal selection. The corps of the EMP was more than 15 percent female, Fisk noted, and this number struck him as substantial, especially in a traditionally patriarchal society such as Mexico. Perhaps they were more progressive in that respect than the United States. Fisk understood now why the chief had let Garza take the lead with Fisk.

Virgilio was a question mark. Assuming Fisk had been given his legal name, the man showed up on none of Intel's many databases. He was registered as part of President Vargas's security team, but nothing deeper than that. Fisk put in a request for more background on Virgilio . . . and realized that he suddenly felt invigorated.

He was onto something here. He could feel it.

Kiser called him back just over an hour later.

"I thought you weren't interested in our little Rockaway Beach party," he said.

"I'm not," said Fisk. "What's the latest?"

"No identifications yet, but it's early. Going at it from missing persons reports, but nothing definitive yet. Not even after the story has hit all the news shows."

Fisk said, "Immigrants or even first-generation Mexicans might not watch the mainstream channels. If you want to use the media, go on Telemundo or Univision."

"Speaking of good advice," said Kiser, "your sweep-the-beach idea netted us something. A bottle."

"*Cerveza?*"

"No, a soft drink named Jarritos. Heard of it?"

"I think so."

"Most popular soft drink brand in Mexico, the country that drinks more sugary soft drinks per capita than any other."

"Good."

"Wiped clean. No fingerprints."

"Oh well."

"But," said Kiser, "inside the bottle was a cigarette butt."

Fisk rolled his eyes at Detective Kiser's dramatic storytelling, even though he got the adrenaline thing of a hot investigation. "You can't wait for DNA. Takes too much time."

"Crime Scene Unit pulls a partial print off the cigarette. Very partial, but the lab thinks they can get something out of it."

"Good," said Fisk. "Meanwhile, where do they sell this Jarritos?"

"We're on it. The flavor is tamarind. Heard of that?"

"No."

"Me neither, but it's the second most popular flavor of Jarritos in Mexico. So, very common. I checked with the Organized Crime Control Bureau, they said you can tell a Mexican neighborhood in New York City by two things, a short woman selling churros at the subway station and a convenience store with a Jarritos sign in the window. I'm trying to get a couple of Mexican American uniforms transferred over to help out."

"Someone is going to come forward with a missing son, boyfriend, or husband," said Fisk. "Let me ask you this. Have you gotten a call from the Mexican consulate or the Mexican president's advance team?"

"No. Why? What am I looking at?"

Fisk smiled at the note of concern in Kiser's voice. "Maybe nothing, maybe something."

"I will say a prayer tonight that it is nothing," said Kiser. "I got enough to deal with as it is."

Cecilia Garza made it to JFK Airport just in time to see the president's Boeing 737 touch down. The aircraft sat dormant until members of the Estado Mayor Presidencial drove out onto the tarmac in black Chevy Suburbans.

Garza stepped out of the silver Suburban, eyeing the airport in the dying light of day. She knew it had been swept, and that all the sight lines had been taken into consideration for President Vargas's brief walk down a flight of wheeled steps and into his waiting Suburban. She also knew that Chuparosa liked to do his killing at close range. But the news of the beheadings had her on edge, and nothing felt assured or guaranteed anymore.

She watched General de Aguilar stand at attention, awaiting his president. She was stirred by the sight of the aging general in his uniform, standing so crisply against the night, dwarfed by the Aeroméxico aircraft. It reminded her that there was purpose and meaning behind such military formalities regarding heads of state, beyond its great expense.

The president's personal EMP soldiers exited first, dressed in suits, eyeing the scene. A few moments of waiting, and then President Vargas appeared, descending the stairs sure-footedly, looking smart and vital as he saluted General de Aguilar and ducked inside his armored Suburban with the twin Mexican flags on the fender.

An aide closed the door and the vehicle started away immediately. It was a warm night, but Garza felt a chill. Why had Chuparosa come to the United States just to kill President Vargas? What kind of statement was he trying to make, if any, by threatening the Mexican president away from his own soil? Was it a message aimed at the United States? And if so—why?

And was the Zeta cartel behind this action, or had Chuparosa gone off on his own? And if he had—again, why?

Jefe returned. "The easy part is over," he said.

"Indeed," agreed Garza. The airplane began taxiing away. "Where will it go?"

"An airfield nearby. It will be guarded, of course." The general removed his hat before climbing back inside the vehicle. "You have a good mind, Comandante," he said, paying her a rare compliment.

She followed him inside the car bound for Manhattan.

isk called ahead to Felix Dukes before heading over to the Secret Service's New York field office, in a secure and anonymous office building next to a major chain hotel in downtown Brooklyn. It had formerly been located with the New York City emergency command center and the CIA station in 7 World Trade Center.

In an average week, the New York field office— the Secret Service's largest away from Washington, D.C.—pursued six protective assignments. United Nations Week had of course multiplied that number many times, with up to two-thirds of the world's leaders—many of them the object of previous assassination attempts—coming to one of the most crowded and yet still most open cities in the world. This in addition to the dozens of counterfeiting cases the agency was working at any given time. Fisk was a familiar sight at the building, and was brought up to the highly secure top floors.

Homeland Security funds had made the Intel Division what it was, and the Secret Service had benefited from post-9/11 expenditures as well. Their new facility was a marvel. The Secret Service did their own phone tracking from a state-of-the-art wire room. Dukes had once shown Fisk a vault filled with disguises, false vehicle decals, and the fake-grass tarps agents hid beneath during both protective and undercover assignments. The Secret Service's polygraphs were considered the gold standard, and the New York field office conducted theirs in a warren of rooms they referred to as "the truth laboratory."

United Nations Week qualified as a "national special security event," in national security parlance. That put it on a level with U.S. presidential nominating conventions, inaugurations, and the G20 summits. Complicating security measures was the fact that many foreign leaders stayed in the same hotels, providing would-be assassins clusters of targets—and they moved in conspicuous, slow-moving motorcades from event to event. Even with NYPD escorts and sirens wailing, New York motorists and cabdrivers were much more reluctant to make room for emergency vehicles than drivers in most of the rest of the country. And it wasn't just the world leaders: almost all traveled with spouses and children, all of whom needed protection.

"Broadside" was the name they had given to the Secret Service's command center. From the secure room, agents tracked the movements of dignitaries and their attendant security details in real time. Many foreign leaders were familiar with their case agent after multiple trips to the United States. Dukes had graduated up from detail leader for former Iranian president Mahmoud Ahmadinejad—one of the biggest of the big-target dignitaries of the past few years—to heading the Dignitary Protection Division at the command center.

He came at Fisk with a meaty hand. "Fisk," he said, trying to kill him with his grip.

"Easy," said Fisk. "What's with the squeeze?"

"Catching me at a bad time, bro," said Dukes. "I got all this shit on me, and my wife is due to deliver our third in nine days."

"Nine days?" said Fisk. "First of all, congrats. Second of all, I think you'll make it through UN Week."

"It's not the birth I'm stressed about," said Dukes, leaning closer. "She's big as a house and feeling every pound. And we got two kids already under four. You hearing me?"

Fisk shook his head.

Dukes looked at him with disgust. "I forget you don't have kids. I've never hated you more than I do this moment."

It was hard to tell sometimes when Dukes was joking, but Fisk was pretty certain this was one of those times. "What am I missing?"

"It's what I'm missing, you son of a bitch." Dukes leaned in again. "Sex, all right? I have to draw you a picture? I'm going out of my skull. But you don't care. Talk to me when you get married, man. When you got little ones running around, climbing in your bed. When your wife's feet are swelled up like a Flintstone's. I ought to shoot you right here."

"Easy, big fella," said Fisk. "Didn't know what I was walking into here."

"I've got two hundred door-to-door details going simultaneously, not including sixty-some-odd State Department security details for lower-level protectees. I've got nine hundred aircraft going in and out of JFK over the next handful of days, all bearing dignitaries. I've got prescouting and security on literally hundreds of events across the city. All of which has to be done safely and expeditiously."

Dukes sat down on the edge of a desk. Even inside the office, he wore the Secret Service uniform: a dark suit with a noticeable paunch, a light blue shirt, a red tie. The paunch, of course, was not the result of a lack of exercise or late-night bowls of sugary cereal. It held his gun, his radio, his handcuffs, and his badge.

The Secret Service was different from any other branch of law enforcement anywhere, in that its most important tool was not handguns but radios. The agency zealously maintained and monitored some sixteen distinct radio channels—an enormous luxury given the limited amount of available bandwidth—each of them encrypted by the National Security Agency. An agent's lost radio was many times more serious than a lost gun. The quickest way to earn a demotion in the Secret Service was to lose one's radio. Any time a radio went missing, every single receiver had to be rekeyed by the NSA, which took a lot of time and effort.

"Hey," said Dukes, suddenly appearing contrite. "Sorry about all that marriage talk, that was stupid."

Again, people walking on eggshells around Fisk because of Gersten. Fisk quickly waved it off, needing to move on. "How's it looking?"

"It's holding together. But that can change in an instant. I don't need to tell you, the last few terror attempts in this city failed not because they were detected by law enforcement, but because the dumb shits made stupid mistakes. With one glaring exception."

Jenssen. Fisk nodded. That was how he and Dukes had met, in the after-action interviews months after the Freedom Tower dedication. The Secret Service was one of the largest consumers of intelligence data in the entire United States government national security complex. Intelligence collection was not in its brief, except as it pertained to improving its own strategic and tactical protective procedures.

Dukes asked, "How is it on your end?"

Fisk looked around. "I always think we have the best of the best until I walk in here."

Dukes nodded. "Federal versus state, man. We have the best toys. What brings you in?"

Fisk leaned back against the edge of the cubicle wall. "So I'm trying to head off any entanglements or anything else that will jam up the city any more than it already is this week."

"Of course."

"You're going man to man, we're looking more at the big picture. Big threats. That said, I had an interesting meeting this evening and I want to follow up with you. You heard about the beheadings in Rockaway?"

"The what in what?" said Dukes.

"Thirteen bodies. Found earlier today."

"I've had my head in the sand of diplomatic security here."

Fisk nodded. "That's what I thought. The Mexican president is flying in tonight."

"Just landed," said Dukes, correcting him.

Fisk nodded again. "You guys are good. What color socks is he wearing?"

"That's classified." Dukes smiled briefly. "Where you going with this?"

"Mexico and the United States have a treaty signing going on sometime this weekend. Mexican president and POTUS signing."

Dukes's eyebrows went up at the mention of the U.S. president. "Now you're worrying me."

"Just putting it on your bulletin board. Got a visit from a Cecilia Garza, a *federale* attached to President Vargas."

"Ah, yes. The comandante," said Dukes. "Came in for a briefing two, three days ago. A man in my heightened state of anxiety does not forget a woman like that. No, quite the opposite. They say Latin women are too volatile? I say bring on the pain. But something went wrong in my Puerto Rican head. I married a nice midwestern girl. White bread. The best. Still, who doesn't like cinnamon toast?"

"Cold shower, man," said Fisk. "Doctor's orders."

"Gotta get someone to hose me down like a mad dog."

"President Vargas's intel assessment bring up anything worth knowing?"

Dukes looked at the ceiling. "Not that I remember." The analysts at the Secret Service's Protective Intelligence and Assessment Division in Washington prepared detailed profiles on all protectees, including threat assessments and sensitive foreign intel. "He was an anticorruption candidate, though in Mexico that's a tough sell. He seems to have upheld his end of the bargain, though it's early days. Fired hundreds of crooked *federales*—hundreds. He's vetting new ones, going after college graduates, bringing in something like fifteen thousand new recruits. He's gearing up for a battle with the cartels. But in a land where everything runs on money—police bribes have their own name, *mordidas*—this sort of thing takes a while to age out of the system. We got a lot of cartel noise, the usual. He probably receives a dozen threats on his life every day. You think our job here is tough. Those EMPs he has watching him have to do more with a whole lot less."

"The treaty is a narcotics and human trafficking agreement of some sort."

"What do you think, was this beheading a warning? Related?"

"I don't know yet. But the visit from Garza . . . something is hinky. She wanted more info from me than she was willing to ask for. She was fishing like she already knew there was a big fish in the lake. This kind of body dumping is way outside the norm for the United States. All I have are question marks, but they are bright red and flashing."

Dukes said, "So you just thought you'd stop by and see how you could make my job even more difficult."

"Exactly," said Fisk.

"Okay," said Dukes. "I'm aware, and I'm on it."

Fisk shook his hand before leaving. "Cold shower," he said again.

Dukes shook his head. "No time." Then, before he released Fisk's hand, "Good to see you back."

The midtown Four Seasons was a fifty-two-story, five-star hotel. President Umberto Vargas was staying in one of the three-bedroom royal suites located on the thirty-second floor, the same floor as delegations from Namibia and the Republic of Georgia.

With the soft click of a door, the frenetic task of transporting a head of state from JFK Airport to midtown Manhattan was over.

The corner suite featured views of the southeast corner of Central Park through floor-to-ceiling bay windows. A balcony offered further views of the city, but the door was locked and the president was expressly forbidden to step outside. Seven plasma HD televisions, three marble bathrooms, handcrafted sycamore furnishings and leather surfaces. In a word: luxury.

"What would the people say?" asked Cecilia Garza, seated on a plush chair near the corner window, holding a glass of water.

"They would be outraged," said the president, nodding to one of his EMP guards to step away, dismissing his valet and his personal secretary and his chief of staff, then sitting on the sofa before a set of briefing papers. "Everyone from the farmer to the banker. If they saw this." He smiled his campaign smile as he slackened the knot of his necktie. "But, if I were to move to a chain hotel without any amenities, they would say, 'Why does our president sleep in a flophouse while the Japanese prime minister stays in luxury?' And in this case, national pride trumps the fear of a trumped-up scandal."

Garza nodded. It was so strange sometimes, remembering her old UDLA law school professor and reconciling that man with the president of her country. He still had his idealism, only now it was tempered by the reality of everyday concessions. It had not hurt his campaign that he had aged so well. Tall, broad shouldered, his thick, dark hair graying at the temples. His expression was intelligent without being judgmental, commanding without being imperious. Looking the part is so important in politics, as in all walks of life, where meeting preconceived expectations gets you halfway to your goal. Garza, herself, had no such advantage as Policía Federal, a woman leading men.

President Vargas waved at the cityscape. "Life. So strange the paths we take. I think that to meet anyone on a crowded city street, even for an appointment, is a small miracle. But for us, for our lives, to intersect again like this, twenty years after leaving the incubator of the university . . . it is not mere fate, it is something richer. Not necessarily fraught with meaning . . . but profound nonetheless. Agree?"

She smiled as he lapsed back into his professorial way of speaking—something the campaign trail had required him to abandon early on, after reports that audiences felt he was bloviating and talking down to them. "I agree it is remarkable, Señor Presidente."

He was in an expansive mood, but could tell that she was not. "Comandante Garza, your eyes are sadder than I remember. The weight of responsibility?"

And fatigue, she might have added. And squinting into the sun whenever she lost her sunglasses, which was frequently. "Perhaps," she answered. "I am quite concerned about the incident."

President Vargas's lip curled a bit at the thought of it. "It is how they see us, no? And how they want to see us. Their inferior neighbor to the south. Violent and unruly. It is all they want to know. What was it Díaz said? 'Poor Mexico . . .'" Garza finished the words of Porfirio Díaz, a former Mexican president, ". . . so far from God and so close to the United States."

"They, who are the cause of all this drug violence, look down upon us for it. That is one of the many things I hope to achieve with this landmark treaty, Comandante. For it is not only to cut down on trafficking and the attendant violence, but to force the United States of America to take responsibility for its role in it."

The so-called drug war in Mexico had claimed well over fifty thousand lives since 2006. Three times the number of murders in the United States, in a country one-third its size. And while that statistic seemed to speak to chaos, in fact the drug trade had become a complex global operation . . . as well as an immensely financially successful one. "A treaty is a great first step, Señor Presidente, but it is just a piece of paper to those who matter."

"And you have faced those corrupt and violent souls, I know. After this trip is concluded and once the treaty is ratified, I would like to have you back in Mexico City. I have not figured out the exact role just yet, but we may need some equivalent of the American drug czar—only, one who can be effective. Someone to oversee the decline—and I say this confidently—the decline of the Mexican drug cartels."

Garza smiled, both at his optimism and at the misnomer *cartel*. Cartels collude to fix prices and/or supply. As the saying goes in Mexico, one wishes the narcotics gangs were cartels. Then they would not constantly be killing each other and driving up the violence.

Garza did not deny the flame of ambition that burned inside her, driving her each day. But she felt instantly that taking such a stance would be exactly the wrong move. She needed to remain in a position to be active and do good, even if on a smaller scale than Señor Presidente foresaw for her.

"I think police work agrees with me," she told him. "I cannot see myself spending the entire day making phone calls and flattering men in neat suits."

"Is that what I am now? A flattering man in a neat suit?"

"You are that when you need to be, I think."

"Don't say yes or no just yet. Think about it. Nothing is set, and as I said, the role itself has yet to be fully determined. It might be something that interests you. And, as I say, it would be nice to have you back in Mexico City, the two of us, working for the national good."

Garza nodded, but inside her head she was spinning. He was coming on to her. She remembered Herrera teasing her, "You would make a fine first lady."

She could admit to a certain crush on him back in her school days—and she was not alone. An idealistic law professor holding forth before a room full of naive young students. And now that attractive man wore an air of authority about him, her magnetic president.

"My focus right now is Chuparosa."

Vargas threw his head back at the mention of the assassin's name. "The damned Hummingbird. Isn't your focus supposed to be on me?"

"It is, Señor. And the office of the president."

Vargas nodded, looking at her with the faintest trace of a smile. "I see. Well, I must say, I have every confidence in you here. We knew we would ruffle a few feathers signing this treaty—to say the least. But you do your job and I will do mine. It helps to have someone close at hand who I can trust."

He smiled again. No malice, no disappointment. If anything, his manner appeared to be saying, *Until tomorrow.*

Garza took that as her cue, swallowing the rest of her now-warm water. "I will leave you to prepare."

The president liked to write his own major speeches. He sat back, pulling his papers into his lap, sliding on a pair of reading glasses. "Perhaps tomorrow night, we can have a late dinner, as our schedules allow?"

She wasn't sure. "Your schedule is my schedule," she said. "Let's see what the day brings."

"Excellent."

Cecilia Garza was also staying at the Four Seasons, albeit in a single room on a lower floor. In-room dining was a tempting option, but she was waiting for a report from Virgilio, who, according to his texts, was on his way back to the hotel. So her work was not quite done for the evening.

She went downstairs into the lobby in search of food. The Garden, just off the main lobby on the Fifty-seventh Street side, was a twenty-minute wait for a table between towering indoor acacia trees. The host suggested that, as a single diner, she try the bar, which Garza was reluctant to do. She went as far as the revolving doors, but she was tired, and the thought of wandering up and down the block looking for something moderately healthy offered no appeal. She turned back, looking into the bar. Lots of beefy American males meeting after work, many in casual clusters at the long bar. A few females in pairs, alternately accepting or fending off attention from the opposite sex. A knot of robed Africans stood around two tables. Garza went a little farther inside, spotted an open chair, second to last along the bar, and made her way to it.

She ordered a very pricey baby shrimp ceviche

with fiery horseradish sauce and a light American beer. The cocktail menu was extremely tempting, especially now that the president was safely ensconced for the evening, but as a single woman seated among high-energy chatter it seemed to her that a martini glass would be seen by others as an invitation to chat. She leaned over her phone instead, the technological refuge of the shy and not-to-be-bothered, though that did not deter two separate approaches by men, one offering to buy her another drink—when she was but two sips into her first, and last, beer—and another clumsily complimenting her on her hair. "I saw you from across the room and just had to come over to tell you that," he gushed, expecting something more than a polite thank-you.

Five minutes, read Virgilio's text.

She cycled through news reports about the beheaded bodies, knowing she would learn nothing new but needing to pursue the matter nonetheless. She was copied on an e-mail from President Vargas's staff, a memo detailing the official response to the incident, should anyone in the administration be asked about it. The preferred response was essentially to defer all questions to the local NYPD authorities, which was the opposite of what Garza was trying to do.

A tap on her shoulder and she turned and it was not Virgilio but yet another potential suitor, asking about her food. Garza, tired and cranky by this time, dead-eyed him until he backed away. Not to say that she preferred the more peacocklike machismo of the Mexican male, but the American gambit of slinking into a conversation left her cold.

She glanced around the bar, glowering, hoping to send a message to any other potential interrupters that she was not there to be picked up. In doing so, she noticed a handful of women who, to her practiced cop's eye, clearly were there to be picked up. Glamorously attired ladies of the evening, young women with clinging dresses, pouty lips, and low-dangling necklaces forming bejeweled arrows pointing right to their cleavage.

Prostitutes. Drawn to the hotel by the promise of United Nations Week, or a nightly occurrence, she did not know. Though she strongly believed that a few of the men talking to them believed themselves succeeding wildly with these women, and had no idea there was going to be a gift request once they repaired back to their room.

Into this scene came Virgilio, walking quickly, compact and muscular. "I was in the lounge looking for you," he explained, when she asked what took him so long. He plucked the last shrimp off her plate. "We got nothing yet."

Garza raised her eyebrows. She showed him her phone. "You couldn't have called with that news? I would be asleep by now."

"Nothing definitive, Comandante. But we did receive word of three men missing. They are illegals, of course. All three are landscapers, and there is a corner in Bushwick where they congregate every morning, hoping to be picked up by the trucks that head for the towns north of the city, where the lawns and shrubs are tended like a movie star's eyebrows. Nothing has been reported to the police for obvious reasons, but the men are four days gone and are unreachable by telephone."

They spoke quietly and confidentially, not to be overheard. "Any link to illegal activity?"

"A sensitive subject, as you can imagine. I only spoke to one direct relative. She said no, but that is far from proof."

Garza puzzled over this. "Killing innocents—if they are—is not at all outside Chuparosa's method of operation. But why fellow Mexicans here in the States? Except to draw attention to himself, and to the Mexican contingent."

"Taunting, perhaps. Announcing himself does seem counterintuitive, but the Hummingbird is half a madman, in my opinion. Highly unpredictable. Part of what makes him so dangerous."

"Next move?"

"I am returning early in the morning to the street corner to try to learn what kind of vehicle might have picked up these three men. Though I fear the trail may have gone cold. I want to offer them money, I believe that is the fastest way."

Garza smiled. "That is why we meet in person. I have almost no American currency. You called Jefe?"

"I did. No answer. I need to be there at the crack of dawn."

"I will pass along your request and the funds will be brought to you."

"Have them find me. I'm not going to sleep tonight. I'm going to have dinner with a cousin. I have too much energy burning inside me now, too much anger. The American press's news coverage of the killings . . . it's a smear. It disgusts me. I am going to find the man who did this and restore our national honor." Virgilio remembered who he was talking to. "I will save a piece for you, of course, Comandante."

"We will get him together," she said.

Garza nodded and Virgilio left. She returned to what was left of her food and signaled for the bill.

She would remember later that she did not watch Virgilio leave. He was one of the most competent, capable men she knew. She thought nothing of him heading off for the night.

Brendan Teixeira, to be quite frank, was not happy about the meeting. It seemed hinky. Wrong.

Brendan's family had been selling fish at the Fulton Fish Market since the 1920s. Almost a century. The family joke was when a Teixeira died, you packed him in ice and put him in a cardboard box.

The Teixeiras' specialty was shellfish: oysters, clams, scallops, and mussels. There was a time when it was just Wellfleets, Blue Points, quahogs, littlenecks, the usual domestic varieties. But the Teixeiras had managed to stay ahead of the curve, flying in fresh varieties from all over the globe: spiny oysters, abalone, sea urchins, nerites. Your Asians wanted all the weirdest stuff possible. And high-end restaurants were always looking for something distinctive, something that not every other restaurant in New York had. Variety and novelty.

So you had to stay on your toes, always looking for opportunities.

Two days earlier Brendan had gotten a call from a guy who said he had a special treat he wanted to show him. A Mexican guy, said he'd be in New York for one day only with a fresh catch of *almeja negras*, a rare clam from Mexico.

Here was the thing: Brendan's dickhead uncle Raphael kept telling him he was going to give him more responsibility with the business. But it seemed like when the crunch time came, Uncle Raphael just wanted Brendan to be a gofer, driving one of the delivery vans around the city. Using Brendan as a glorified intern. Finding a new variety of clam, something the company could potentially sell for big bucks to select high-end restaurants in Manhattan, that might get Uncle Raphael to see that Brendan was good for more than just driving.

"Here is the situation," the man had said, his accent thick, though not hard to understand. "I represent a fishing cooperative of Yucatec Mayan fishermen. They got a special monopoly on this particular location based on Mexican law respecting Native Peoples. I'm bringing in half a pound of oysters by air, packed in dry ice. Four hours from the docks in Ciudad del Carmen, seven hours from the ocean. At this point in time, I'll be straight up with you, I have no permits, no paperwork, no nothing. Okay? I'm not gonna sell them to you, we not gonna do any sort of transaction that could make problems for you with Customs, Department of Fish and Wildlife, none of those guys. We meet in a parking lot over in Hunts Point, you taste the merchandise. You like the freshness, the firmness, the consistency . . . we gonna work out all the permits, the importation, make it legal going forward. You don't like the merchandise? You don't like the price? Hey, no hard feelings, my friend. That is how confident I am. Everything starts and ends with the fish, I know you agree. If I don't deliver a great product, we have nothing to talk about, am I right?"

The way the guy talked, Brendan Teixeira could tell the man had some background in the wholesale seafood business. It didn't matter what you sold— shark, tuna, mussels, octopus—in the business it was all "fish."

Brendan wasn't wild about rendezvousing with some Mexican dude he'd never met in a parking lot away from home. But what was the downside? Sometimes Customs would indeed run a sting on people in the fish business, try to sell them smuggled fish, entrap them. Or the New York State Department of Fish, Wildlife and Marine Resources would sometimes try to sell you endangered species or whatever. Big fines for that, even jail time.

But if there was no transaction, some guy just handing you a fish saying, "Here you go, taste this . . ."—nah, there was no bust in that. And since Brendan wasn't carrying cash, there was no worry about a heist. Brendan had told him that on the phone. "I don't carry cash to meetings, I just want you to understand that up front. No cash, and no merchandise in the truck."

The guy reassured him and seemed to have no concerns. A taste test, he insisted. Brendan could not see any downside for him.

The point was, you did not get to be the leading shellfish wholesaler in America by tiptoeing around worrying about shit all the time. Boldness paid off. If a guy wanted to meet you in a parking lot with a piece of smuggled fish, you had to be flexible. Everybody's got to start somewhere. He would see where things went.

BRENDAN DROVE HIS FORD Econoline van through the parking lot on the north side of the Co-op terminal, out into another parking lot. At the far end, over near the piers jutting out into the East River, he saw a man leaning against a Mercedes. A short guy, trim, compact, wearing a Yankees cap. Arms crossed. A wide smile on his face.

Brendan was not so wild about the other guy there behind him, leaning against the hood of their car: he was a big guy with a gut, wearing a Cuban-style shirt, untucked, hanging off his waist.

"You didn't tell me there was gonna be another guy," Brendan said.

"How are you, Mr. Teixeira?" the man said. He introduced himself as Ray. "This gentleman here, I told you about the Indian tribe I'm representing? I did not think I needed to inform you that I would be bringing them. Don't worry, he's a very good man. He speaks very little English, and understands not much more, so I will do the talking. Oscar here is the head of this fishing cooperative I talked about. He's the head of the tribe, Yucatec Maya. I front for them. As I told you on the phone, they have certain exclusive monopoly rights based on Mexican law, which allows them to control this species one hundred percent. Very interesting opportunity, in fact, what these people—"

"Yeah," Brendan said, not liking this as much as he did when it was a voice on the phone with an opportunity. "I'm not trying to be an asshole, but can I see the fish? I get calls like this all the time. End of the day, like you said on the phone, if the fish ain't there we're just three guys wasting time in a parking lot."

"You are correct, absolutely correct," the Mexican said. Then he turned and said something in Spanish to the guy with the gut.

Brendan had seen shows on Discovery Channel about the Mayans, these guys in the jungle down in Mexico, El Salvador, wherever the hell it was. Those men didn't even vaguely look like the guy with the big gut. They were little guys, with distinctive hooky-looking noses. This guy, he looked nothing like that. More like a football player from Texas. Plus, something about him seemed vaguely threatening. His eyes, that was what it was, they had a dead look that made Brendan nervous.

But then he supposed being an Indian in Mexico was probably like being in one of these tribes that ran casinos in the United States, a bunch of scam artists, blond guys from the suburbs in Connecticut, cashing in on the fact they had one sixty-fourth part Narragansett Indian blood or whatever.

The only weapon Brendan had was his shucking knife, which he carried at all times, day or night, in a little holster on his belt.

"Oscar is the fish expert, you understand. Head of the fishing cooperative. His people have been eating these oysters for a thousand generations, and yet never sold a single one of them. They have some sort of religious significance to his people, whatever it is. Recently, though, Oscar here came up with his own way of farming them. Suddenly they had many more of these things than the locals could eat. He decided he would cash in. That is where my involvement began. The point is, Oscar is very protective of the fish."

"I can see how that'd be," Brendan said. "You gonna show me or not?"

"Come around the trunk here. I know you will be very impressed. I have been in the fish business for a long time, and I have never tasted anything like this."

Ray went over and opened the trunk, leaning in to pick something up. Oscar, the tribesman with the gut, was just standing off at the front of the car, looking out at the river, not even paying attention to what was going on. Which made Brendan feel better. The guy didn't seem nervous or worked up. He was just waiting, looking like he was ready to go home for the night, sleep in his own bed.

"Here," said Ray.

Then he put his hand out. But instead of an oyster, he had a small black plastic thing with two shiny points protruding from it.

The shiny points flew out and struck Brendan in the chest. A wave of electric agony ran through his body. Suddenly he was lying on the ground, his arms crooked and stiff, legs straight out, his body a shivering spasm of pain.

He had been hit with a bolt of electricity from a Taser.

He stared up in the air, his vision filled by the side of his family's van. TEIXEIRA BROS. SHELLFISH—NEW YORK'S FINEST SINCE 1921. Big gold letters edged in blue, ornately scrolled. Brendan saw Oscar cross from his vehicle to Brendan's truck, yanking open the sliding door.

Sometimes trucks got heisted. A truck full of albacore could be worth eighty, a hundred grand.

But his truck was dead empty. He'd told the guy on the phone, very specific about it, he was bringing zero merchandise, zero cash to the meeting.

So why, he wondered, would these guys go to all this trouble to steal an empty truck?

Then he saw Ray, his eyes shadowed by the brim of his Yankees cap, standing over him, staring down. The look on his face was one of curiosity, not menace.

Brendan could not do anything, neither move nor scream.

The man lifted his foot, a cowboy boot with a scuffed heel.

He brought it stomping down on Brendan's head . . . and everything went black.

Detective Kiser returned Fisk's call within ten minutes, catching him before he got in to work.

"Detective Fisk," said Kiser. "You calling again about the case you don't have any interest in?"

"Exactly right," said Fisk. The details had been gnawing at Fisk all night. "Thanks for the call back. I know you're busy, so give me the one-minute download."

"No identifications yet. Working on the tattoos, going through the database. Fingerprint on the cigarette butt is a true partial, and I'm told it might not be enough to help us pull it up through latents. The 'friction ridge analysis' is inconclusive, but could be enough to tie a perp to the scene, just not vice versa. There's not enough to reliably put through the system. They are going to run some tests on how specific the partial is, but it doesn't look great."

"Okay," said Fisk.

"We're canvassing stores based on the bottling code on the Jarritos. We don't have any outstanding missing persons reports that match our headless beachgoers."

Fisk said, "Probably illegals then. More afraid of the police than trusting."

"Yup," said Kiser. "And we have no faces to put out on the news. There's some internal debate about going out with the tats, but that seems like a desperation play to me. I don't think we'll get that far. Somebody's going to come forward . . . if we don't match up one of these bodies first."

"Where are the bodies now?"

"Queens morgue. I don't think they're cutting them. Cause of death is self-evident."

Fisk said, "They may want to know if they were dead before they were beheaded."

"Maybe so," said Kiser. "Thankfully, we're getting out of my area of expertise there. Now give me the one-minute download on what this means to you."

Fisk smiled. He didn't know how to answer that exactly. The beep on his phone told him he didn't have to. A second call coming in, this one from the office. "I've got another call I have to take."

"No, you don't," said Kiser. "I need to know what I might be looking at—"

Fisk dumped him, switching over to the other call. "Fisk."

"Where are you?" It was his boss, Dubin.

"Almost there," said Fisk. This did not sound good.

Dubin read him an address in Bushwick. "Eight-three Precinct is on scene. They've got one DOA in a car in a cemetery."

Fisk frowned, wondering how this mattered to him. "And?"

"The car is registered to the Mexican consulate."

Fisk's pulse rate jumped. Comandante Garza. "Is it a female?"

Dubin said, after a pause to read his alert, "I don't have that."

Fisk said, "Give me the address again."

Bushwick was a neighborhood in Brooklyn, just on the edge of Queens. After a very rough end of the twentieth century, which saw a spike in the drug trade and violent crime, the "Bushwick Initiative" and a concerted effort from the local precinct's Narcotics Control Unit had started to revitalize the neighborhood. It was ethnically diverse, made up of Puerto Ricans, Dominicans, and Salvadorans, but the fastest-growing group in the area was Mexicans.

Fisk badged his way through the police tape at the main gate of the Evergreens. The westernmost corner of the cemetery was right on the border of Queens. For Fisk, it was a long walk back to the crime scene, and he was moving quickly. The side gate the vehicle had entered through—the area that was geographically still in Bushwick, in the Eighty-third Precinct—was closed for crime scene processing. The lanes along the graves were hilly and well groomed. He passed a towering monument of a winged angel, came to the top of a rise, and saw the black vehicle in the distance.

The incident had drawn a nice crowd. As he drew closer, he recognized a captain, an assistant chief, two Secret Service agents, a gaggle of cops and crime scene techs, and a trio of Mexican body-guards who looked ready to kill somebody.

Fisk was some thirty yards away when he spotted Garza, her black hair jumping out among the green-ery and the gray headstones. Fisk's pace slowed a bit. Not her. He felt a small measure of relief that he dismissed as simply a result of having met her the day before, and not wanting some harm to come to a person to whom he could put a name and face.

She was getting into it with the deputy inspector from the Eighty-third. It looked like a good squab-ble. The captain had six inches on her, but she was more than holding her own.

Fisk came up behind the captain, and when Garza saw him she paused just a moment, a dis-tracted beat, before continuing. "This vehicle has diplomatic plates and is the property of the Mexican government."

"This is a New York Police Department crime scene," said the deputy inspector, a black man wear-ing rimless eyeglasses. "A homicide. That trumps any claims you or your government might have—"

"Not so, sir," said Garza. "The homicide occurred within the vehicle, which is Mexican property, and we, as Mexican law enforcement officers, are autho-rized to investigate this crime. We will call on you for assistance, as needed."

"Assistance?" This word was spat out by the im-posing plainclothes woman standing shoulder to shoulder with the deputy inspector. She was a homi-cide detective in the Eighty-third. "We don't assist in these matters, Officer . . . ?"

"Colonel Garza," said the comandante, giving

the American equivalent of her rank. "Mexican Federal Police, under assignment to President Umberto Vargas's security detail. I have phone calls in to the Mexican ambassador in Washington, D.C., who is contacting the State Department."

The tall homicide detective turned to her deputy inspector. "Sir, this smells to me like a goddamn cover-up."

The deputy inspector wisely—and gently—forearmed the detective back and away. She looked mystified at the treatment, but then Fisk stepped up beside her.

"Stand down, not your fight," he said.

She looked at him, saw the badge on his belt. "Not my fight? It's my job."

Fisk nodded to her confidentially, leading her back a few more steps. "It's a fight the Eight-three is going to lose. I know that pisses you off." He was referring to the three Mexican bodyguards standing near the vehicle. The NYPD was not used to being muscled. "Can you catch me up? Fisk, Intel Division."

She gave her name as Sue Escher. Leading him toward the car, she couldn't help but seize upon his being an Intel cop as a way to get back into the case. "They're trampling all over my crime scene."

The car was a black sedan. The rear license plate was bordered in blue on top, red on the bottom. Inside the red field were the words ISSUED BY AND PROPERTY OF THE UNITED STATES DEPARTMENT OF STATE.

"Right there," said Escher. "Property of the United States!"

"That's just the plate," Fisk explained to her, smiling at her earnest tenacity.

The Mexican bodyguards—more likely plain-clothes EMP agents—moved near them in an attempt to cut them off. Fisk shook his head at the nearest one. "We can look, partner."

The Mexican said nothing, his eyes hidden behind Oakley shades.

"We have a problem?" asked Fisk.

Again, no response.

"Good," said Fisk.

The body lay lengthwise in the front seat, keeled over from behind the steering wheel. A male in his thirties or late twenties, Fisk guessed, with close-cropped black hair, wearing blue jeans and a thin, hooded sweatshirt.

Blood spray was splashed against the interior of the windshield, probably arterial. There was blood on the man's cheek, his hands, and the seat beneath his body.

Fisk did not recognize the man, only knowing that it was not the other man he had seen with Garza and General de Aguilar the day before, the man known as Virgilio.

"Knife wounds," said Escher. "Could be as many as ten or twelve. Gate was chained, links snapped by bolt cutters. We're confirming with the groundskeeper, but looks like no cameras on the gate, none in the cemetery."

Fisk nodded. "Good place to dump a body."

"I'm thinking he was forced to drive in here. Not a lot to go on in terms of tire tracks and footprints, but he didn't clip the chain and drive himself in here with multiple stab wounds. There's no blood outside the car at all. The engine was cool, the car ignition turned off."

"Wallet? ID?"

"Nothing in his pockets. Glove compartment is clean. Wears a shoulder holster. It's empty."

Fisk shook his head. "Not good."

"If I had to guess, I'd say he's one of these guys here." She thumbed at the Mexican plainclothes bodyguards. "Somebody attached to the Mexican contingent. It stinks to high heaven, Fisk."

Fisk nodded. "Something's going down. No knife found, I'm assuming."

"You assume right. Nothing found yet. We were about to remove the body and work the vehicle when this shit fight started."

Fisk looked around. "Did you call the Mexicans or did they happen to show up?"

"No, we called. Not me, the deputy inspector. Called Intel. Your people went to the Mexicans. Then little miss Colonel Bitch showed up."

Fisk smiled again. "She's tough."

Escher turned on him. "You know her?"

"Know of her. Let me get in there, see what I can do. You're not going to win the jurisdictional issue. My guess is somebody's going to slap a temporary injunction on the NYPD and seal this thing until somebody on the federal level works out who's got what. If he's in New York on a diplomatic passport, they'll claim there's some kind of diplomatic immunity."

Escher shook her head in disgust. "The guy's dead, he's beyond needing immunity. Are they going to fly up an entire crime lab to process this, too?"

Fisk nodded, showing her his open hands in a gesture of calm. "Let me see."

A skirmish erupted to their left, as a Secret Service agent got into it with a Mexican PF bodyguard who was trying to enter the vehicle. The Secret Service agent was physically restraining the man.

Fisk hustled over, and with others separated the two men. That brought the deputy inspector over, coming around one end of the car. Garza marched around the other end.

Fisk said to the Secret Service agent, "You know better than that. Get Dukes on the phone."

Then he went to head off Garza.

"You're going to need the NYPD on this one," he told her.

"Detective Fisk," she said. "I don't have time to debate this. I have lost a man—"

She was going to say more, but stopped.

Fisk said, "Could I have a word with you over here, Comandante?"

Garza looked at the other officials, then stepped to the side with Fisk away from the others.

She looked even more pale than she had when he met her at Intel headquarters yesterday—though her bearing, perhaps exacerbated by the turf argument, was more erect, her chin higher, her eyes more imperious.

"Look," he said. "I don't give a shit about any of this squabbling here. It's only holding things up. I'm playing a much longer game. I want to know what is going on here."

She did not hesitate with her comeback. "I wanted your help yesterday. You refused. You want answers for what has happened here? I don't have them yet. But when I get them, they will remain with me."

"Okay, we got off on the wrong foot yesterday. Get my meaning? It's an American idiom. We didn't hit it off right. I'm ready to apologize and move forward if you are."

"No."

"I see." Fisk looked back at the others, who were standing around waiting to see what came of this head to head argument. "I imagine General de Aguilar has official duties to attend to. I'm wondering where the other man is at this hour. His name was Virgilio."

He read distress in Garza's refusal to answer.

"I'm telling you right now, my Intel Division can help you better than anyone. If your man is missing, we can mobilize and follow his tracks. But—and that's a big goddamn but—you need to be up front with me about what is going on here."

"I accept."

"You . . . what?" Fisk all but scratched his head. "Didn't you just refuse to apologize a moment ago?"

"You were rude yesterday. But I am more than willing to put aside pride in order to draw upon your full resources in order to—"

"'Full resources' is a matter to be decided. We move predicated on the level of seriousness."

Garza said, "It is of the utmost seriousness, but the focus is President Umberto Vargas."

"Who is going to be signing a treaty with our president in a few days." Fisk reset, thumbing his pockets, checking her eyes for signs of untruth. "What do you think happened here?"

Garza said, "This man was with Virgilio last night."

"He is part of the Presidential Guard?"

"Yes," said Garza, her eyes narrowing just a bit. "And no."

"Where is Virgilio now?" asked Fisk.

Garza swallowed. "I believe he has been taken."

In Fisk's car, on the way back into Manhattan, Cecilia Garza finished a telephone call with General de Aguilar, the head of the EMP, updating him on the discovery of the dead man. She was cognizant that Fisk understood Spanish, and did not go into full detail. She hung up and looked at Fisk, watching him drive.

At first she thought he was still wearing the same clothes as the day before, but no. This was a fresh blue shirt, red necktie, and gray suit tailored to his athletic frame. He had about him a look of solidity, as though nothing that happened around him was going to move him from what he intended to do. He was quite handsome. This was something she generally distrusted in a man.

She felt a wave of vertigo as he cut across two lanes of traffic. The possibility of losing Virgilio made her sick. She might never be able to convince a foreigner what kind of man he was.

"I know this man," she said. Her voice came out strident and high-handed, as it always did when she felt stressed or defensive. Sometimes it was useful to have that quality. But she was not sure if this was one of those times. "We have been in a state of war, of civil war. Nobody trusts the police, and often with good reason. I would put my life in his hands."

"He is not a *federale*?"

"He was a member of the Centro de Investigación y Seguridad Nacional. The CISEN. Do you know what that is?"

"Mexican CIA. The equivalent."

"There is a new group forming . . ."

"The CNI," said Fisk. It was a new national intelligence agency within CISEN, created by the newly elected President Vargas, aimed at centralizing and coordinating efforts against organized crime, part of an overall movement to centralize Mexico's security apparatus."

"Calderón was focused on attacking major criminal groups," said Garza, referring to the previous Mexican president. "It was effective at times, but at a great cost. We saw massive waves of violence unleashed all across the country. Vargas's strategy is to prevent violence through intelligence gathering and improved communication within the Interior Ministry."

"Sounds like you voted for him."

"I did."

"So what was Virgilio, if that is his real name, doing here as part of Vargas's advance team? I know he did not register with our people."

"No, he is here under deep cover. Brought in on my recommendation."

"Because of a threat to your president. Why didn't you alert the United Nations, the State Department, Secret Service . . . ?"

"Is that what you would do when your president

visits a foreign power? Even a close ally? Do you turn his welfare over to them? No. We are his security force, and we are best suited to safeguard him against any threat."

They were on the bridge, crossing over into Manhattan. Garza looked for landmarks, spotting the Empire State Building spire to the west. The sight of that icon should have set her mind at ease, should have demonstrated to her that she was beyond the reach of the man who had filled the plaza in front of the Palacio de Justicia in Nuevo Laredo with headless corpses. But apparently now nothing was beyond his reach.

She was certain now. Chuparosa was here.

Fisk asked, "Which drug cartel is it? The Zetas? Sinaloa?"

Garza shook her head. "None of the above."

Fisk looked at her. "Colombians?"

"Can you drive any faster?"

She was not ready to explain it fully. And there was no way to explain it partially. She knew that questioning a man's driving was the surest way to get him to speed up and to distract him from the issue at hand.

Fifteen years ago, Cecilia Garza wouldn't have felt even a ghost of shame at feeling vulnerable in front of a stranger. In fact her twenty-year-old self would have been ashamed *not* to feel deeply, would have considered it almost a moral imperative, a necessary affirmation of her own humanity. But now? Sometimes she hardly even recognized the person she had become. A decade and a half ago she had been an outgoing, lighthearted, maybe even somewhat frivolous person. University life, ditching early classes, taking weekend trips with girlfriends, singing karaoke when that craze was new. Dancing with strangers and drinking with friends. That girl wouldn't have had a moment's regret about feeling insecure. In truth, she had been proud and even protective of her volatile artistic temperament, nurturing it: thinking of herself as someone alive to the rhythms of the world, her skin raw and sensitive to every change of wind, every frothing wave washing across the surface of her life. Like her mother. And her young sister.

Would that girl have recognized who Cecilia Garza was today? No. No, she wouldn't.

Because of course she knew the answer. She had become the Ice Queen almost as an act of pure will. Between her first and third years at university, she had not spoken to her father even once—other than an occasional exchange of meaningless pleasantries when she came home to visit her mother and her sister. Her father had disapproved of her choice of career and friends and lifestyle. So they had become . . . no, not precisely estranged. Almost worse, they had become infinitely distant from each other, irrelevant to each other somehow.

So when the phone had rung at her squalid little hippie-student-chick apartment in the Coyoacán district near UNAM, and she had answered and heard her father say, "Cecilia, it's Papi"—she had known something terrible had happened.

And yet it turned out to be worse than anything she could ever have imagined.

That had been the beginning of the cocoon

phase—a metamorphosis that had resulted, even demanded, the replacement of the frivolous and emotional girl of a decade and a half ago, emerging not as a beautiful butterfly, but as the lady Ice Queen, a woman without weakness, without pity, without fear.

She said suddenly, "I should not have left the crime scene."

Fisk shook his head. "We're good at that. We know some things. I can guarantee you that nothing will be withheld—fingerprints, trace evidence, nothing. Let the professionals do their work. This is what we can do."

She appreciated his professionalism. Even if what he was saying was just for her benefit, she acknowledged the gesture as one she herself would have made.

"Focus on when you saw him last," said Fisk, speeding north toward Fifty-seventh Street and the Four Seasons. "Because if someone had wanted to pick up his trail, they would have done it at President Vargas's hotel."

The head of security for the Four Seasons was an African man named Nnamdi Nwokcha. He wore a much nicer suit than Fisk's, and had evidently spent a great deal of time shining his shoes. But inside the security room off the rear of the lobby, he ran the complex hotel camera system like he'd been born for the job.

"I was trained in IT," Nwokcha said as he began fiddling with the buttons on the console that ran the hotel security camera system. "During the downturn, I wasn't able to find work in my field. Drove a cab for a while, then ended up in security." He punched in some numbers. "Good system. RAID array, saves data to the cloud every ten minutes. We're in the process of replacing all the cameras, but over seventy-five percent are now high-def."

Garza said, "We were at the bar, he came in alone."

"Do you have a photograph of the man?" Nwokcha asked.

"No," said Garza.

"Was he a guest?"

"Yes, but unregistered."

Nwokcha switched from the lobby door camera to

a camera just inside the bar, focused on the entrance. Garza gave him an estimate of the time. "The real heart of this system is the software. It's absurdly sophisticated. Full facial recognition, AI search functionality, and a threat assessment, object-oriented database. We have the capability to run every returning guest's face as they walk in the door and greet them by name by the time they reach the front desk if we wanted to. Management decided that is a little too presumptuous and creepy, though."

Nwokcha stopped the playback so that the image of each guest's face flickered on the screen. "That's him," said Garza.

Nwokcha reset the playback, showing Virgilio entering, glancing around, spotting someone, and starting toward them.

A new angle showed him greeting Garza. Nwokcha improved the zoom function. There was no sound, but Fisk would not have been surprised if it existed somewhere on this system.

"What am I looking for?"

Garza said, "I don't know. Maybe someone at the bar."

Fisk could tell she was searching for a particular individual.

Nwochka said, "Male? Female? Be specific."

"I don't know him by sight. I am told he is neither short nor tall, neither thin nor fat. His age should be late forties."

Fisk said, more to Garza than the security head, "That's not much to go on."

Garza said, without moving her eyes from the screen, "I know the methods more than the man."

"Then we are looking for somebody looking at Virgilio," said Fisk. "And maybe you."

Nwokcha found another camera angle which seemed to be situated above the bar itself. As Virgilio left, and Garza turned to request her food bill, a young woman turned her head, tracking the man back across the lounge to the exit.

"There," said Garza.

The young Latin woman excused herself, disengaging from the heavy gentleman she had been in the process of flattering. On high heels and in a snug black cocktail dress, she started out of the lounge after Virgilio.

"Aha," said Nwokcha. He switched back to the lobby camera.

They watched as Virgilio walked directly to the revolving doors, pushing through to the street.

The young woman followed, not quickly but casually.

Nwokcha picked them up outside, just in front of the entrance, under the overhang.

Virgilio waited, then jogged across the street to his waiting car.

The young woman just stood there on the sidewalk, holding the strap of her handbag, looking intently in Virgilio's direction. A bellman approached her, apparently inquiring if she needed a taxi. She did not answer or even acknowledge him, and he turned to a late-arriving guest.

After almost a minute or so, she turned and walked east, as though nothing had happened.

"Any more?" asked Garza.

"That is our only outdoor camera."

"It cannot pan up?" She wanted to see Virgilio get into his car, apparently.

"No, it is fixed."

Fisk said, "She was marking him."

Garza straightened. "Yes."

"Marking him?" said Nwokcha.

"Signaling someone," said Fisk. "Someone who is not on camera."

"Pointing him out," said Garza, doubly anxious now.

Nwokcha had isolated her face from the bar and was running it through their system. "The system has her flagged as a hooker."

"It does?" said Fisk.

"There's an algorithm for that. Young women in short dresses who come and go frequently and aren't tagged to a specific room . . . the system flags them as prostitutes."

"So you can blackball them?"

"Hardly. A hotel without working girls? We'd be out of business in no time. No, we just want to know who is coming and going." He tapped a few more keys. "Her first visit to the hotel, apparently. No additional information."

"She's Mexican," said Garza.

Fisk said, "You're sure?"

"Of course I am."

Fisk asked Nwokcha, "Is that the best image?"

"The computer automatically displays the clearest facial image, the one most suitable for further analysis."

Fisk said, "Could we get a printout?"

"Not from here. But I can e-mail you the image."

Fisk gave him his Intel address and waited for the e-mail to arrive at his phone. Garza had stepped away to call in an update.

Fisk asked Nwokcha, "Does the system do anything for people who don't show their faces?"

"It isolates them. Here's the trick if you don't want to be photographed. Use this." He pointed to Fisk's phone. "You pretend to talk on a cell phone, you see, with your eyes down. Wear a baseball cap or something similarly common that will obscure your face from a high angle. Then you add in sunglasses, of course, hunch up your shoulders a little. Put your finger in your other ear as though you are having trouble getting reception or hearing well in a crowded area. People do it all the time who *aren't* hiding from cameras. Looks perfectly natural."

Fisk's phone hummed with the arriving e-mail. He opened the attachment and looked at the photo image of the woman. On his phone, she looked even younger, maybe nineteen or twenty. He forwarded the image to Intel.

Back in his car, before pulling out, Fisk turned to face Garza. "We need to issue an alert about Virgilio."

"He's already dead," said Garza.

Fisk studied her. Her jaw trembled a bit, but her eyes remained fierce, focused. "You're saying he wouldn't have allowed himself to have been taken alive?"

"Only if incapacitated. I realize there is always a chance . . . but if the aim is to extract information, about President Vargas's movements and security, he won't cooperate. He will be killed when he refuses."

"Then there is no reason not to issue an alert. It might give us a lead."

Garza looked through the windshield at busy Fifty-seventh Street. She had already resigned herself to Virgilio's fate.

Fisk continued, "If you are reluctant because of showing your organization's vulnerability, or disclosing his true identity . . ."

Garza turned to Fisk. "He was a good man. I cannot accept that he is gone . . . and yet I have to."

Fisk was checking his mirrors.

"What is it?" she asked.

Fisk said, "I'm making sure nobody picked us up at the hotel to follow us."

Garza's eyes narrowed, and she looked at the hotel doors as Fisk pulled out into traffic.

"All right, Comandante," he said. "I think it is time for you to tell me who this guy is you're looking for."

She looked off into the distance as though she was trying to decide whether or not she could trust him.

"You need help here," said Fisk, more pointedly this time. "And if I'm going to marshal resources, I need a damn good reason. Who is he?"

"Two months ago, Detective Fisk, a row of headless corpses was left on the plaza of the town of Nuevo Laredo, just across the border from Laredo, Texas. The man I am chasing was responsible for those killings and numerous others. We finally tracked him back to a compound in the mountains that was his home. His refuge. He was gone. But before leaving, he killed every one of his servants and even his own men. He was making a statement. He left this behind, just a few feet away from a dead boy we believe to be his nephew."

She thumbed her phone screen, waiting for Fisk to be able to take his eyes off the road and look over. He saw the image of a newspaper photograph of President Vargas, over which was a peculiar reddish brown design.

"That's blood," she said. "And if you were able to look at it closely, you would see that it is not just a random stain. It is a drawing. It is the mark of an assassin known as Chuparosa. It means Humming-bird."

Fisk glanced at the image again. He could see it now, the wings, the needle-shaped nose.

"Why a hummingbird?"

Garza looked at the image herself before darkening the screen of her phone. "It is a symbol of vigor and potency. But specifically? I don't know. He was notoriously aligned with the Zeta Cartel as something of an inspirational figure, cherishing violence over all else."

"And you've never seen him?"

"No confirmed photographs exist. I have been tracking this man for two years now, Detective. He existed like a legend for years. In a country of dangerous men, this man is the most dangerous, by far. So brutal that his exploits were denied by many, out of sheer disbelief. Last July was the closest I have ever come to catching him."

"Why did the Zetas need to rely on one man?"

"He aligned with them early. To give you an example . . . in searching his compound after we secured it, we discovered six metal barrels below a trapdoor in a storage shed about a half kilometer from the main house. Outside the shed was a fire pit covered by a grill. You see, disposing of bodies is problematic, especially in the heat of the desert. Scavengers will dig up anything that is buried. And cadaver dogs can track the scent of the long dead. For every beheaded victim of the drug war, there are another dozen victims who simply disappear. In one particularly horrifying case, a man who reported the abduction of his family was himself kidnapped the next day."

She paused a moment, and Fisk knew she was thinking of Virgilio.

"What we believe is that Chuparosa would fill a barrel with water and two large bags of lye. He would set the barrel on the grill and light the fire, bringing the liquid inside to a boil before submerging the dead body. Over the next twenty-four hours, the body would liquefy. We found remnants of a pinkish gunk that resembled posole. Do you know what that is?"

"No."

"It is a stew. Later he would dump the liquefied remains into a nearby stream. We learned this by digging up soil samples and testing them for traces of human remains. But our forensic teams could not identify even one victim. He is as diabolical as he is thorough. Hundreds of families have no answers, and will never know the true fate of their loved ones. He has no regard for human life, Detective."

She turned to him.

"Let me see the bodies dumped in Rockaway yesterday. There may be something of value there."

Fisk had some more questions to ask before answering her. "Why does he now want to kill the president?"

"I don't know. It must have something to do with the trafficking treaty."

"That seems somewhat extreme, doesn't it? Why take this on by himself? It seems like he would be motivated more by a personal grudge."

"It is terror. I believe that is his motive. He is striking at his homeland, our country. He seeks to destabilize and disgrace. Like a . . . a bad seed, an evil son. He wants to destroy."

"So killing him, or attempting to, in the United States is easier . . . ?"

"No, but it is more profound. It is more unsettling. It shows his reach, his power."

Fisk remembered the file on Comandante Garza. "So he is certainly aware of you then."

Garza nodded. "He is."

"What if you had left the hotel last night?"

She dismissed this outright. "Virgilio left in a state of distraction. The shame of the beheadings had soured him. I believe it was a momentary lapse of attention."

Fisk frowned. "You've never had a momentary lapse of attention?"

"Not when it comes to Chuparosa."

Fisk said, "It is not a good sign when the Mexican president's protection needs protections herself."

"I need no such thing," she said, indignant. "I need cooperation. I need to see the dead bodies. It is connected, I promise you."

Fisk said, "What you need is to go to the Secret Service with this information. You need to tell them there is an active plot to assassinate President Vargas in New York City."

"Yes," said Garza. "Led by a man who no one can prove actually exists."

Fisk conceded that.

Garza went on, "Based upon a drawing in blood made over a photograph in a newspaper. See, Detective, there is a difference between what I know and what I can prove."

Fisk said, "You're right. If we go to the Secret Service with this, they'll assign you another agent, maybe two. There's too many people to watch in New York this week. And when I spoke to the head agent, asking him about the brief on Vargas, he mentioned nothing about a 'Hummingbird' or any active threat."

Garza was quiet a moment, and Fisk realized she was looking at him.

"So you did follow up, after all. After dismissing me yesterday."

Fisk shrugged. "Maybe I did."

She said, "You feel it, too. You sense it."

"Whether I do or not, the problem is getting you the support you need. A threat to your president is one thing. It's serious, and it's actionable. But a threat that might involve our president? That brings out all the big hunting dogs. That's what you want."

She crossed her arms. "So take me to Rockaway. As I asked you to do in the first place."

"You demanded it, actually," said Fisk. "And besides, the bodies are long gone from Rockaway."

Fisk slid his phone out of its dashboard mount and found Detective Kiser's number.

Detective Kiser shed his suit coat and his tie, his white shirt soaked with sweat. He looked exhausted.

Fisk said, "Appreciate you taking the time."

"Are you kidding?" said Kiser. "I welcome the professional help."

Fisk nodded. "If we're right—and I'm not saying we are—but if we're right, this has got an international dimension. And she supposedly knows more about the doer than anybody on the planet."

Cecilia Garza returned from her phone call. "Nothing still."

Fisk nodded. He understood her drive to keep moving ahead, to not dwell on the unknowns regarding her disappeared comrade, but to look for answers wherever she could find them.

Even if it was in the Queens Office of the Chief Medical Examiner.

Morgue floors were always shiny. They cleaned them every other night. A morgue attendant wearing a mask and gloves—dressed almost like a hazmat worker—pulled the wheeled tables out of the walk-in cooler. Each one held a zipped body bag.

Kiser offered Garza his three-ring binder. "We have everything photographed if you'd prefer."

She shook her head, stretching latex gloves over her hands.

"I'd very much prefer . . ." said Kiser, his voice fading to nothing.

The attendant went about opening all the black rubber bags. Kiser pinched his nose.

"Everything's been bagged and tagged," Kiser said, nasally. "One guy's got no feet. Where do you put a toe tag on a guy with no toes?"

If the attendant was aware the question was directed at him, he did not answer.

Fisk pulled on his own gloves. He waited while Garza made a careful inspection of all the bodies, helping the attendant flip them over so she could see their backs, too.

When she had looked at every single corpse she said, "Help me move these stretchers in order."

Fisk said, "Order?"

"For narrative clarity," she said. "These eight, here . . . this one here . . . this one down here . . ." When she was satisfied, she stood back. "There are three major drug cartels in Mexico at the moment. The Zetas are at war with the Gulf Cartel and Sinaloas. The Sinaloas are primarily a West Coast operation, while the Gulf is on the East Coast. The Gulf Cartel has been almost eliminated now, absorbed by the Zetas. So what's left, mainly, is the Sinaloas, the largest and strongest."

"Okay," said Kiser.

Garza pointed at the first eight bodies. "Let us

call these corpses one through eight. Fairly pedestrian tattoos, in my opinion. These are men with perhaps Mexican heritage, but so far as we can see, no evident gang affiliation."

She moved to the next three bodies. "Here, I'm guessing these are all Mexican gang members or affiliates. Their tattoos include Santa Muerte—the Lord of Death—which is often believed to be derived from the Aztec god Mictlantecuhtli." She pointed to a large tattoo of a robed figure with a skull for a face. "There, this one actually says 'Sinaloa' here, but there are various other symbolic references to the cartel which are a good deal more cryptic. Bottom line, though, these three are all almost certainly Sinaloa Cartel members, ex-members, or affiliates. As you can see, all of these men have all been tortured or mutilated or abused in one way or another."

She went to the second-to-last body.

"Here we have a man covered with tattoos . . . but tattoos of a very different character. First, you will note from his skin tone and body hair color that he appears to be a Caucasian. Also, all of the words tattooed on his body are in English rather than Spanish. But more importantly, you will note that these are well-executed tattoos, composed in rich color, with complex and varied detail. I would go so far as to classify these as highly artistic, wouldn't you?"

"If you say so," said Kiser, still plugging his nose.

Fisk was impressed with her review of the bodies: crisp, well reasoned, and unflinching.

She continued, "And other than the head and fingertips being removed, there is no evidence of torture or desecration on this last body."

"*Other* than the decapitation," said Kiser.

"Yes—setting that aside for the moment." She pointed at the last man. "Finally, we have this last body. Again, head and fingertips removed. His skin was apparently quite pale, even before death. And there is only one tattoo on his body."

Fisk saw it. A black hummingbird.

"It's him," said Fisk.

"Taken together, these bodies constitute a sentence, a phrase, a grammar, a message. This message announces that an assassin is here, someone of substance, someone whose work must be taken seriously. Someone capable of sophisticated, ruthless, extreme violence. Moreover, the manner in which they were killed draws a connection to other killings in Mexico.

"Now, we turn to these two. Let us focus on this man with all the tattoos. These are of a higher artistic quality than the others. None of them are gang related in the least. No flaming skeletons, no broken chains, no skulls or AK-47s, no Blessed Virgins. Now, if you examine the orientation, several of them appear to be turned at peculiar angles."

"What do you mean?" said Kiser.

"Just look. Normally a tattoo is intended to be viewed while a person is standing. But this one . . . and this one . . . and this one . . . are oriented sideways. So that if he were standing at rest, you would have to crane your head all the way to the side in order to look at them properly. Odd, right? But . . . consider this. If he crossed his legs, you see, this tattoo of the duck . . . it would be oriented toward his face. Now, here, this one is a Buddhist image known as Fudo Myo-o. The flaming bodhisattva with the rope and the sword. If he crooked his arm—as for instance laying it on a desk in front of him—this Fudo Myo-o tattoo on his forearm would also be oriented toward his face. And these oddly oriented tattoos are among the most intricate and beautiful on his body."

Fisk nodded. "This guy did himself. He's a tattoo artist."

"Putting his best work on his own body. And not because he had to, by the way. A competent tattoo artist transfers a picture onto the skin and then just fills in the lines. Paint by numbers. No, he oriented them this way for his own enjoyment. He wanted to see the fruit of his own labor."

Kiser said, "That's something I can work with. And what about this last guy? The pale one. He's got nothing except that bird."

Cecilia Garza looked at the last corpse, the one with the small tattoo of the hummingbird between the shoulder blades. Her face momentarily showed . . . not sadness exactly, Fisk thought. But something close. More like a soul-deep weariness.

"I have seen this design before. Many times. This one was traced from an original design. Always drawn by the same hand. And this tattoo is a very accurate, careful representation of that design. It's a faithful copy, if you see my point. It captures the gesture, the expressiveness of the original."

Kiser looked skeptical. "I'm just following along, hearing what you're saying. But I'm not sure I'm getting it yet."

"He's unusually pale," she said. "No other blemishes. He is, if you will, a human canvas. See the sand from the beach still lodged in the design?"

Kiser cocked his head for a better look. So did Fisk.

Garza went on, "See where the hair was shaved, from just below the neck? A corona of redness beneath the skin around the design? That is not lividity. The blood has settled on the front."

"It was a brand-new tattoo," said Fisk, straightening. "He got this hummingbird right before he was killed."

"It is a cartel signature, usually a 'Z' for Zetas, a '13' for MS-13, something like that. The whole point of this . . . display . . . this work . . . whatever you want to call it, is to show us this tattoo. To frame it, to underline it."

Kiser said, "And this bird means something to you."

"Something," said Fisk, going back to the presumed tattoo artist. He rolled him back onto his stomach, hairy buttocks in the air. "Look at this."

Fisk pointed at his right shoulder. It was a tattoo of an attractive woman, the image rendered in impressive detail.

Fisk said, "He couldn't have done this one himself."

"No," Garza said. "Most likely he did the drawing and had a colleague paint by numbers."

Fisk snapped off his gloves and took out his phone. He snapped a picture of the tat.

"You don't need to do that," Kiser said. "I told you, forensics got photos of all the tats already."

Fisk just nodded, returning his phone to his pocket.

Garza said, "I need to run those images through our database back in Mexico City."

Kiser looked at Fisk. "What say you?"

Fisk said, "I don't see any need for you to get any special authorization. This is about solving crime, right?"

"Well," said Kiser, "actually it's more about keeping my job. Kidding. Anything that puts me one step closer to understanding what I'm looking at is good. Can we go now?"

They stepped out of the morgue proper, into the outer offices. Fisk stopped Kiser. "As soon as we start pulling this together, you'll know as much as we do. Meantime, not a word of this to anybody who doesn't need to know, okay?"

"Sure. You got it."

"The president of Mexico is in town to sign a major antinarcoterrorism accord. Today we find we have the top Zeta hitter—former top Zeta hitter—in town. I'm not going to draw any straight lines for you because I don't know yet if they're there to be drawn. But you can see where this is going, right?"

"Holy shit," said Kiser.

While Garza was pushing through the photos of the tattooed corpses to her people in Mexico City, Fisk e-mailed his photograph of the woman's face to Intel.

His phone rang almost right away. It was Nicole. "What is this now?"

Fisk explained the photograph's source. "It's so photorealistic, I think you need to run it through the facial recognition program."

"Well, it's more detailed than a criminal sketch, but—"

"It's worth a try. It's never been a one hundred percent unique metric, but it can narrow down the pool of potentials. Bounce it through FBI and State. State has something like seventy-five million faces in their system, FBI not nearly as many. Every single American who has walked through a major airport in the past decade is in the database, for starters. They've got this new next-generation software that creates a three-D projection from an image. Maybe we get lucky."

Nicole said, "If I can get tagged in all my friends' photographs on Facebook, why can't this work, too?"

Fisk said, "Exactly."

Garza came back with some information on the hooker, including a picture on her phone.

"Silvia Volpi. Missing since last February." Garza looked up from her phone. "Trafficked up north."

"Forced prostitution," said Fisk. "She's going to be tough to find."

Fisk had her send him the photo, which he then submitted to Nicole at Intel.

Fisk said, "I think you should have your president moved from the Four Seasons."

"Already have," said Garza. "Plans are being made now. The problem is finding a suitable location last minute."

"Tough week for hotels," said Fisk.

Garza said, "We are doing it very quietly, while maintaining our reservation at the Four Seasons. We are running a program to make it seem as though President Vargas is still there, and swapping out agents on bogus errands in hopes they will be tailed. Maybe we can trap someone."

Fisk nodded his approval. "Good one." Fisk received the information on Silvia Volpi. The photograph was apparently from her *quinceañera*, the celebration of her fifteenth birthday. She was wearing a pink, promlike dress with a matching bouquet of pink roses, the photograph taken professionally. Fisk shook his head as he forwarded it along.

Fisk's greeting upon his second visit to the Secret Service's New York field office in two days was not as cordial as the first. Dukes was even more tense than the day before.

"Christ, Fisk."

"I know. I think we need to brief ICE, Customs, State, DEA, maybe Carlisle at the UN. Along with the Mexican contingent, of course."

Dukes looked at Garza. "This guy Virgilio, why didn't he register with us coming in?"

Fisk intervened. "Let's work that out after we find him, okay?"

Dukes backed off after a moment, raising his hands, conceding the point. "We *will* get into it later, though," he said to Garza. "We are, after all, the world's premier agency at protecting government representatives. I get national pride and all, but . . ."

"Dukes," said Fisk.

"All right, all right. Let's get your man back, and let's protect your boss, Señor Presidente."

Fisk knew why some said that the Secret Service was difficult to deal with. They were very smart and hard-nosed, but by the nature of their mission, they also tended to be myopic and high-handed. If you weren't part of the solution, well, you were part of the problem—that kind of thinking.

Garza was not intimidated by Dukes. "My sole priority is to protect the president of Mexico," she said coolly.

Dukes said, "All the stuff we have on this Chuparosa is related to drug gangs. You're convinced he's a legit threat?"

"Entirely convinced," she said. "Based upon my examination of the corpses from Rockaway Beach, as well as certain information which is confidential to my agency. It is my belief that an attempt on the life of President Vargas will be attempted while he is in New York, and I further believe that Virgilio's disappearance is connected to that attempt."

Dukes said, "What is Virgilio's real name?"

Garza shook her head. "I cannot see how that is a concern right now."

Dukes smiled. "That's exactly the attitude I don't want, Comandante. Certain information which is confidential to your agency? I trust you will reveal the pertinent aspect of that information so as to make it possible for us to incorporate specific and credible threats into our planning scenarios?"

Fisk knew that her credible information consisted of a bloodstained piece of paper clipped from a newspaper.

"Not at this time," she said.

"Not at this time." Agent Dukes gave her a strained smile. Fisk could see the wheels turning in Dukes's head. He had no dog in the turf battle over the crime scene in Queens, and no reason to doubt her suspicions about the missing Virgilio, but he suspected that Garza's reticence was part of an attempt by the Mexican government to cover up some potentially damaging or embarrassing news about the murder of a Mexican spy operating in the United States.

Dukes's dilemma was clear. If Garza was bringing him a bogus assassination plot, it would create a vast amount of work for him—work which could potentially make it difficult for him to fulfill his duty to protect the dozens of other world leaders on hand, never mind the heads of the United States government. On the other hand, if he failed to properly prepare for a legitimate threat, he would be committing career suicide.

"Comandante Garza," he said, "I would be pleased to offer the full resources of the Secret Service's Threat Assessment Division to assist you in determining if such a plot is, in fact, imminent."

"That will not be necessary. The threat is imminent."

Dukes gave her a wincing smile. "Perhaps I'm not being clear enough, Comandante. If you expect to have our fullest assistance and cooperation in the protection of your president, it is imperative that you present us with any actionable intelligence you might possess with respect to any imminent assassination plot."

Garza sat silently, looking at Dukes as though he had not spoken at all. Dukes shook his head, exaggerating a shrug.

"Are you refusing to accept our assistance?" Dukes asked.

"My agency, along with assets of the New York Police Department, is following up on several leads at this very moment, Agent Dukes. We will bring them to you the moment that we have reached more solid and actionable conclusions."

Dukes folded his arms across his chest. "That is absolutely unacceptable, Comandante Garza."

"You may take it up with my boss."

"General de Aguilar? I'll call him right away," said Dukes, the wincing smile still frozen on his face.

"I was referring to President Vargas," said Garza, producing her phone and ready to press a speed-dial button. "I'll let you speak with him directly."

Dukes frowned, unimpressed by this power play, but having to stand down anyway. "That won't be necessary at this time, Comandante."

She tilted her head a few degrees to the side, then thumbed her phone off. "As you wish," she said.

Dukes gave Fisk a look, as though to say, You fucking owe me for this.

"The way I see it, three things need your immediate attention," said Dukes, speaking to Garza. "One is already taken care of, and that is the hotel move."

Garza looked perturbed. "How did you know?"

Dukes smiled flatly. "We know," he said. "The second is the Mexican Independence Day celebration in Woodside, where Vargas is due to speak. An outdoor daytime event, that's an obvious red flag. And the big one is the dinner with POTUS, currently scheduled at that Mexican restaurant . . ." Dukes snapped his fingers, trying to recall the name.

"Ocampo," said Garza.

"It's almost too late to reset and rescreen everybody for that event."

Fisk was shaking his head. What was this?

Dukes said, "A dinner at a small restaurant in the West Village, on Waverly, a half block off Seventh Avenue. It's already a nightmare, that venue. Now with the thermostat turned up even higher, I don't know if it's going to fly."

Garza said, "President Vargas will not alter his schedule—"

Dukes didn't let her finish. "Well, it may get altered for him. I'm going to set up a fresh walk-through at this Ocampo, my office will let your people know when. Try to talk him out of the festival. The earlier he cancels, the better. For him."

Fisk's telephone and Garza's telephone buzzed almost simultaneously. They were answering theirs when Dukes's phone rang.

St. Michael's Cemetery on Astoria Boulevard in East Elmhurst is one of the oldest cemeteries in the New York metropolitan area. The cemetery is open to all faiths, though it is owned and operated by St. Michael's Episcopal congregation on the Upper West Side of Manhattan. It is the final resting place of Granville T. Woods, better known as "the black Edison," and ragtime composer Scott Joplin.

Again, a secondary entrance gate had been breached overnight. But the gate had swung back to its usual position, making it appear closed as usual. The bodies had been discovered by a groundskeeper removing dead flowers from a nearby grave.

Silvia Volpi lay floating in a small pond on the southeastern corner of the property. She was facedown, only her back and shoulders out of the water, but Fisk recognized the dress from the hotel security camera. He could see abrasions and blood on her neck and shoulders.

They were pulling her to the bank as he arrived. That she was floating indicated that she was dead before she was put in the water. A drowning person swallows water, expelling oxygen from the lungs, usually resurfacing a day or two later as gases build up inside the body. An already dead body in still water generally remains buoyant due to its air-filled chest cavity.

The other body floated closer to the bank on the other side of the pond. Fisk could tell by the way Garza looked at the body that it was Virgilio, even before they hauled him to dry land and turned him over.

He had been beaten, but the wounds were barely swollen, indicating that he had been in a fight and died soon after. His shirt was torn and bloodstained. The way the fabric lay against his chest, Fisk could see multiple stab wounds in his chest, a half dozen or more. His hands were also cut with defensive wounds. His eyes stared at the sky, but lacking the supreme blankness of most corpses Fisk had seen. He wondered if knowing he was dying for a cause—choosing death over betrayal—informed Virgilio's steadfast expression.

Garza stared down at the man. Fisk could only guess at their relationship, but felt it had been purely professional. Perhaps she saw in Virgilio a dedication to lawful order complementary to hers, but which, as a woman in Mexico, she felt herself unable to fulfill as completely as he had. Perhaps she envied his easier road to success . . . and perhaps it was this ease that had allowed him to let his guard down at the worst possible time.

Fisk went around backing off arriving law enforcement. There is, even in veterans, a human impulse to get close to the scene of a crime. He wondered why they had chosen two different cemeteries.

He came back to Garza, who was on the phone with General de Aguilar. "Yes, General . . . It would be most proper for you to come, I think. I cannot remain here a moment longer than is necessary . . . No, too many things to do. Yes. Thank you. . . ."

She hung up. Fisk watched her. She seemed to be okay. Maybe too okay.

"No cameras in a cemetery," said Fisk. "I'm thinking they dumped the other car and body first, hoping to get something out of your man. Looks to me like he went down fighting."

"Of course he did," said Garza quietly.

"And the girl? Probably killed because she was a link to them."

"Exactly why," said Garza. "No witnesses. Ever."

"We should key on her. I know she's an illegal, but she had to live somewhere, sleep somewhere. Know someone."

Garza nodded, still looking at the ground.

Fisk said, "There are enough traffic cameras in the areas surrounding both cemeteries that we should get some images of them. License plates, maybe faces. It will take time, but we will have something."

Garza nodded again, saying nothing.

Fisk said, "I'm not going to ask you if you are okay, because I know you are not."

"I am fine."

Fisk waited for more. "We're going to get this guy. This is New York City, not Mexico."

She looked up at him with heated eyes, as though taking offense.

Fisk said, "What I mean is, this isn't his native

country, he doesn't know how everything works. He's going to screw up."

A crime scene tech came over. "We checked his pockets, no phone."

Garza stared at the young man, then nodded. She e-mailed this news back to her people. "He will have cloned the phone by now, disabling GPS and cellular service. He wants to know what Virgilio's schedule was . . . and by extension, President Vargas's."

Fisk said, "I'm sure he had it encoded. It was a secure phone?"

"It was," said Garza. "But how can we assume anything except that he has that information, or will have it soon?"

"It's mostly public, I imagine."

"It is something to check. To make sure. We should go now."

"Go where?" asked Fisk, surprised.

"To go over the president's itinerary."

"Hold on," said Fisk. "Take a minute here." He pointed to the body, just a few yards behind her. "It's okay."

"I am fine," she said. "Let's go."

She started past him. Fisk hooked her arm, spinning her around . . . and raising her ire.

"Take a moment," he said. "Pay your respects."

Garza glared at him, all fire. "I will pay my respects when I have time, Detective. Let go."

Fisk let go. She walked around to the girl's body, speaking to the arriving Mexican EMP agents, then continuing on to the car.

Fisk followed, watching her climb inside while checking her phone. He knew he should let it go, but he could not.

He climbed in behind the wheel, leaving his door open. "Look," he said, "maybe this is none of my business, but you should—"

"It is entirely none of your business. This is the business of the Policía Federal and the Estado Mayor Presidencial."

"Use this anger, this pre-grief. Don't run from it."

Garza did not look up from her phone. "Is that your professional advice? Is that what you did when your comrade was killed by Jenssen?"

Now it was Fisk's turn to stare at her. Garza was tapping out an e-mail with her thumbs.

"You know about that?" he said.

"Of course," she said, clipped. She tapped in a few more letters, then said, "I suppose you were sent to therapy and pursued a talking cure."

Fisk said, "I did. I had no choice. It is built into the system."

"If we did that in Mexico, there would be no time for work. No time at all. You tell me to honor my fallen comrade? I will do so by pursuing the man who killed him."

Fisk nodded, still digesting her attitude. "And by pretending not to be distraught over his death?" he said.

Garza did not look at him, did not say anything.

Fisk started the engine and said, "I can see you come by your reputation honestly."

Garza resumed typing out her e-mail as she

opened her door and got out of Fisk's car, walking back to the cemetery gate.

Fisk did not follow her. And she did not want him to. She was going to ride with someone else.

Fisk returned to Intel headquarters. He fed more money into the vending machine and ate another chicken salad sandwich on damp white bread from a triangular plastic carton. He badly needed a long run or some gym time, but couldn't foresee either one happening until after United Nations Week was over.

He filed the forms to get eyeballs on corner cameras within a four-block grid of each cemetery. He narrowed the window of time from 10:00 P.M., when Virgilio departed the Four Seasons, and 7:00 A.M., just after dawn.

He had a long list of e-mails, which he was able to cull by two-thirds without too much effort. The rest pertained more directly to his desk duties. A few of them he was able to pawn off on others. The rest remained, needing to be addressed.

Two of them were from the U.S. Attorney's office downtown. Those he did not even open.

Fisk went back to the break room for a bag of barbecue potato chips. He sat at the only table, brushing away the last person's crumbs, and finished the large bag in about ten handfuls. He crumpled up the evidence and tossed it into the trash, stopping to buy a Coke Zero before returning to his desk.

Nicole had gotten back to him. Nothing yet on the tattoo sent for face recognition. He checked his phone and found he had a missed call from Kiser.

"I heard there are more dead Mexicans," said Kiser, answering on the first ring.

"There are," confirmed Fisk.

"These ones have heads?"

"They do." Fisk gave him the details, just generally. "There is a link, but I would pursue your own case independently for now. You don't want a piece of this interagency morass."

"That's good advice I already gave myself," said Kiser. "You can thank Comandante Garza for me."

Fisk exhaled. "I could if she were here. Thank her for what?"

"The break. You don't know?"

"Not unless you tell me."

"Her agency used the tattoo photographs to identify four of the headless horsemen. Two of them they got from Mexican driver's licenses, no criminal histories. They were illegals, but apparently not bad guys. Bystanders who got caught in this Hummingbird guy's nest. The other two are illegals linked to the Zeta Cartel. And the Terrorist Screening Center has both on the No Fly List."

The little-known Terrorist Screening Center is a division of the National Security Branch of the FBI, though it is a multiagency organization including representatives from the Department of Justice, the Department of State, the Department of Homeland Security, the Department of Defense, and the U.S. Postal Service. While the No Fly List began as strictly a register of terror suspects not permitted to board a commercial aircraft for travel into or out of the United States, it had since grown to include other more generalized criminals, including known traffickers.

"I'm writing," said Fisk, grabbing a pencil and paper.

"A Mexican national by the name of Carlos Echaverria. Nickname Carlito. Big huge guy, one with the gang tats. I guess Carlito translates as Little Carlos. Kind of like calling a big guy Tiny. Unless there's a bigger Carlos in his family."

"I get it," said Fisk, not in the mood for Kiser's banter. "Stay on point here."

"Anyway, this Carlito guy, he's Zeta Cartel connected. U.S. No Fly, but okay to board in Mexico and land in Canada, apparently. He flew into Montreal on July twenty-third, Aeroméxico Flight 269 from Mexico City. Payment for his ticket was on a credit card, a prepay Visa from a check-cashing store in Laredo, Texas. Presumably somebody bought it for him and carried or mailed it to him."

July was when Chuparosa would have fled Mexico after the beheadings, Fisk remembered.

"The other corpse's name is Elias Rincon—also a No Fly—flew in to Montreal the next day, July twenty-fourth. No hotel registrations in Montreal under those names, at least none that we can find. No record of either of them entering the United States, obviously."

Fisk said, "Flying into Montreal . . . it's a pretty good bet they snuck in across the border into upstate New York."

"Right. Of course."

Fisk remembered the smoky-bomb fiasco. "It happens to be an area I have some expertise in," he said drily.

Kiser said, "The only other charge on the Visa prepay was a rental car picked up on the twenty-third and never returned. Surprised they haven't found that yet."

"It's not a priority," said Fisk. "Most rental companies would prefer the insurance money to the return of another beater with twenty thousand miles on the odometer."

"I'd like to push this a little further," Kiser said. "You think you could help me out? I know you Intel detectives have deep contacts. Maybe you can even do it yourselves. And a lot faster than I can."

Fisk said, "What are you thinking?"

"Airport surveillance photos for those dates. Maybe a few dates on either side also. If you think your Hummingbird man might have come into the United States the same way."

"It's a good bet." This guy had shown he was more than willing to kill those around him to preserve his anonymity. Chuparosa guarded his secrets ruthlessly. But at the same time, his circle was drawing ever smaller and smaller. It didn't make sense.

Fisk told him he would get into it with the Canadian Security Intelligence Service. "No promises, but I'll keep you in the loop."

"Do that," said Kiser. "And again—thank Ms. Garza when you see her."

"Uh . . . yeah."

Fisk hung up. He wrote up a memo with the dead men's names and a request that they be searched for on Montreal-Trudeau's CCTV system via the CSIS.

Then he checked his e-mail and text messages again, looking for at least a CC on the No Fly List discovery Garza had forwarded to Kiser.

There was none.

Having no messages from Garza at all angered Fisk, both professionally and personally. That was when his phone rang. An unfamiliar number, though he recognized the exchange. Somebody from the U.S. Attorney's office. Probably the same guy who'd e-mailed him twice already. He listened to it ring, thinking about pressing the red circle that would kick it to his voice mail . . . but he knew how U.S. attorneys were. This guy would call again and again.

Instead, Fisk thumbed the green button on his cell.

"Fisk."

"Hi, Detective Fisk? Kevin Leary, U.S. Attorney's office. How are you?"

"Super busy. What can I do for you that won't take more than one minute?"

"Oh. Um . . . look, I don't know if you got my e-mail . . . ?"

"I have not, no."

"Okay, sir, well, here's the thing. I'm looking at Case Number S Dash Seven Six Four One Three? Exhibit Number Three One One Nine? Anyway, Detective, the thing is it weighed out at a one hundred and thirty-nine point two five three grams. And it weighed in at one hundred and thirty-nine point two five one grams."

"Is this supposed to mean something to me?" asked Fisk.

"It's the polonium," said Leary. "From the smoky-bomb case. You didn't see the subject line of my e-mails?"

The prosecutor was starting to get that *I'm getting irritated because I'm smarter and more important than you* tone in his voice. This was always Fisk's cue to start stalling, just on principle.

"No," said Fisk, trying to find a way out of this.

"The evidence sheet has a weigh-in and a weigh-out line."

"I gather that. I'm sure you must have a question, Kevin. I just haven't heard it yet."

Leary said, "The weight change is a problem."

"The point zero zero two grams?"

"The defense has filed a brief about there being less polonium-210 than when originally booked into evidence. This is your case."

"It is my case. But I'm not responsible for the evidence handling. When I left it, it was in a sealed steel container inside a sealed evidence envelope."

"Where do you think it went, then?"

"The point zero zero two grams? Are you sure you calibrated the machine correctly? What is that, half a grain of salt?"

"Detective, the defense is trying to exclude the evidence by claiming evidence tampering. If we don't have the evidence, we have no case."

Fisk said, "Was the evidence envelope still sealed?"

Leary said, "No, the envelope was not still sealed. Defense had to open it to weight it."

"Was the steel container still sealed?"

"Is that a trick question?" asked Leary. "I assume it was, they didn't say otherwise."

"Well, then?" said Fisk.

"I don't know," said Leary. "Can those envelopes be duplicated?"

"I doubt it," said Fisk. "But you should pursue that with someone responsible for handling said evidence. For example, the defense."

Leary sighed. "You see, this is the sort of thing that brings down otherwise ironclad cases. A little bit of doubt in the jury's mind . . ."

". . . and O. J. Simpson goes free, I get it. Why don't you reweigh it yourself? Maybe the mistake is on their end."

"I did reweigh it. Pain in the ass. It says one thirty-nine point two five one grams. That's pretty damn exact."

"Kevin, no offense," said Fisk. "But this doesn't seem like my problem."

"Your signature is next to the larger amount, so it is potentially your problem. I weighed the evidence on a scale called a Lyman Micro-Touch 1500. It's intended for weighing bullets. Because normally bullets are the only evidence that small that needs to be weighed with any degree of accuracy, it happened to be the only scale in the evidence lockup that weighs in fractions of grams. Now the thing about the Lyman 1500 is that if it's been out of service for a while, you have to let it warm up for up to twenty-four hours before it stabilizes for final calibration. Up to that point, it varies by a couple of thousandths in either direction. That gives a potential range for error of point zero zero five grams, top to bottom."

"Okay, so, there we go."

"This is all lawyer talk I'm doing now. This is how we'll have to counter this. The machine's accuracy is affected if you don't have time to warm it up for twenty-four hours and then calibrate it."

Fisk said, "I didn't weight it in myself. I did sign for it."

"Okay," said Leary.

"In lawyer speak," said Fisk, "no matter what kind of scale you use, there will always be some level of error. So the only scientifically supportable approach is to round the observed figure to a reasonable, scientifically supportable number based on the published accuracy of the machine."

"One hundred and thirty-nine . . . uh . . ."

"One hundred and thirty-nine point two five grams, correct."

"But still . . . if it says in your logbook—"

"The logbook will not be entered into evidence," said Fisk. "Here's what you do. You put a little footnote in the filing that says, quote, 'All exhibit weights expressed to published limits of machine accuracy.' That's a scientific term that you can look up in any manual of bench chemistry. If it ever comes up—and it won't—but if it does . . . then I'll have to get on the stand and explain that I've taken all these courses in evidence handling and scientific measurement and blah blah blah, and that scales have inherent levels of inaccuracy, that they have to warm up, calibration, blah blah blah, and that's why we round the number to one thirty-nine point two five, that this number is the scientifically correct number despite the fact that the machine has a higher level of recordable and observable resolution."

The line was silent.

"Kevin. A hundred and thirty-nine point two five grams."

Leary said, "Okay."

"I should not have to be telling you how to do this. Okay? This is stuff you're supposed to know."

Leary said, "Okay. I'll get back to you."

Fisk said, "No rush," and hung up.

He darkened the screen and sat there a while, looking at his phone.

Secret Service agent Dukes said, "Fisk, I only have a minute."

"It's the Mexican president's itinerary. There's one blocked-out period of time that isn't accounted for."

"Okay."

"That doesn't concern you?" asked Fisk.

"It might if I didn't know what it was."

"So you do know what it is."

"I didn't say that."

Fisk waited a breath. "So what is it?"

"Some things I'm not allowed to share, Fisk. Even with a friend. That's my job."

"Not even if it might affect your job. That is, protecting visiting heads of state."

"If I knew there was an immediate need to know, maybe. Why not ask your girlfriend?"

Fisk winced. "That's funny."

"It's smart. I'd help her out if I could, too. And if I wasn't otherwise married."

Fisk scowled. He was tired of this. "What time is the restaurant walk-through?"

The Waldorf was fully occupied," said President Vargas, watching his bags being unpacked on the seventh floor of the Sheraton. "I guess I'll make do."

He seemed to regret the attempt at humor almost as soon as he uttered it.

"I didn't know the man well," he said. "But I know he was your personal hire."

Garza nodded, wanting to move past this. "It is a terrible loss. Do you understand my concerns now?"

"I have understood them from the beginning," said the president. "But I cannot see any way to curtail my activities here."

"The festival for Independence Day," said Garza. "That has to be left off the schedule."

Vargas stopped, sitting down on his bed. "This visit is where we set the tone for my entire administration. I understand that the treaty has angered the cartels. That is its purpose, in large part."

Garza said, tamping down her impatience, "This is not a cartel. This is a lone assassin. I am sure of it."

Vargas clapped his hands once. "Who is dead set on making an example of me? If you know he is here, and know his intent, is it not that much easier to forestall him?"

"Not this man. He is killing everyone who has aided him in coming here. I believe there is no way to deter him from his goal."

Vargas said, "I have not known you well for many years now. But your reputation is such that I would think you could not back down from such a challenge."

Garza bristled at this second reference to her "reputation" in a matter of hours. "It is quite a different matter when the life of the Mexican president is at stake."

"Granted," he said. "Which do you want more? To save me? Or to catch this Chuparosa?"

"I want both. They go hand in hand."

"And trust me, I have no desire to be a . . . a piece of bait. But allow me to do my job, and I will allow you to do yours. Tomorrow will be a great day, signing the treaty on the anniversary of our country's independence." He checked his wristwatch. "Now, if you will excuse me, I am due at the UN for a meeting with the Costa Rican ambassador and I am already running late."

Elian Martinez was looking in the mirror, straightening his black bow tie, when he heard the door buzz.

"You expecting anyone?" he called to his wife, Kelli.

"No," she called back.

"Guess I better get it then," he said.

There'd been some push-in robberies in the neighborhood lately, the same guy in every case, forcing his way into women's apartments, stealing their stuff, beating them up. Elian figured it was always better to have a male voice answer the buzzer.

He came out of the bathroom, pulling on his coat. He was going to be late for work if he didn't get lucky with the traffic.

He pushed the button on the intercom. "Yes?"

A voice in Spanish came back, "Señor Martinez, it's Sergeant Benividez with the Policía Federal. We're here for the credentials inspection."

"The what?"

"I'm sure the Secret Service informed you. We're part of President Vargas's advance team. We're validating the credentials of everyone who'll be—"

"Ah, sí, momento, momento!" He pressed the button

releasing the lock down in the vestibule. He could hear the buzz of the lock mechanism right through the wall.

"What is it?" Kelli said. She spoke no Spanish. Elian was getting his Ph.D. at NYU, moonlighting as a waiter. He and Kelli had met the first day of grad school and they were both finishing up their dissertations in Econ. He could practically taste the money he'd be making on Wall Street come this time next year. But in the meantime, they were currently clipping coupons and pulling nickels out of the couch cushions, just trying to get by.

Elian said to her, "I told you about President Vargas, right?"

Kelli said, "Only about twenty times."

"Hey, give me a break. I think it's cool, I might be personally serving the president of Mexico."

"Why don't you slip him your résumé inside his oysters?"

"Ha ha. Though actually not a bad idea."

There was a knock on the door.

Elian opened the door and let two men into the room. They were both wearing dark suits, sunglasses. A big guy and a medium-sized guy. The big guy seemed a little out of shape to be presidential security, but this was Mexico, maybe their standards were different than the United States.

"Come in, come in," Elian said, ushering them in. "Sorry about this . . . the mess."

The smaller man entered first, looking around. He acted very official. "We'll make this nice and quick," he said. "Sorry for the inconvenience. We just need to see your credential documents yet again, to log you into the database. This won't take but a few minutes."

Elian frowned. "The Secret Service said they were taking care of everything. Is there some reason why—"

"We have to double-check every detail," the man said, smiling broadly. "It is a redundancy, I agree. But that is our job. Be assured, you will see us at least one more time before the event. You understand how it is."

Elian nodded as though he did. "Sure, sure, no problem." Elian just wanted to get it over with so he could get to work. He went back into the bedroom, pulled out the manila envelope they'd given him the other day, and carried it back into the main room. He emptied the contents onto the hall table. "Is this what you're looking for?"

"*Exactamente.*"

Elian hadn't really looked in the envelope yet. There was a plastic ID with a hologram running across his photograph, plus some kind of itinerary with a big official-looking seal on it and a letter of instruction. The big man picked up everything from the envelope, then nodded to the other man. The other man took out a small digital camera and snapped a picture of each item, front and back.

"*Muy bueno,*" he said, when he was finished. "*Muchas gracias,* my friend. Your cooperation is most appreciated."

"*De nada,*" Elian said. "Is that it?"

"That is all for now, señor."

Elian nodded, thinking, That was easy, and opened the door for the men. They departed without handshakes, walking straight to the hallway elevator.

After Elian had closed the door, and heard the elevator door open and close, he felt oddly relieved. Something about authority figures, especially such humorless ones as those, always bugged him.

"Are they gone already?" asked Kelli, coming out of the bathroom with her head tilted, sliding a small pearl earring into her right earlobe. She tended bar in a midtown hotel three nights a week and was also getting ready for work. Kelli was a beautiful woman, with porcelain skin, red hair, and very green eyes that had a skeptical expression. Even now, after he'd known her for four years, she still seemed impossibly exotic to him. "That was super quick," she said.

"Just checking up on me, I guess," said Elian.

"Well, wouldn't they have copies or something? Why would they need to take pictures of it?"

"He said it was just a verification process." Elian shrugged. One thing he did know was that you didn't get anywhere by bugging Mexican cops with a bunch of questions. He was lucky they left without demanding a bribe. Plus, beneath his grin, the shorter man gave Elian the impression that nothing would give him more pleasure than having to tune up a reluctant civilian with a nightstick. And the guy with the big gut . . . he looked even worse.

"Huh," Kelli said.

"It's fine," Elian said, stealing a kiss from her. "I gotta go, baby."

"I'm coming with," she said.

He opened the door and slipped his arm around her narrow waist, feeling like the luckiest guy in the world. She wore a green dress that matched her eyes, tight as a glove on her slim torso. All those jerks at the hotel bar would be perving over her, hitting on her, trying to get her phone number. And every night Kelli came home to him. *Him!* It amazed him sometimes.

By the time he got to the bottom of the staircase, he had forgotten all about the men from the Policía Federal.

The essence of executive protection, as performed by the Secret Service, is to examine an event and its location in excruciating detail, then to provide a plan for every contingency. Every conceivable form of attack is imagined and planned against, with backups and backups to the backups and fallback plans and worst-case scenarios. The direct ring of protection around the principal is provided by a protection detail that moves with him or her. Around that ring is a secondary layer of protection primarily composed of Secret Service agents whose position is generally stationary—but which may include special local law enforcement assets—bomb-sniffing dogs and their handlers, snipers and executive protection specialists. This ring secures the facility rather than the individual. Then around that is the largest ring of security, which is generally composed primarily of local law enforcement. This third ring is responsible for the lowest-level functions like traffic control, running metal detectors, and guarding barricades—but also includes specialty units like SWAT, air units, bomb squads, and so on.

New York City has the deepest law enforcement bench on the planet, and more highly trained specialty units than any other law enforcement agency in the country—with the exception of most of the federal law enforcement agencies—and long experience handling security at large, complex, high-value sites. It's a rare day that the NYPD isn't blocking off a stretch of road for some visiting potentate or a posse of finance ministers.

None of which made Fisk's job any easier. The head of every specialized unit in the NYPD outranked Fisk, and was guaranteed to be jealous of his or her turf and distrustful of Fisk's perceived lack of a defined jurisdiction. There were a lot of egos to be juggled, a lot of phone calls to be made, a lot of memos to be sent.

On top of that, the UN is a particularly complex protection assignment. Inside the UN, protection is supposed to be provided and coordinated by the UN's own people. This meant that every time anybody walked in or out of the UN building, a handoff had to be made between UN security and the NYPD. The personal security details of the Mexican president accompanied them onto the property, while the main shell of protection had to remain outside the perimeter of Dag Hammarskjöld Plaza.

As much as Fisk looked down on this sort of assignment, it had demanded every ounce of his energy and attention over the past few days.

THERE IS MORE THAN one New York. Most cops live in a New York of parochial schools, family-owned garbage-hauling businesses, cars with sticky doors and dinged fenders, cramped little houses, outer borough accents.

Ocampo was not part of that New York. It was part of the other New York, the one many see only in the movies, the New York of their daydreams, the one full of hipster artists and supermodels and hedge fund managers and celebrities.

Fisk lived in an odd sort of middle ground—in both worlds—having been raised as the son of a diplomat. And yet he was not really of either world. Fisk had grown up all over the map, going to American schools full of very privileged kids who thought the world was theirs by right. It was a world Fisk could have lived in if he'd chosen to.

But for reasons he'd never quite understood, he'd walked away from that world and had chosen to work in a blue-collar world populated by people who didn't expect the universe to shower them with glory and money, beauty and fame. The truth was, the world favors very few with all of that. For most people—even the hedge fund managers and hipster/model/actresses—life is mostly a lot of hard work, bad deli sandwiches, trips to the dentist, coaching the kid's soccer team.

As he walked in the front door of Ocampo, he felt a bittersweet sense of recognition. The restaurant was designed to make people feel like they'd risen above all that quotidian crap and ascended into some broader, more powerful, more amped-up world. You went to Ocampo and you felt like a star, like somebody. This was the clientele they catered to. This was the experience they worked so hard to give you.

He found Dukes standing with his cadre of Secret Service agents, ready to do the technical security clearance. He did not seem very impressed with the establishment.

"You know what we call this kind of place in the Secret Service?" said Dukes, in regard to the restaurant where American president Obama and Mexican president Vargas would be dining the following evening.

"Overpriced?" Fisk said.

"A kill box," said Dukes.

GARZA ARRIVED MINUTES LATER with a contingent of EMP agents and the agency's head, General de Aguilar, now dressed in a dark suit rather than his military uniform.

Garza slowed a bit when she saw Fisk, and something like a look of regret passed over her face like a shadow. Fisk remained impassive. He noticed she had changed her clothes and perhaps had a shower, and wished he had done the same.

The chairs were large, the tables were heavy and very shiny, the art on the walls was just Mexican enough to feel edgy, but not so much as to make the would-be rich feel like they'd walked into something that could be described as a "Mexican restaurant." There were plenty of those in Manhattan and across the country. Here at Ocampo, there would be no steaming fajita skillets, no spicy chorizo, and, most especially, no mariachi band crooning and bumming tips at your table. Entrées started at seventy-five bucks and went up steeply from there.

Dukes said, "What do they serve here, dollar bills?"

"A 'kill box,' huh?" said Fisk. Fisk was no trained

bodyguard, but even he could see that the restaurant was a less than optimal place to bring someone you wanted to protect, starting with the wide span of plate-glass window in front. There was one door in front, one in the back. No internal stairs, no basement, no elevator. If things went sideways here, there was no place to run except through the kitchen and there was no place to hide.

It was four thirty—a time when most New York restaurants are empty and preparing for dinner—and yet at least half of the tables were full, diners drinking out of clay cups, munching raw shellfish artfully positioned on huge plates with Mayan-themed designs painted on them. The host was a smiling young man who seemed determined from the first moment to let you know that while he might be working the door at a restaurant right now, he had graduated from an Ivy League school and was cut out for far bigger things than this.

Dukes said, "Where's Delgado?"

The young man picked up his phone, dialing nervously. He turned away from them, speaking in a hushed tone, then hung up, almost dropping the telephone. "Coming right now."

Out of the darkness in back came a trim man with a thick mustache and a professionally hospitable expression.

"Agent Dukes!" he said, with a generous Mexican accent—so generous, Fisk wondered if it was less than 100 percent real. "What a great, great pleasure to see you again! And your . . . friends."

Dukes stood with his hands on his hips and looked around the restaurant with an expression of disdain. He said, "What are these people doing here, Mr. Delgado?"

"Pardon me, sir?"

Dukes tapped his watch with his index finger. "You said this place would be empty until seven."

Mr. Delgado smiled widely beneath his ample mustache and said, "I apologize if I conveyed that impression to you, Agent Dukes. I cannot recall my exact words, of course . . . though I am sure what I would have said is that our clientele is thin until about—"

Dukes clapped him on the shoulder, warmly but forcefully. "Nope. You said 'empty.'" He smiled at the diners, some of whom were now looking at the large number of suited men—and women—in front. "Mr. Delgado, would you kindly get these fine folks out of here."

Delgado looked appalled. "Get them . . . out? You mean . . . ?"

"I mean instruct them to leave."

"All right, I . . . certainly. If you could give us maybe fifteen or twenty minutes, we should be able to wrap this up in a manner that's not too egregiously—"

"Right now," said Dukes, giving Delgado the sort of stare a man might give you in the prison weight room before he took your barbell away from you.

For a moment Delgado looked helplessly around the room. "Agent Dukes, please. Ten short minutes."

"Mr. Delgado, you are hosting a pair of heads of state tomorrow night. It will make for a nice little photograph of you and Mr. Obama and Mr. Vargas, something that will hang on the wall here long after each man has ended his term. Unless you want to explain to the owner why this venue had to be scrapped at the last minute . . . ?"

Mr. Delgado rallied then, snapping his fingers impatiently at one of the waiters, calling him over for a quick conversation full of angry, whispered sibilance. Soon a rush of waiters emerged bearing takeout cartons and checks, followed by a parade of indignant customers.

Within just a few minutes, the restaurant was empty. Once the overfed men and their beautiful women were gone, the place appeared somehow hollow and gloomy, almost like an abandoned movie set, the quiet majesty of the place having vanished the moment its glamorous occupants did.

Ten minutes later, Dukes, along with a member of the Secret Service's Technical Security Division, began his presentation, which continued for nearly an hour without a break. That the venue had already been cleared by the Technical Security Division hardly mattered, now that a new and substantial potential threat had been identified. Dog teams would sweep the restaurant at least three times in the next twenty-four hours, sniffing for explosives. Dukes went over fire safety inside the establishment, discussed where the various chemical, biological, and radiological sensors would be placed, and discussed how a layer of bulletproof glass and blast webbing would be constructed over the front windows.

He noted where the jump teams would be hidden across the street, where the counterassault team would be stationed, addressed roof security and air cover of the entire block in the West Village. Approximately ninety minutes before the dinner, the entire four-block radius would be put on "POTUS freeze." An agent in the presidential protective detail then stepped forward to briefly discuss his goals and duties. The "package" was what he called the protective detail, whether in or out of the motorcade, as in,

"Nobody moves to the package unless they want to get shot in the heart. The package will move to you."

Dukes resumed, pointing out choke points on a map, talking transitions and shift changes, none of which interested Fisk. He stole a glance at Garza a few times, found her staring off, somewhere else mentally. Fisk's ears perked back up when Dukes addressed obscure but persistent threats: poison gas, mortar attack, suicide bombers. It was no wonder that the Secret Service was regarded as a clan of hard-nosed paranoiacs. The job rewarded incredibly hardworking, detail-oriented, humorless people, who expected the worst from humanity and took no shit from anyone.

Accordingly, Dukes did not take questions.

"I will say—not for the record, but just so that you will understand the level of extra effort that will need to be exerted here—that this location was chosen against the very strenuous objection of my agency. Let me explain what the Secret Service likes in a venue. We like large steel-framed, low-rise buildings on high ground, with underground ingress and egress, substantial interior walls that can be used as defensive fallback and rally points, multiple elevators and multiple stairs, concrete or stone exterior walls, land buffering the building from the street, separate and easily controllable mechanical rooms with backup generators, modern fire suppression and security systems, fully redundant and high-bandwidth communication connections, exterior walls which are not shared with adjoining properties, and ten thousand square feet of controllable floor space on the event floor. Rural is good. A perimeter fence is super nice. A twelve-foot blast wall with razor wire . . . even better."

Dukes smiled tightly.

"As you can see, this Mexican seafood restaurant has precisely zero of these features. None. It's a relatively small restaurant in a row of typical four-story, wood-frame commercial buildings constructed over a century ago. Charming windows looking out on a pleasant view of a heavily traveled street. Unrestricted sight lines extending to higher buildings along Seventh Avenue and several blocks down Waverly. A minimally competent sniper could engage the front of the building with effective aimed fire from any of over three hundred different vantage points. An RPG could pass from the front of the restaurant to virtually any interior point of the restaurant. A truck bomb could level the place."

Dukes folded his hands at his waist.

"Also, while not publicly part of either president's schedule, the event is known, and we are monitoring chatter on the Internet. As such, you can only imagine my level of enthusiasm for this venue. But the choice has been made above my pay level, and so we are going to make it work. We in the Secret Service never, ever question the wisdom of our superiors, or second-guess the political choices of those we protect. We just shut up and do our job.

"So what's our strategy? All traffic functions en route will be conducted on a need-to-know basis. NYPD will prepare for a rolling street blockage with minimal notice. We will have intersection control for both presidents' motorcades, and will have two lanes of setback—that is, space between the motorcade and other traffic—whenever possible. We will bring our principals in through the alley in the back, and we'll close and barricade the street between Greenwich and West Tenth. The upper floors of the restaurant's building include residential space, and will be evacuated and occupied by counterattack agents starting three hours before the event is to start."

He surveyed the room, hands on his hips.

"There's your site prep. If I failed to cover anything . . . well, it was not an oversight. You know as much as you need to know, and more than enough to assist without getting in our way."

His last remarks seemed aimed at the Mexican security contingent.

"Good day."

Fisk stopped Dukes before he left.

"I notice the owner is not here."

"Guess not," said Dukes.

"C'mon," said Fisk.

Dukes just shook his head.

"You vetted this guy? I don't like the caginess."

Dukes sighed. "I know you're not presuming to tell me how to do my job, Fisk," he said, giving Fisk a borderline hard stare. "Here's the thing, Fisk. Your job is all about the *Why*. Lot of gray areas—why a guy kills somebody, does this, does that. Lot of questions to be answered. But for us, for me . . . it's all black and white. The principal lives or the principal dies. *Why* is just a distraction. *Why* kills."

Fisk grumbled, "So President Vargas just loves a good fish taco then."

"That must be it," said Dukes. "Look, when you start telling me everything you know about your job, I'll start telling you everything I know about mine."

"Point taken."

"Point *made*."

Dukes went off out of the restaurant. That was when Fisk saw a deputy U.S. marshal standing near the door. A short woman with squat hips and straight brown hair, wearing a dark-jacketed suit. He went over to her. "Graben, is it?"

"Detective Fisk."

She did not offer to shake his hand.

"It's been a while," he said.

"Heard you were out of action. Put up on the shelf."

"They pulled me back down. Can I ask you a question?"

"No," she said.

"What is a deputy U.S. marshal doing here?"

Graben shrugged. "I'm not here."

"Really," said Fisk. "That old thing."

"That old thing."

The U.S. Marshals Service is charged with protecting and supporting U.S. federal courts, as well as conducting fugitive investigations. Another thing they are known for is the Witness Security Program, protecting, relocating, and assigning new identities to witnesses and other high-threat individuals.

"Good to see you back in the game, Fisk," she said, turning and following Dukes out the door.

Fisk stood there a moment, processing the interaction, then followed her out.

He watched her get into the vehicle behind Dukes's sedan and follow him away, heading uptown.

Fisk was unsure of his next move as he turned around, and found himself facing Cecilia Garza.

She was looking, not at his eyes, but at his chin.

"Thanks for the update on the No Fly boys," said Fisk. "The dead Zeta hitters."

"Dead traffickers," she said. "I assumed someone else would forward you that information."

"Detective Kiser did, wholly by accident."

"I am not a person who apologizes," she said. "But I want to." Her eyes came up to his. "For what I said about your former partner, your girlfriend. That was uncalled for. I think you are right, I was distraught, I did not handle it well. You were right about my emotions, and I lashed out. Will you accept my apology?"

Fisk watched her. He had the feeling that if he said yes right away, she would walk on and never look back.

He said, "I'm trying to figure out how much of your personality is a mask and how much is real."

She nodded as though she had expected some pushback. "I am so tired of never being able to trust," she said. "Anyone. It derives from work. I have so few people I can truly trust in Mexico, in the PF and elsewhere in law enforcement. Virgilio was one of those people. Corruption is so rampant, it is a part of doing what we do, it is deep within the system. The men in my unit are the cleanest in the force . . . but beyond that I have to assume that every cop I deal with is on the payroll of the cartels."

"I'm not."

She waved that away. "Of course, I am just trying to explain. The pay is so low that bribes have become part of the system, like gratuities. Part of the pay scale. Never for me. But for many. If not most. You do not have to murder someone, or smuggle drugs, or break into evidence lockers. Thousands of pesos just to look the other way."

"I get it. It's hard not to be cynical."

"And the truth is that I see something in you, something that I like. And that is a complication. I do not like complications."

Fisk felt a little heat at the back of his neck. ". . . I see."

"I have no time for complications right now."

"No, of course," he said. "Me neither."

Garza nodded as though something had been agreed to. "Do you accept my apology?"

Fisk said, "If I say yes, am I ever going to see you again?"

Nicole?" said Fisk, entering Intel headquarters. "Why are you still here?"

"Work to do," she said.

"Can you push those traffic camera captures to my secure laptop?" he said, passing quickly, heading for his office. "This is Colonel Garza."

Nicole nodded at her a little strangely. "I remember her from yesterday."

"Good evening," said Garza.

Fisk grabbed his laptop off his desk and carried it into one of the briefing rooms, closing the door. He opened it up before them.

The high-angle videos showed split-screen versions of the same scene, one in regular exposure and one shot with night vision. The automobile, a Ford Explorer, had tinted windows, but the night vision picked up some images through the glass.

One video showed a bulky man driving, only from the chin down. In the backseat, on the left side, a man wearing a Yankees cap glanced out the window as the Explorer passed the camera.

Two videos offered different perspectives on the same car, but the first one offered the only true glimpse at the man in the backseat.

Two other traffic videos, each of much lower quality and taken from a higher angle, showed the sedan they had found being driven toward the first cemetery. In the front passenger seat, the bulky man was again visible, only from the shoulders down, due to the extreme angle. But the knife in his hand was plain to see.

That one was taken at 11:43 P.M. The other video was captured four hours later, at 3:51 A.M.

As ever, there was an eeriness inherent in viewing the confusing final moments of a doomed human being. The driver, Virgilio's cousin or friend—it mattered little to Fisk now—looked as though he were in conversation with someone in the backseat. Someone unseen.

Perhaps the man in the Yankees cap.

Fisk said, "We have the license plate of the Explorer. Stolen four days ago from a parking lot in Ozone Park."

Garza was transfixed by the image. "He has changed vehicles by now."

Fisk watched her watch the screen. "You think that's him? The Yankees fan?"

She nodded curtly. "I think it might be."

"Okay," said Fisk. "Now take a look at this."

He pulled up stills from an e-mail from Canadian Intelligence. The first showed a series of color images of a man with tattooed arms walking through an airport.

"First U.S. No Fly Zeta goon," said Fisk. "Back when he still had a head."

He clicked to open up the second attachment.

Another man, this one wearing a tight gray

sweatshirt and sunglasses, walking through the same airport corridor.

"U.S. No Fly Zeta goon number two," said Fisk. "We think they crossed into the country through the border into New York State, either through the woods, which is better attempted in winter, or by vehicle, traveling with false papers. But we have no border-crossing photos, at least not yet."

Fisk opened up the third attachment.

"Voilà," he said.

A man of medium height, wearing a thin navy suit jacket and trousers, moved through a different corridor in the same airport, a travel bag slung over one shoulder. He held a cell phone to one ear, covering the other with his finger as though trying to hear someone over a bad connection. He wore sunglasses and a ball cap that further obscured his face.

The cap was black with a white Yankees logo on it.

"Chuparosa."

Garza stared. The series of images cycled through on slideshow, the man walking down the corridor among other disembarking passengers. His face was mostly covered, but he certainly resembled the darker figure in the backseat of the Explorer near St. Michael's Cemetery.

She glanced once Fisk's way, in disbelief, then back to the screen. Memorizing his gait. The shape of his body. Burning it into her memory.

"It's all circumstantial," said Fisk. "But I'd lay odds it's him. The question is, why did he off his own guys?"

"He's killing anything that links to him," said

Garza. "He wants to succeed at any cost." She turned to Fisk. "Based on what I saw back at his compound, I believe he understands this to be a suicide mission. It is the only way he can succeed. And, for whatever reason, he has accepted that fate."

Fisk nodded. "All we need to know now is where he is."

Octavia Clement?"

The door to apartment 231 was barely open more than a crack. Garza was a block from Brookville Park in Rosedale, standing with Fisk in front of the door to a walk-up apartment situated over a store called Tats 'n More.

Garza could not see much through the crack: a single eye peering back, the door still on its chain.

"Who are you?" It was a woman's voice.

"Octavia Clement? My name is Colonel Cecilia Garza." Garza knew that the American equivalent of her rank sounded more impressive to the English-speaking ear, and less confusing than comandante. "I am here with Detective Fisk of the New York Police. I am with the Mexican Federal Police. May we come in and speak with you?"

The eye looked at her with unconcealed suspicion. "Mexican?"

Garza nodded. "We very much need to speak with you. It is very important."

The eye blinked. After a moment the door closed, the chain came off, and then the door opened wide.

Standing in the doorway was a slightly plump woman wearing a thin T-shirt with a black bra showing through underneath. Her bare arms were covered with tattoos.

Her face was the face from the dead tattoo artist's upper arm. A little older, a little more weathered, her hair dyed red now.

But the resemblance was plain. The facial recognition search had worked. This was the same woman.

"You are Octavia, correct?"

"Are you here about Gary?" Her mouth hung open a bit. She seemed to know what was coming.

Garza and Fisk stepped inside. The apartment reeked of cannabis smoke.

"Where is he?" the woman said. Garza noticed her tongue stud, the twin silver rings through her left eyebrow, the multiple loops in both ears. She looked petrified with fear and suspicion, her skin ashen, her hands trembling.

"May we sit down somewhere?"

The woman shook her head. She might have been indicating no to the truth she knew was about to come, but they did not sit. "Is Gary okay?" she asked.

Cecilia Garza pulled her cell phone from her purse. She had the photo of the tattoo ready. She thumbed the display button and turned it around so that Octavia Clement could see the picture of herself taken from the arm of the dead man on Rockaway Beach.

Octavia Clement stared at the picture. It was just the arm, not the entire dead body . . . but Garza could see that she knew. You didn't show a candid picture of a tattoo on a person's arm and then tell the person looking at it that the person in the phone was just fine.

Garza hated this part of her job. It was one hundred times easier looking at decapitated bodies than it was talking to the families of victims. "This is Gary?" asked Garza.

The tattooed woman let out an awful howl and sagged against the doorframe, clutching onto it as though she were holding onto the edge of a cliff. Fisk caught her before she could collapse completely and strike her head on the floor. He helped her into the front room of the apartment, setting her on a futon covered with homemade blankets.

It was a good minute or two before the woman could get enough breath to speak. "I knew he was gone," she said, wiping her tears on her tattooed wrist.

"His full name?" asked Fisk.

"His name is Gary Lee Clement," she said. "He's my husband. Did those men kill him?"

"Those men who?" said Garza. "Please tell me what men you're talking about?"

Garza sat so close to the woman on the couch, she felt the woman's leg against her own. The apartment was lit by lamps with colored shades—red, amber, yellow. Large bright photographs of flowers hung on the walls, and there was a tripod and other camera equipment in the corner of the room. The furniture was old and mismatched, but the place appeared to be in perfect order, every surface clean. Amazingly clean. The scent of cleaning solution, bleach and ammonia, came through behind the lingering marijuana smoke. Bohemian, but without the squalor. A TV played a news channel on the other side of the room, turned so low it was barely audible.

The young woman waved a hand around the apartment. "I've been cleaning for twenty-four hours straight. Just trying to keep my mind focused on something . . . something else." Her lips were pressed tightly together. "You still haven't told me what happened to him. He's dead, isn't he?"

Garza nodded. "I am very sorry to be the one to inform you."

"And it was those men?"

Garza was patient with Octavia Clement. The bereaved required forbearance. Sometimes they were quite helpful; sometimes they were no help at all. "Tell me about the men."

Octavia Clement closed her eyes for a moment. "Me and Gary, we grew up in McCool Junction, Nebraska. Population three hundred and seventy-two. Can you imagine that? We were the only people in our town who were like this." She ran her hands down her body, showing off the tattoos, the hipster clothes, the eyebrow rings. "And it was subtle then, compared to now. Gary, he had such a gift. He was such a beautiful soul . . ."

She collapsed into tears again. Fisk went off in search of tissues and thankfully returned with some. Octavia blew her nose and balled the tissue in her hand.

"He was an artist. From the very first time I saw him, he could draw these amazing pictures." She pressed her fingers against her wet eyelids, as though pressing and activating these happy memories. "I fell in love with him the very moment I saw him draw for the first time. Ninth grade! He was everything I wanted out of life. Everything." She smiled gently, still with her fingers on her eyes. "It took him maybe a little longer to see me. But eventually he came around. I got him. We got married on my nineteenth birthday, March the twenty-third. On March the twenty-fourth, we loaded up his pickup truck and drove out here. Knew nobody and nothing. And we made it our home."

Her voice trembled momentarily, but she held it together. Garza wanted to pounce on her, to drag the information out of her, but had to sit and listen.

"We were so happy together. The tattoo business has taken off so big, the past ten, twelve years. People could see it, you know? His talent? His gift? It just . . . it shined out of everything he ever did." She paused. "But he was sweet, too. You could see that in the work, too. The sweetness."

Garza saw an opening. "And the men?" she asked. "Please tell me about the men."

"Too sweet maybe," said Octavia, going on without hearing Garza. "He would never have gone with those men if he hadn't been too naive, too trusting for this world. I didn't like them. I told him that. There was something about them. Something dark. Something evil. I could just see it."

A siren screamed outside suddenly, a passing ambulance. Octavia went silent until the sound faded away.

"There were three of them," she said finally. "Last week we got a call from a man who said he had a special order. Said he'd pay four thousand dollars cash for a good afternoon's work. Gary had to come to him, though. That was the only catch. But for the price, it was good for him. Four thousand." She looked from Garza to Fisk, stressing the impact of that much cash. "Gary asked where he should go, and they said, 'Don't worry about that, we'll pick you up.'"

She sat forward suddenly, as though she was about to get up. But she was just stretching out so that she could swallow more easily, craning her neck as though for extra air.

"Gary was so excited, but I didn't like it. I truly . . . I'm not just saying that now. I did not like it at all. I don't like different things. 'Whatever it is,' I said to Gary, 'it's not worth it. Don't do it.' But he was like, 'It'll be fine, Tavy. It's a gig. Nothing's going to happen.'" She smiled a sad, fond smile. "No one else ever called me Tavy. And now no one ever will." Her smile turned pinched, and tears sprang from her eyes. "Gary's folks farmed wheat. That was the difference between him and me. You stand out in a field of wheat, looking out at all that bounty, and you think the world is bounteous and gentle and generous. But me? My old man ran a meatpacking plant. You spend your young years near a slaughter-house, you realize on a deep level that things won't always be fine. Just the opposite. You understand that beneath all our good intentions and bad pretensions, we're just meat on the hoof." She stared at Garza. "All that killing. It does something to you. Makes you cold."

Garza looked at her own hands for a moment. Fisk was standing to the side, giving them space.

Octavia said, "Maybe that's why I needed Gary. I needed his light."

Garza hesitated before saying, "Please, Octavia . . . so when did the men come?"

"Three days ago. Not to the house, they came to the store downstairs. I was up here working when they came. I sure never talked to them or anything. I do Photoshop work, mostly advertising, but some glamour, some fashion. Taking the ugly off people—that's what Gary calls it." She smiled faintly. "Anyway, Gary called me from the store downstairs to say he was leaving. Said he'd be back that night. So I went over and looked out the window. Set back a bit, so they couldn't see me."

She was quiet for a moment, her eyes looking into the past, not seeing what was around her.

"There was something about them," she said quietly. "I instantly wanted to run down and tell him not to go. Three men. There wasn't anything necessarily remarkable about them. It just . . . it wasn't right."

"Can you describe them in any way? Did anything happen?"

"Not really," she said. "It was up here, looking down. Gary, he's one of those guys who never met a stranger, you know? He was talking away. All the way into the back of the truck." This time her smile was angry, angry at her husband for trusting the men who'd killed him. "It was an SUV they got into. Brown." Her hands balled into fists and she pounded her thighs. "Why didn't I stop him? Why?"

"You couldn't have known," Garza said. "May I ask a leading question?"

"Whatever that is," said Octavia.

"Did any of the men wear a hat?"

Octavia thought hard. "Yes. A sports team hat. Baseball. I don't give a shit to follow any of that stuff. Does that help you? Can you catch them?"

Garza took the woman's hand. "Two of them are already dead themselves. One remains."

"You find him," said Octavia, then buried her head in her hands. "My Gary . . ."

"I will find him," Garza said. "I will."

Where are you staying now?"

"The Sheraton," Garza said. She was checking her messages on her phone. "Tomorrow is the big day."

"I don't like this feeling," he said. "The feeling of running out of hours in a day."

"I'm so exhausted. And keyed up at the same time. I can't believe I lost a man today. Two."

Fisk nodded. There was nothing to say to that.

IT WAS NEARLY TEN by the time Fisk and Garza reached the Sheraton. He pulled up outside under the overhang, watching theatergoers trickle in from Times Square. A homeless man stood praying and singing to a streetlight.

She opened her door and extended one leg out, her foot reaching the curb before a valet could arrive. "Did you eat?" she said, without looking back.

"I've been dining out of a vending machine pretty exclusively."

She nodded. "Cop cuisine."

"Are you offering to buy me dinner?"

"No," she said, rising from Fisk's car. "But you can join me if you like."

THEY FOUND SEATS TOGETHER at a table near the lounge. But when the time came to order, neither one wanted food.

Garza said, "What do you think of a Chilean Malbec?"

"Love it."

"You didn't seem like a shot and a beer kind of man."

"Oh, but I am. Just not tonight."

The server came and Fisk ordered two glasses. The San Felipe Garza had wanted only came by the bottle. She tried to make him change the wine, but he refused, and the server went away to get a bottle.

Then Fisk felt strange. He hadn't drunk wine with anyone, never mind an exotically beautiful woman, since he was with Gersten. Suddenly he was moved to keep the conversation about work.

"Tell me about Vargas, your president."

Garza's eyebrows lifted and she fiddled with the cocktail napkin the server had left in front of her. "President Vargas is a good man. A courageous man. And I believe the presidency will break him."

"How?"

"He is still a man of principle."

"You say 'still'?"

"I knew him when he was a law professor."

"Oh," said Fisk, not sure if he wanted to know more.

"I believe the accord is built on a good foundation. In the past, cooperation between Mexico and the States has focused on equipment, police funding, communications protocols, all sorts of law enforcement tools. Gifts, I call them. As from a parent to a child. Your country saying, 'Here, play with these, and keep quiet and out of our way.' I like more guns, more breaching explosives, more trucks, more helicopters, more body armor, better radios. But it is just money. There is no working relationship. No sense of responsibility."

"As your number one importer of illegal substances."

" 'The giant nose to the north,' we say. It is just confronting violence with violence. In an illegal market, the natural tendency is toward monopoly, and beyond the rule of law, all that is left is violence. On the other hand, this is also a big fat check for corrupt Mexican military and police to stuff in their pockets. Most *federales* make less than a worker at McDonald's. Drug cartels pay no taxes, but more than the equivalent in bribes to mayors, prosecutors, governors, state and federal police. I'm forgetting the army and navy."

Fisk said, "This accord will cut the purse strings."

"You have to go after the money. The product is plentiful and cheap. Very cheap until it gets across the border, when the cost of doing business rises and rises. It is the money coming back—often in the same shipping containers the drugs go north in—that needs to be intercepted. The blood flowing back to the heart—that is where the knife blade must go."

Fisk's eyebrows shot up at the gory image. Garza winced.

"Sorry," she said. "What about you?"

"About me? You can look me up on Wikipedia."

"Yes?" She smiled. "Is it accurate?"

"No." His turn to smile. "What about you?"

"Am I on Wikipedia?" she asked.

"I don't know. We could check."

"Don't," she said.

"So?"

She squirmed a little.

"You don't like talking about yourself. I imagine there's quite a story in there. How you ended up doing this kind of work," he said.

Her eyes darkened. She actually looked pained.

"I'm not putting the thumbscrews on you," he said. "We're just making conversation. I think."

She seemed to be trying to maintain her formidable front. But cracks were forming, as though she was getting tired of the strain.

After a moment she said, "Okay. Yes. There is a story."

Then she clammed up again.

"Waiting." Fisk let a hint of a smile appear on his lips.

She seemed to be considering whether she wanted to open up to him or not. Before she could make up her mind whether to answer him, the server arrived and showed Garza the label, unscrewed the cork from the bottle of San Felipe, poured a bit, let her taste. She smiled and nodded, and he completed her pour, and Fisk's. He asked about food, but they demurred. He came with a bowl of glorified Chex mix and left them talking over a hissing candle.

Fisk watched Garza drink. She appreciated the vintage, closing her eyes for a moment. When she opened them, there was the barest gleam showing.

"Your English is very good," said Fisk, trying to start her off. "Schooling?"

"My father went to graduate school here. University of Illinois at Urbana-Champaign. So he sent me to the American school in Mexico City."

Fisk took another sip of wine and then set the glass aside so he could focus on her. "It must be hard, though. There can't be many people like you in the Mexican police."

"Like me?"

"Female. Incorruptible. At your level."

She shrugged, tossing that away.

"I get it," said Fisk. "I'll stop. I'm not in the habit of talking about myself much either. That counselor I mentioned, the therapist. Like pulling teeth with pliers. Something about it. As though once I start talking about myself, I'll overindulge and that will be all I talk about."

"It's lonely."

"Therapy?"

"No. The job. For me. You asked."

"Lonely, yeah." He nodded. "It's lonely as hell sometimes."

"You found someone on the force you could confide in."

Fisk nodded, trying not to look forlorn. The candlelight, the red wine, the lounge chatter around them.

"I envy that very much," she said. "I have never found such a person."

"Never?"

"I've dated. A few men in Mexico City over the years. But they were always lawyers, dentists. Once a political functionary—never again." A brief smile. "Somehow they all seemed like boys—smooth, soft, talky—but when it came right down to it, barely competent to cross a street safely. You can say what you will about the men in my unit, the ones I surround myself with . . . but they are men."

"None for you?" he said.

She shook her head strenuously. "I cannot. It is hard enough maintaining my position. To do that would weaken me irreparably. Once they see me as anything other than their boss, I will lose command. That is my trap."

"Trap? That sounds harsh."

"I may look like a born cop, but . . ." She shook her head, her hair shifting around the sides of her face. "When I was at university, I was going to be an artist. Until I realized I had no talent. I shouldn't say that. There was talent. But there was no *talent*. I had a bit of a crisis. Who am I? Why am I here? Difficult questions, even at that ridiculously young age."

"True," he said.

"I switched to law. I finished my degree, all the while knowing that I would never be happy as a lawyer. But I had gone too far down the road by that time. I worked briefly in the Justice Ministry. One day I went out with the Policía Federal on a raid. The first time I went out, I thought: This is it! I quit my job that day and signed up for the police academy."

"Really?" said Fisk. Her story seemed to take some abrupt turns. "How was that?"

"Honestly? Awful. It wasn't being a woman that was the worst. You are operating under a misconception there. There are actually quite a few women in the PF."

"Then what was it?"

"In the United States, you maintain the fiction that there are no class divisions in your country. But in Mexico, there's no fiction, no papering over the fact that some people are rich and some are dirt poor. Working people are very happy to hate the rich down there. My father is an affluent man. I suppose you could even call him rich. He was in the electronics assembly business. Owned a couple of *maquiladora* factories up by the border. Circuit boards for refrigerators and toasters and things like that. Eventually he sold out to a big Korean company." For a moment she looked sad. "We are not close. He's getting on in years now, but he's on his second marriage. Has a couple of young kids. His wife is younger than me. We speak . . . but only occasionally.

"Anyway, to return to my story—the other girls in the Policía Federal, they all hated me. Constant hazing. One time they held me down at night and beat me up a little and shaved my head. That sort of thing. I got my revenge by beating them at everything. I shot straighter, I trained harder, I studied more diligently. And once I was out of the academy and on duty, I was the first one into every room, the first one to grab a perpetrator, the first into the line of fire. I was like a tiger." She looked grimly at the bottles on the other side of the bar. "I progressed very quickly through the ranks. But I never let my guard down. Not with anyone. Not ever."

Fisk studied her carefully. He couldn't quite figure it out—but it seemed to him that some facts had gone AWOL here. There was some part of the

story that she wasn't telling him. It was the inter-
rogator in him. He wanted to push, but could not.

"Eventually they started calling me the Ice
Queen. They don't say it to my face, of course. At
first it was an insult. But I think that over time they
have come to have a certain fondness for me. I hope
so, anyway." Her eyes were hooded. "It's so hard to
maintain your integrity in Mexico. The corruption
among the police is unimaginable. But men have a
hunger for purity, for goodness. It preys on their
souls to take money, to do things for evil men. So
I think—I hope—that they are able to look at her,
their Ice Queen, and say, 'If she can do it, if she can
remain pure . . . then so can I.'"

"Her," Fisk said. "You referred to yourself as
'her.'"

She frowned, looking at her half-empty glass
as though blaming it. "Yes. Well, in a manner of
speaking, she is a character I invented." Her frown
went away and she smiled, but without warmth. "If
you had known me fifteen years ago, you wouldn't
have recognized me. I was . . . she was . . ." Cecilia
Garza looked at Fisk sharply. A sudden change had
come over her, a stiffness, a defensiveness, like the
armor was suddenly clanking into place again. "I
don't like this conversation."

Fisk could see what it was that angered her. There
were two versions of this woman hiding inside one
body. She and Fisk might have shared similarly unusual cop biographies. But they weren't the same.
Fisk had never really felt the way she obviously
did. Had he avoided certain topics of conversation
once he joined the force? Had he concealed the fact

that his father had left him a trust fund—however modest it was? Had he been slow to parade his ability to speak five languages in front of other cops? Sure. There were things he didn't talk about when he went out for a drink with the guys. He skipped the stories about vacations in the south of France when he was a kid. But he'd never felt like Jeremy Fisk was an invented character. Quite the reverse. In a lot of ways he felt like he'd only discovered the true Jeremy Fisk when he'd left the world of Ivy Leaguers and jet-setters.

It must have been very difficult to be Cecilia Garza.

She drew herself up very straight in her chair. Suddenly she seemed distant. "Look, perhaps this was a mistake, Detective. Virgilio is gone, and . . . here I am, drinking wine. With you."

Fisk said, "That doesn't seem like a bad thing, necessarily. We're not going out dancing."

Garza shook her head, as though to say, *This is not what I do*. "Again, I want to apologize for my rudeness earlier. It was uncalled for."

Not only had her words gone formal, her voice had gotten hard. Even her accent had gotten stronger, as though her entire being were drifting back toward Mexico.

She pushed back her chair and stood.

"It's getting late, Detective."

Fisk extended his hand, motioning for her to stop. He almost pulled it back again, once he realized that . . . he did not want her to go.

"Don't rush off," he said. "Finish your wine, at least."

She dug into her handbag, pulling out a twenty-dollar bill.

Fisk said, "You better not leave that here."

She started to, then put it back inside her bag.

He said, "I think you're running away, not walking."

Her face grew masklike. "Is that therapy talk?"

"It's real talk."

"Good night."

Cecilia Garza was so angry, she was trembling.

Standing there, waiting for the elevator, not even remembering what floor her room was on. Tasting the Malbec on her tongue.

For a moment there, she'd thought that he was different. For a moment, she'd thought that they shared something. Two cops. Two people with similar burdens. Two people on opposite sides of the same border.

And then there had been the expression in his eyes. It was as though he was looking through the surface of her skin, like her face was made of glass and he was seeing right through it, seeing deeper, seeing the real Cecilia Garza.

She was no fool. She knew how men looked at her—how they had always looked. Women, too. The thing that made men gravitate toward her, she had found a way to make it useful. To counteract their hunger with starvation. To give them nothing and make them accept it.

One of the great reliefs of being in the PF was that once you were geared up—vest, helmet, mask, gun, boots—everyone looked the same. Inside the helmet and the mask, she was just a cop.

So she never took it off.

Not even when she saw Virgilio's body floating facedown in that wretched cemetery pond.

She felt a tear reach the corner of her eye. She pushed the elevator button frantically.

Virgilio was dead. The man in the New York Yankees cap, the one on the cell phone: it was Chuparosa. He was near. She was close.

The elevator car arrived and she darted inside, waiting for the doors to close again. As soon as they did, she let out all her breath, trying to remember which floor number to press.

What had gotten into her with Fisk? Normally she did not allow herself the luxury of regretting that she had offended people. She never cared.

And now she felt she had offended him again.

Those dark, intent eyes . . . listening, actually listening, to every word she said. For years she had told herself that she was looking for a man who could look past her face, who could see the real Cecilia Garza. Not the Ice Queen. Not the cop. Not the beautiful woman. Past all of that.

And here he was. He'd looked past all of that, probed down into something underneath. And what had she done?

Thrown dirt in his face. Squandered it. Sabotaged herself.

Maybe the sad truth was that she truly did not want anyone looking into her soul. Maybe it was too late.

Fisk sat there looking at Garza's half-empty glass, finishing his own, and trying to find the server so he could get the hell out of there. Then he felt a hand on his shoulder.

"Okay," said Garza, her hand leaving his shoulder as she settled back into her chair. "I'll tell you how it really happened."

It was impossible to say what the difference was, but the woman sitting across from him now barely resembled the woman who had left. She seemed younger, softer, less certain. It was still Cecilia Garza, still the same slim neck, the same high cheekbones, the same glossy black hair. But there seemed nothing of the comandante left in her.

Fisk shook his head. "How what happened?"

She drank another sip of wine. "My father was a very stern, practical man. He indulged me in certain ways, the way rich men do when they have a daughter. He was proud, but that pride came out in such a way that I believe he wanted a daughter who was . . . what? . . . an ornament? I don't want to be cruel. But that was what was expected of the girls I knew back then. Grow up and be respectable, pretty, marry a guy whose dad owns a bank or a telecom company. Have multiple children. Put on nice parties."

She shrugged, as though gesturing, *Here I am*.

"I never quite fit the mold. I tried to please him at first. I was a good student, didn't drop out of school and smoke pot with American dopers or anything. But I started getting in trouble because I wouldn't shut my mouth, drinking, staying out too late, jumping in the swimming pool naked."

"Really," said Fisk.

"Believe it or not. My father had a place in the country, and when we would go out there I would ride dirt bikes and shoot guns and climb rocks, or steal the Jeep and ride off-road. I broke my leg once. I was always smashing something I wasn't supposed to or generally scaring the hell out of my parents. I was acting out, I suppose. I was an adrenaline junkie. Still am.

"Anyway, I felt like I spent my entire childhood trying to fight my way out of this correct little box that my mother and father had built for me. I always enjoyed drawing. So when I went to university, I thought I would be a painter. You know, I read all the books about Frida Kahlo and I thought I'd be this rebel artist genius fighting the conventions of society and . . ."

She sighed.

"As I said, I loved the ideal of the artist. The life! Sitting around in cafés, running counter to the prevailing culture, nobody to tell you how to live or how to dress or what to do. But that's not reality. Reality is, you have to paint pictures. You have to make something profound and beautiful, not just

nice and interesting. And after a few years of painting pictures, I could see in the eyes of my teachers
. . . that they were not *excited* by my work. They
weren't even very stimulated. My goal was to set the
world on fire with my art, not be a mere candle on
a cake.

"I still wanted to crash cars and ride dirt bikes
and shoot guns. So I went into this sort of funk. I
knew that I wasn't going to finish the art degree.
So if I wasn't that cool artsy girl, smoking filterless
cigarettes in the café, who was I?"

Fisk smiled. "You were young and no longer idealistic."

"In Mexico you study law as an undergrad. It's not
just a graduate degree like it is here. So I took a class
with Umberto Vargas. He was the big star teacher
on campus. All the girls thought he was so great, so
brilliant, so handsome . . . and he was. Made quite
an impression. But he made practicing law come
alive. There was a flavor of art to it, at least the way
he taught it. Of ideals, of protecting interests rather
than exploiting them. Typical lefty rich girl, I was
going to take on the vested interests, all the big rich
jerks like my father, change the system, make the
world better . . . all the naive things any girl in law
school should think she's going to do."

She finished her first glass and slid it toward him
to be refilled.

"Now, my father was deliriously happy when I
switched to law, and yet whenever I came home we
would argue. He, too, had originally trained to be
a lawyer, so we argued stupid abstruse points of the
law. But really it was about the same old thing. Was

I going to be the conventional little ornament to my father? Or was I ever going to be my own person?"

She shrugged sadly.

"Over time we just stopped talking. Then one day I got a phone call. It was my father. I knew something bad had happened because . . . he never called me. My mother had a minor heart condition—I thought maybe she had suffered a heart attack. But that wasn't it."

He slid her refilled glass back to her, but now she just looked at it.

"You read about the cartels and you think that crime in Mexico is just drug gangs blasting away at each other. But that's only the tip of the iceberg. There is also, as you may or may not know, a terrible epidemic of kidnapping."

Fisk nodded, hanging on her words now.

"My father called . . . and all he said was, 'It's your mother. And your sister.'"

"My god," said Fisk.

She shook her head once, violently, as though trying to expel the memory from her brain.

"I drove straight home. My little sister and I . . . we never had much in common. Seven years between us, and she was a sort of flighty girl. Pliable. Indulged. Whatever her friends did, whatever my mother and father said, whatever the teachers said—she went along with it." She closed her eyes. "Anyway. I drove so fast that I almost wrecked my car. I arrived at the house, and my father was absolutely beside himself. Underneath his sternness, he was a very emotional man. And he loved my mother just unimaginably. So he didn't care about the money, didn't care about anything. He just wanted my mother back. And of course my sister.

"But a kidnapping is a process. It's a kind of game. And my father, he thought he understood the game. So he played the game the way you have to play it. Certain brokers are hired. Certain corrupt police who play both sides of the street are called. There's this theater that's played out where you pretend that you're negotiating with people at a distance through honorable intermediaries. But in truth, the intermediaries are working for the bad guys. Or sometimes they are the actual ringleaders and the kidnappers are simply working for the cops. You never really know which is the tail and which is the dog." She smiled sourly. "You just have to trust in the goddamn process."

She was silent for a moment, staring at Fisk.

Finally she continued. "In a perfect world you go back and forth, there's a certain amount of shouting and screaming on the phone . . . all to scare you. A few false alarms to squeeze the maximum figure out of you. But these guys are businessmen. They just want the money and they are rational creatures. That's what everyone hopes, at any rate.

"So eventually there's a handoff that's shepherded by the crooked cops. It's the one place where the cops are of value, you see—because their credibility in this process is predicated on their ability to reliably assure the safety of kidnap victims. If a cop gets a reputation as a man who can't control the crazy assholes who actually do the kidnappings, then word will get around. People won't trust him. They want this to work.

"Funny thing. I was at my father's side the entire time. And you know what? We never argued, there was never a harsh word between us. Normally we argued constantly. But when the chips were down . . ."

For a moment her eyes welled up, and she fought back tears.

"The only time in our lives—before or since—that we got along, was while the most horrible thing was happening to us. If my father and I could have spent our lives fighting a horrible, grueling, vicious war, we might have been great friends."

She blew out a long breath, centered herself.

"Eventually it all fell apart. As time went on we could feel the negotiations going wrong. The go-between cop was a fool, incompetent. Too stupid even to be properly corrupt. At the very end, we were supposed to make the swap. When you do these things, you hire a man to carry the money. We paid. My father paid something like six hundred thousand U.S. dollars. An incredible amount. And we never saw them or the money again."

Fisk said, "Never?"

She shook her head. "Not alive. They were identified two years later, after their deaths. Drug addicted, infected with hepatitis, bodies covered in sores. They had been sold as sex workers and held captive in a city eighty miles south of Mexico City. They had been kept inside security houses known as a *calcuilchil*, or "houses of ass." Mirrored glass for windows, so outsiders cannot see who is living inside. They were both shot in the head. Perhaps trying to escape, perhaps . . . I'll never know."

She was nodding slightly to mask her trembling.

Fisk said, "I don't know what to say . . ."

"Or what to think, I know. It's my hell. Each of us, we've been through something, we've been marked, scarred, changed. I tried to go on, maybe like you are now. I took a job at the Ministry of Justice, filing papers, doing all the things junior prosecutors do. But I was insane inside, crazy. Doing reckless things. I was not cut out for the work. I may have had an appetite for the mission. But not for the job itself.

"Then, as I said earlier, one day I arranged to go out with the PF . . . something I had been thinking about for some time . . . and everything fell into place. I was no more built to be a lawyer than I was an artist. Not for the girl who used to wreck dirt bikes in the country. So I joined the PF and you know the rest of the story, the one I told you earlier."

Fisk was processing this. "Please tell me this doesn't link up somehow to Chuparosa."

She looked puzzled. "No. I know who took my mother and sister. Who sold them like drugs to men who treated them like nothing."

"Who?"

"Ochoa. Do you know the name?"

Fisk did. It was a moment coming to him. "Vaguely."

"German Ochoa. He ran the Guerrero Cartel. Guerrero is close to Central America, and he was tapped into Colombian cocaine. But that wasn't enough, of course, and his crimes extended into human trafficking, among other things. But soon

after the kidnapping of my mother and sister—
perpetrated not by him directly, of course, but
by his men, operating under his protection and
control—his empire began to crumble. He was fan-
tastically rich, of course. You realize that the goal of
these cartel leaders is not to sell drugs. It is to make
money and remain free to spend and enjoy it. That
is why he essentially bought the former iteration of
Mexican Intelligence. He was worth billions."

Fisk got it. "He's the plastic surgery guy."

She nodded. "He underwent extensive surgery,
including a full facial reconstruction, liposuction,
everything. And died on the operating table. Heart
attack, or anesthesia overdose—it's not known.
Your DEA identified the body using DNA recov-
ered from his house. Six weeks later his doctors
were discovered in barrels encased in concrete,
their corpses showing evidence of torture. 'Uncle
Ochoa.' Disgusting."

"And the Guerrero Cartel?"

"The cartel names are fluid. One disappears, another rises immediately to take its place. So no . . . my
revenge has no direct outlet. But Chuparosa, above
all others, reminds me of the brutality of Ochoa,
who died before I could do anything about it."

Fisk sat there, not knowing what to say. He
wanted to refill his glass, and yet he had lost his taste
for the wine.

Garza said, "You will look at me differently
now, you will think of me differently. But here is
the thing. It could have been me. If I wasn't away at
school . . . it would have been me. That is my reality. Ochoa would have served me up just like he did

my mother and my sister—who were not rag dolls, by the way. They were not fighters as I am now . . . as I have made myself to be . . . but they must have fought, as much as they could. They were brutalized. They were victimized. And here I stand on the other side. A woman of the law, who looks out for the victims now. Who acts for those who cannot."

"And your father?"

"He suffered, too. And then he moved away from Mexico City, to California. Remarried."

Fisk said, "You resent that."

"Sometimes," she said. "Sometimes I envy him." She leaned closer, speaking so that no one else could ever hear. "You faced down the man who murdered your lover. You saw your revenge."

Fisk said, "I arrested him."

"You faced him and you stopped him. You won. There was an ending. For me, there is no ending."

Fisk sat back. She had touched something deep inside him, and he wanted to express this correctly.

He said, "All I can tell you is that it is never the victory you think it will be." Fisk was remembering Jenssen's words to him in that prison room, about America's tolerant system of justice. Its weakness for the rule of law. "We have to be better than those we hunt. It is the very thing that defines us. We lose that . . . then we are lost ourselves. This cycle of murder and retribution, be it personal or international . . . it sickens us a little, just being exposed to it. Like radiation poisoning. There is no end. There is no cure."

Garza listened, but it seemed to Fisk she was trying to understand how these words related to him—rather than giving any thought to how they related to herself.

"Aren't you glad you asked?" she said. "About me?"

"Yes," Fisk said, and meant it. "I want to know more about you."

Her eyes narrowed a bit, shadowed by the candle flame. "You know the worst, and still you want to know more?"

Fisk nodded. "I think I want to know everything."

She looked confused for a moment. Almost amazed. Then—as always—she pulled back. "Maybe we are too much alike. Maybe we have found our counterpart and simply want to ask it questions. Maybe we are a two-person support group."

"Maybe," he said.

"Maybe it's the Malbec."

"Maybe. And exhaustion. And overload." He conceded all those points. "And maybe it's more than all that."

She smiled as though he might be right. "Tomorrow," she said. "I won't be distracted. I cannot be distracted. Not until . . . after tomorrow."

"After tomorrow," Fisk said.

Her eyes had gone dark again, her expression hard. He could tell she was picturing the image of Chuparosa in her head, visualizing him. Wondering where he was at that very moment, what he was doing, what he was thinking.

She stood, and so did Fisk.

"To be continued," she said.

No handshake, no good-bye. He watched her walk out of the lounge and into the hotel lobby.

BOOK THREE

Dubin called him into his office at Intel first thing in the morning.

He did not look happy. He stood immediately as Fisk entered. "You're dropping the ball on UN Week."

"I'm not," said Fisk. "I'm doing my best—"

"I hear from Secret Service you've been running down this threat to the Mexican president, which is all well and good, but we've got other potential targets out there, and that's the Secret Service's brief. Your job is to protect the city of New York. Not one of its visiting dignitaries."

"This is a serious threat, and it may—I say, may—involve our president. The background we have on the potential assailant is that he is a potential suicide risk. This could involve a crowded event, something public . . ."

"Who is this Comandante Garza?"

Fisk put his hands on his hips. "I think you probably know who she is."

Dubin said, "Did you forget that there were something on the order of a dozen eyes on you last night? While you were getting gooey eyed and wine-drunk with Miss Mexico in a bar at the Sheraton?"

Fisk pulled back on his anger. Gooey eyed? If anything, it was the opposite. But he understood how their talk, her confessional, might have looked. Then his anger came out anyway. "What the hell does that have to do with anything?"

"First there's an imminent threat in New York. Then there's a wine date at a hotel bar."

Fisk boiled. "The Mexican president was tucked away safely. We went there to eat and instead . . . we had a talk. Did your tattlers tell you we went our separate ways after?"

Dubin waved that away as though it did not matter—though, if he had gone up to her room, it would certainly have mattered. "You've been off your desk escorting this Garza around—"

"Escorting! Jesus, Barry."

"You've been AWOL chasing an alleged cartel hit man who many people think is a legend, not an actual person. A cartel fiction, a bogeyman—"

"This is total bullshit."

"You're getting caught up in one woman's personal crusade instead of doing your job here. Now, I don't know if this has anything to do with the other thing, but for appearance's sake alone—"

"What other thing?" said Fisk.

"The other thing," said Dubin, adopting a softer tone, stepping forward. "Gersten."

"God," said Fisk. "Is that the talk? Nobody has any time to do any police work around here?"

"It's in your after-action file from Dr. Flaherty. A caution about repeating patterns, trying to replay the past. About saving this Garza from a similar fate as Gersten."

Fisk laughed out loud. In that moment, he was embarrassed for Dubin. "I'm working a case here," said Fisk.

"Exactly. When you are supposed to be liaising with UN security and making sure everything in this city that employs us is running smooth."

"You know what?" said Fisk. "I've got an employment file with quite a few victories in there, and now suddenly this therapy report is the number one thing about me."

"You are a pipeline between the NYPD and the United Nations. You are not to be gumshoeing around the five boroughs with the head of security for another country's president."

Fisk tried one more time. "This involves New York. This is New York. There is an assassin here now. He's killed three people in the last forty-eight hours. Dumped thirteen bodies in Rockaway, none of them with heads."

"Believe me, I know all that." He held up the *New York Post*. The headline screamed, in the *Post*'s usual fashion, CARNAGE. Then, below that, MEX DRUG WAR HORROR COMES TO NYC.

Fisk said, "You see?"

"I see it. We have people on this. I got a call from a supervisor in Rockaway saying that you authorized one of his homicide detectives working the headless thirteen to share evidence with the Mexican *federales*?"

"It's how they made these guys!"

"Chain of command, Fisk. Not the first time I've uttered those words to you. Now listen up. You're just back on full active duty. You want to stay that way? Distance yourself from Comandante Hottie. Okay? I don't care how nice her ass is. Do your job. Show up at the UN briefings you are supposed to go to, and let the Secret Service do their duty."

"Dukes, right?" said Fisk. "He call you direct, or have someone else do it for him?"

"Stay out of the way."

Fisk sat at his desk for a while, waiting for the usual thoughts of resigning to subside, so he could focus on the task at hand.

A couple of days ago, Dubin was singing his praises, worried Fisk might leave for another intelligence agency. Today Fisk was a liability, apparently.

He should have followed his gut. He should have quit after the Freedom Tower incident. After catching Jenssen and losing Gersten.

He should have walked away then. This was so obvious to him now.

"Hey, Nicole?"

He called to her from his desk. In a moment, she was in his doorway.

"Will you please get me the Mexican president's full itinerary for today?"

Her mouth opened, but nothing came out. She went away, then came right back. "Don't you want your schedule for the day?"

Fisk said, "Dubin spoke to you, too?"

She shared a pained expression with him. Fisk was not angry with her.

"President Vargas's itinerary. I know he's got a stop at the Mexican Cultural Institute sometime this morning, then a stop in El Barrio, then the independence parade and festival and the dinner tonight."

Nicole nodded. "And you have a field briefing at the UN at eleven thirty this morning . . ."

"No," said Fisk. "I won't be going to that."

"You won't be . . . ?" She waited for further instructions. "So I should cancel you."

"No, you can keep it on the books. I just won't be there."

"Okay," she said, looking a little sick.

"Don't worry, Nicole," said Fisk. "You tell me what I'm supposed to be doing, and if I don't do it, it falls on me, not you."

President Umberto Vargas's motorcade exited from the garage beneath the Sheraton New York Times Square Hotel and rolled south down Seventh Avenue. Cecilia Garza was in the first SUV with General de Aguilar and two EMP agents. President Vargas rode in the middle car with a reporter for *The New Yorker* who was doing a long-range article on the bold new Mexican administration. More support rode in the third SUV, and an NYPD motorcycle cop led the way.

The streets were busy that morning, faces turning toward the dark-windowed motorcade of shiny black and silver SUVs but nobody reacting with anything more than a passing curiosity. The motorcycle cop up ahead bleated his siren at traffic lights and slow crossings so that the SUVs did not get held up. At the Fortieth Street intersection, Secret Service agents had shut down traffic so the motorcade could turn left without stopping. The SUVs drove to Park Avenue, where they turned right, then right again onto Thirty-ninth.

The Mexican Cultural Institute was located at the Mexican consulate, just off Park Avenue, across the street from a row of low-rise brick buildings and brownstones. The institute had been founded in the early 1990s as part of a "Program for Mexican Communities Abroad," in order to nurture a sense of national identity among people of Mexican origin living in the New York metro area. They ran programs to strengthen awareness of Mexico's history and rich traditions "as a democratic, plural, and creative nation," read the press release in her hand.

A press release. She crumpled it. Why was the consulate publicizing Señor Presidente's visit? Were they not aware of the security threat? Or were they just so overly confident of security in and around the consulate?

Blue wooden NYPD sawhorse barricades had been set up at Park Avenue, but sidewalk traffic was allowed to pass across the street from the consulate, behind a barricade fence. The barricades had evidently been up for some time, because a small crowd had gathered across the street from the consulate, drawn by the promise of an event of some sort.

Garza reviewed on her iPad a surveillance video taken from the second floor of the consulate, panning the faces in the crowd they were about to encounter. Garza went over it once very quickly, looking for Yankees caps, then admonished herself for looking for the obvious, the expected. She went back through each face, looking for anyone who might resemble the Chuparosa from the Montreal airport and Queens traffic cameras. She spotted a cluster of photographers wearing press credentials camped behind some TV news cameras on tripods, and saw that the headlines in the morning newspapers were going to dog them all day long—exactly as President Vargas feared. The antitrafficking-treaty signing might be overshadowed by the usual narrative of Mexico's drug cartel violence.

Garza checked her phone one last time. No contact from Fisk. She had expected to see him with the security contingent as they left the hotel, but he was nowhere to be found.

She accepted this. Upon further reflection after a night's sleep, perhaps he realized that her past marked her as too complicated. She had to admit that, upon waking, the night before in the hotel lounge seemed to her like a dream, in which a different version of herself unburdened her personal side to a man she had only recently met.

She needed to get back to Mexico. To get out of New York. She wanted to return to the familiar confines of the PF, to go about her business and leave the concerns of presidential politics and security behind.

But first she wanted to get Chuparosa.

Her lead car pulled just past the limestone front of the five-story consulate building. There were two entrances. One faced the sidewalk, beneath a giant black globe housing the consulate's security cameras. The other was inside a very small, gated courtyard, not much larger than a limousine. That was the public entrance, reserved for consulate business, such as visas, passports, immigration paperwork, and the like.

They idled and waited for the second and third vehicles to fall in behind them. An EMP agent in the backseat was monitoring the radio.

Garza grew anxious, watching more bystanders

arrive, drawn by the police presence and the idling motorcade. What was taking so long?

"Visto bueno," said the EMP agent.

Garza was out of the vehicle quickly, striding around to the rear, ready to escort President Vargas over the few yards to the entrance, which was controlled by security from inside the consulate. A small knot of consulate employees, including Consul General Francisca Metron, awaited him near the entrance.

Vargas exited through the door to the sidewalk, as planned, buttoning his jacket once he emerged and turning to wave blindly at the gathered crowd. Voices were raised, questions being shouted by reporters across Thirty-ninth Street, a one-way street with two traffic lanes and a parking lane. A number of Mexicans in the crowd cheered, and Vargas slowed to further acknowledge them, flashing the smile.

The gathered media misconstrued this action as an opportunity to shout more questions, which frankly neither Garza nor Vargas could hear above the din. Garza was sweeping her eyes over the crowd on the other side when she heard a voice yelling.

"Stop! Stop! Stop!"

A man wearing a heavy black backpack had hopped the barricade fence and begun striding quickly across the street toward the president. The perimeter EMP agents were the ones yelling at him to halt.

The man wore a dark ball cap with no insignia on the crest. As he came, he readied a Nikon camera strung around his neck, as though to get a picture.

At the same time, he swung his backpack forward off one shoulder, as though he were about to throw it.

Garza perceived all of this as happening in extreme slow motion.

Both items—the camera and the backpack—were potential weapons.

Her reaction time lagged just a second. Because to her eyes, this man did not match the video image of Chuparosa she had been playing and replaying in her mind since yesterday evening.

A Secret Service agent broke from the rear SUV of the idling motorcade and drew his weapon, a SIG Sauer P229. Into his suit jacket cuff, he shouted, "Breach! Breach!"

Garza was also drawing, her Beretta coming out of her shoulder holster as she jumped in front of President Vargas. She shouted, *"Amenaza! Amenaza!"* Threat! Threat!

A third individual sprang from the crowd behind the side barricade, wearing a dress shirt with rolled-up sleeves and dark pants. He was aiming a Glock at the man and shouting, "Get to the ground! Get on the ground!"

The man with the camera stopped, momentarily mystified by the triumvirate of armed people yelling at him. Then he recognized the weapons in their hands. He went down to one knee, then the next, half collapsing, half complying.

The Secret Service agent was on him first, grabbing a free hand and driving his knee into the photographer's back.

The gunman from the crowd was a close second.

The Secret Service agent, not knowing this man, pointed his gun at him.

Fisk's hands went up quickly. "Fisk! NYPD Intel!"

"Jesus!" said the agent.

Garza kept her grip on Vargas, watching the photographer grunt and try to explain himself on the ground. When the Secret Service agent rolled him over, there was a wet spot on the pavement where the photographer's groin had been.

Garza did not remain to watch any more. She turned and pushed President Vargas's head down and ran him to the consulate entrance, past the stunned greeting party, getting him inside as fast as possible.

Once safely inside, she scanned the interior of the consulate entrance. She began to relinquish her grip on the president's suit jacket when she felt it pull away from her.

"It was only a goddamn photographer!" he said behind her.

Garza turned. She saw the flash of anger cross the president's face as he fixed his jacket. It stunned her.

"Have we not had enough bad press!" he said. "A photographer. Not an assassin!"

Garza was stunned. It was all she could do to walk away from him, quickly, before she said something back to him. She left him to the watchful eyes of her EMP compatriots, striding back out through the door to the sidewalk.

The photographer was being led to a police car by two uniformed officers. Every photographer in the media throng was still snapping away.

Fisk had turned his face away in an attempt to avoid them, but it was much too late. The Secret Service agent was huddling with his compatriots. One of them held an M4 carbine.

Garza went to Fisk, pulling him behind the president's SUV, blocking them from view.

"What are you doing here in disguise?" she said.

He billowed out his shirt, trying to air out his sweat. "It's not much of a disguise. I left my jacket in the car and rolled up my sleeves."

"Why weren't you at the hotel this morning?" she asked.

Fisk frowned. "I'm not supposed to be here at all. Dubin—my boss—thinks I'm spending too much time on one visiting dignitary. I think he got a complaint from Dukes about us. And if I'd gone to the hotel first, I would have had to check in with them."

Garza said, "They know you're here now."

"Yeah," he said. "It's not good. Thanks to that idiot with the camera."

"What's going to happen?"

"I don't know," said Fisk. "Got any openings in Mexico?"

Garza smiled. "Depends. Can you be corrupted?"

"Only by red wine," he said.

Garza grinned, then backed off.

"What is it?"

She shook her head. "Vargas. He didn't like the way that looked."

Fisk sighed. "Believe me, he would have loved it had that idiot had an explosive device in his backpack."

Garza was steamed.

"Interesting start to the day," said Fisk.

"Was that urine I saw on the road?" she asked.

"Oh, yeah," said Fisk. "Looking into the business end of a handgun does that to people."

Garza took a moment to scan the crowd. They were starting to disperse now that the show was over.

"I was feeling good about having an image of Chuparosa," she said. "But now suddenly I feel we are no closer to him. No how, or where, or when."

"He's killed off everybody who could answer those questions."

"He couldn't have killed everybody," said Garza. "He is staying somewhere. Someone is helping him."

Fisk said, "I had a look at the seating plan for the dinner tonight. Obama and Vargas are seated at separate tables, which I guess is a power hosting thing. It gives the gathering two prime tables for guests to sit at, and by guests I mean donors."

Garza nodded. "So?"

"Obama's seatmates were all named on the diagram. As were Vargas's seatmates . . . except for one. One was left empty."

"Why?"

"I was hoping you could tell me."

Garza shook her head. "I haven't seen the chart."

"Well, then two other things came to mind. One was the mysterious presence of a U.S. marshal at the security review. I recognized her on the way out. She gave me a very vague nonanswer about what she was doing there. As you may know, they handle fugitives and federal witness relocation. And where was the restaurant owner? Two heads of state are coming to your establishment for an important dinner, and you're not present at the security review? You're not overseeing every little detail?"

"Fair point," she said. "Who is the owner?"

"A limited partnership. Some shell corporation. But even shell corporations have to file legal papers and tax forms." Fisk crossed his arms, looking down at her over his sunglasses. "I think we need to go pay this fellow a visit, Comandante."

Garza nodded. "I think we do, too."

Chuparosa entered the garage dressed in a pair of light coveralls. He lifted the rear door of the fish truck with the Teixeira Brothers logo on the side and loaded in the deep tray of finely chopped ice.

He opened the four cases of shellfish, kneeling on the floor of the van. Blue Points, Chincoteagues, littlenecks, and Wellfleets, one box each. He spread the fresh ice in and around the oysters.

Packed in the ice beneath several layers of Wellfleets were the plastic frames of two Glock 17s. The trigger guards of each frame had been ground off, and all of the straight edges of the frame and handgrips had been modified with a Dremel tool in order to mimic the shape and roughness of an oyster.

Both guns had been fieldstripped, their slides and magazines distributed in the lining of a box of oyster knives. Each handle of the sixty-eight knives contained a single 124-grain 9mm Hydra-Shok hollow-point round sealed inside a lead lining so that they could not be detected by X-rays.

The barrels of the Glocks had been inserted inside the handle of a hand truck he had bought at the Home Depot on DeKalb Avenue in Brooklyn.

Silencers were the easy part. The two AAC

Ti-RANT cans were top-of-the-line military-grade suppressors, slightly modified. Each had been disassembled, the tubes and pistons painted the same color as the hand truck and attached to the cross member, the baffles disassembled and slid onto the handles of the truck in place of the original rubber grips and painted matte black.

The locking blocks of the Glocks, too, had been painted and attached unobtrusively to the frame of the hand truck with Loctite. All that was left of the Glocks were the trigger groups, the trigger bars, the sears, and the trigger connectors—all of which were small pieces containing little more metal than a ballpoint pen. They were installed inside a tablet computer labeled ORDER TRACKING MODULE, effectively immune from detection.

The most distinctive parts—the gun barrels—had been set aside. They would have the most distinctive X-ray profiles, and so they would have to go in through an entirely different route.

Chuparosa heard footsteps and grasped the handle of the knife he carried in his belt, just as a precaution. He turned and waited.

Tomás Calibri came around the corner carrying two formal-looking outfits on hangers, wrapped in dry cleaner's clear plastic. Tuxedo shirts and black pants.

Servers' uniforms.

From his pocket Calibri pulled out two black bow ties.

"I hope you know how to tie a real bow tie, *patrón*?"

Fisk and Garza spent some time out of his vehicle at the security station before the gate built into the twelve-foot-high stone wall. It was a beautiful, blue-sky day on Long Island. Their respective credentials were examined by a security guard while a second guard, a backup, remained inside the booth, watching them carefully.

The first guard carried their identification into the guard booth and spent a considerable amount of time on the telephone. He finally returned, again checked their faces against their identification cards, and only then signaled the second guard to roll back the gate.

When they were back inside his car and rolling up the wide driveway, Fisk said, "Getting on an airplane is easier than that."

The lawn was beautifully landscaped, the main house not coming into view until the wide driveway took a leftward turn.

The mansion was slate roofed, with multiple dormer windows set symmetrically between red-trimmed gables. It was three stories and wide, fronted by a large circular driveway ringed by perfect green shrubs, offset by a pond with a fountain in its center. Picture perfect against a clear blue sky on a warm September day.

"My goodness," said Fisk.

"How much would you say?" asked Garza.

Fisk said, "Seven million. The upkeep alone would be beyond any cop's reach."

"All from one tiny restaurant?" said Garza.

They parked outside the front door. The door was opened by a butler, who welcomed them inside. He was Mexican by appearance, stern looking, in his fifties. "Comandante and Detective, Don Andrés insists upon a strict no-gun policy inside his home," said the butler.

Fisk said, "That is simply not possible."

"I am afraid I will have to insist. Or else Don Andrés will not be available to sit with you today."

Fisk checked with Garza to be sure he was speaking for both of them. "You tell your boss that we wear our weapons wherever we go."

A woman stepped into the entrance from one of the three rooms that fed into it. "Then I will have to insist," she said.

Fisk smiled. "Marshal Graben." The U.S. marshal he had seen at the restaurant during the briefing.

"Good to see you again, Fisk. You shouldn't be here."

"Why not?"

"Because it's no concern of yours. But since Andrés León does not object, I am making it happen. But not with your service pieces. Again—his house, his rules."

"Fine," said Garza, unsnapping her holster and removing her Beretta.

Fisk, after a moment's consideration, pulled out his Glock.

The butler was waiting with an open box. They laid them inside.

"And any electronic devices," added the butler.

Fisk glanced sideways at Graben before relinquishing his phone. Garza laid hers inside the box next to Fisk's.

The butler closed the box and set it on a table near the door. "Thank you," said the butler. "Now, if you don't mind . . ."

He did not give them a chance to mind. The butler frisked Fisk, thoroughly and professionally. As a courtesy, Graben walked over to pat down Garza.

Garza stared at the marshal during the frisking.

"Satisfied?" said Fisk.

Graben said, "He is on the patio in back."

Fisk said, "Care to draw us a map?"

Through an open glass door in the back, they stepped down onto a brick patio arranged in a wide circle with inlaid tiles set to resemble a glowing sun. Beyond the patio, trees rose before the wall that circled the property. Above the patio was strung a thin netting that did little to block out the sun.

From one of three deck chairs set before a table containing the remains of a fine breakfast, Andrés León set down his iPad and stood. He was an older man, his hair long, held back in a gray-black braid that came halfway down his back. He wore loafers with no socks, linen pants, a loose, long-sleeved shirt, and a wide straw hat. He smiled in a grandfatherly way, greeting them.

"Welcome!" he said. He took Cecilia Garza's hand politely, almost as though he were about to kiss it, then shook Fisk's hand.

"Mexico City and New York, working jointly," he said, having been appraised of their identities in advance of their appearance. "It is rarely a pleasure when police appear, but to what do I owe it?"

He offered them the other two chairs, but neither Fisk nor Garza sat.

Garza said, "We are preparing security for a special dinner tonight between two heads of state—"

León said, "Of course, of course. At my restaurant. But I believed all security matters were being seen to already."

Fisk said, "We were curious. We hadn't met you personally and wanted to come by ourselves."

"Curious, I see. You won't sit?"

They did, reluctantly.

"Anything? Orange juice? So fresh?"

"No, nothing," said Fisk.

"I might have some," said Garza.

"Wonderful." He waved to a servant standing off to the side, and she departed.

"As you can see," he said, "I live in a beautiful prison here."

Fisk nodded. "We were going to ask you about that."

"That was my assumption. Inspector Fisk, I followed your exploits in the news last year."

"It's Detective," said Fisk.

"And you, too, Comandante Garza. I follow Mexican news most closely. You have made quite a name for yourself. I am not surprised you would seek me out here, due to my involvement in the dinner tonight. I am happy to answer all questions."

Garza said, "Who are you?"

"Who I am now is a protected individual living under the careful watch of the United States government. A retired Mexican financier. An expatriate. A man in self-exile."

Garza's orange juice arrived in a crystal glass, sunlight glinting off the facets and sparkling. As the servant leaned forward to hand Garza the juice, Fisk saw the strap of a shoulder holster beneath his white jacket.

When the servant retreated, León said, "*Who I was* was a money manager for certain interests in Mexico, many years ago. I was heavily involved— you might say, desperately involved—in many illegal enterprises, as an accountant and a banker, laundering many millions for fifteen cents on the dollar."

Garza said, "for the cartels."

León tucked his chin and set his lips, looking resigned. "Corruption always begins with small things, Comandante. It comes at you sideways. I was a legitimate banker once. A long, long time ago. The movies make what I did look daring and exotic. It was hell. Daily hell. Ulcers. Paranoia. No sleep."

"Not everyone is corrupted," said Garza.

León opened his hands as though to concede the point. "The age I am now, I think more and more of *mi papi*, my poor father. I can never forget the expression on his face when he got himself out of bed every day. His back had been broken in an industrial accident. He was a wreck of a man physically. He was never treated properly and spent his life in physical agony. Still, every day he dragged himself out of bed and worked twelve hours a day selling newspapers in a little stand near the Palacio Legislativo. Every day, politicians came by his newspaper stand. They called him by name. I would see this, I would help him, hawking. This was back in the day when the PRI monopolized Mexican politics, of course. They all wore sparkling rings and fine suits. And they would flip me a ten-centavo piece because I was the broken newspaper vendor's son. You know, ten centavos . . . it was worth less than nothing. They knew it and I knew it. And my father would always say to me, 'That was Deputy So-and-So. He made sixty-three million pesos in bribes for putting a road across Oaxaca.' Papi never said it, perhaps never even thought it, but to me the lesson was that, in a just world, those sixty-three million pesos would have gone to fixing the broken backs of the unfortunate men who hurt themselves in an industrial accident, and not to lining the pockets of politicians."

His face looked almost clownishly sad, but that was his manner. León was a man of broad expression.

"But I never hated Mexico. My father made sure I would never follow his fate, and I did not. I built myself. But I was too ambitious at times. Too eager to meet with the wrong people. I had a bit of self-destruction about me. It seemed so remote, the violent source of the funds I was entrusted with moving and investing. I was willfully ignorant, I fully admit that." He patted his knees, wanting to be done with his own story. "And so now I am trying to repay a debt."

"You do not seem to be suffering," said Garza.

"Not in the least. That offends you."

"Yes," she said.

León nodded.

"Which cartel?" she asked.

"The unofficial name was the Sonora Cartel, but these things change. People make pronouncements, naming this and that, but it is so fluid. I started low on the pole, I had my fingers in many pies. It was a different business thirty years ago, and yet very much the same. What knowledge I learned—I was always a good student—I have tried to put to good use here from the other side of the border."

Fisk said, "You are an informant?"

"Bigger than that. I know informants. I still have several well-placed contacts in Mexico. I am an aggregator of information, Detective. I have assisted the Mexican government in curtailing the cartels' activities, inasmuch as anyone can. The United States offered me this sanctuary in exchange for my offer of help in keeping such outrageous drug violence from drifting north, over its borders. And so I defected, though that is not the word that is used between friendly countries. To this end, I have been most helpful, I think. Until these past few days, that is."

Garza nodded. She seemed to be hanging on the man's every word.

"That is the language of Mexican crime now, is it not, Comandante? Atrocities. Meant to shock. It is terror."

"Chuparosa," said Garza.

Fisk felt she was uttering his name in order to watch León's reaction. Fisk saw nothing in the man's face to indicate anything out of the ordinary.

"I have heard the name," said León. "Whispered, most often. Friends speak of him as though he is not real."

"He is real," said Garza.

"And he is here? He brings you to New York?"

Garza gave him a very brief summation of what she knew: nothing privileged, nothing revelatory. Fisk noticed a softening in her manner here, which confused him at first. Then he began to think it was a cultural thing, brought on by a conversation with this older, grandfatherly man.

Fisk admitted that there was something impishly likable about León, his blarney and bluster. But he needed to know more.

"He sounds like quite a gentleman," said León. "Do you have a photograph, by any chance?"

"No," said Garza.

"One wants to see the face of a man who could do such things, no?" León swiped at his mouth with his linen napkin, tossing it back upon the table. "Do you have any insight as to why he wants to bring down President Vargas? And perhaps die in the process? It seems so . . . extreme, no?"

Garza was appropriately cagey with León. "He holds a grudge, I believe. He is wedded to the old ways, the old Mexico. The one you seem to know. This treaty could—I think—effect real change in our country."

León nodded, deep in thought. "You give me pause, Comandante. I wonder if it is wise for me to attend tonight." He shook his head. "Forgive me, I am not a coward. But I am certainly not a brave man either. How I would hate to miss it."

Fisk said, "Security is going to be incredibly tight. You can feel confident."

"But nothing is ever guaranteed, Detective Fisk. You know that as well as I. My position here is precarious. In fact, I rarely leave this home. By rarely,

I mean no more than once a year. I am a paranoid man, and rightly so. The restaurant is my only commercial enterprise. I miss the tastes of home, you see. These dishes I used to have prepared here, we started serving at Ocampo. Have you read our Zagat review? I'll have someone hand you a copy on your way out. Extraordinary Mexican seafood cuisine! Others scoffed when it opened. We have three stars from Michelin! I am sorry to brag, food is a weakness." He patted his belly. "I live too well. Living well is addictive."

Fisk said, "So why is it that the president of Mexico chose your restaurant for his celebratory dinner?"

"It should be obvious to you both by now," said León. "Umberto Vargas got his start in politics as a prosecutor, after leaving academia, roughly around the time I repatriated here. He made his name going after organized crime and the cartels." To Garza, he said, "You know that started him on his stunning trajectory toward the presidency. He has been an anticorruption, antidrug guy all the way. And I, in my own manner, have been of some help to him. Some prosecutions, I helped make possible. Even from afar. I was his secret weapon, in a sense . . . though I do not want to be thought of as taking too much credit. President Vargas is the one whose face is out there. He is a man of valor, of principles. I have been, so to speak, his counsel in the shadows. Not to overstate it, but we have become . . . I don't know what you want to call it. Friends? Associates? Neither. Strange bedfellows, perhaps. I have been very, very useful to him, and for that I feel wonderful. I still love our country, Comandante. I love it like . . . like an ex-wife I once wronged, who is still raising my many, many children. President Vargas is . . . an expression of my penance. I supported his campaign in every way, including financially. I honestly believe that a man like him comes once a generation. Now is the time to do great things."

León grasped Garza's hand for emphasis.

"You must keep him well and safe. We cannot afford to let these forces of evil stop the progress we have made. This antitrafficking accord with the United States is the greatest attempt Mexico has made at stemming the tide of violence, corruption, and terror. This treaty is a great step forward. And, in many ways, I am its crux."

With their service pieces and phones returned to them, Fisk and Garza waited until they were outside León's gate before speaking.

"Okay," said Fisk. "Now we know who he is."

"You don't like him," said Garza.

"Not especially. He put on a happy face, but a guy who made who knows how many millions laundering blood money has an epiphany and gets a golden parachute into the United States to live off the taxpayers' money in secret? He's either a genius or a piece of shit."

"Or both," said Garza. "I had a great-uncle like him. A rascal."

"What about your president, though? Secretly in bed with this guy."

"I don't have to like it. It affects me not at all."

Fisk's phone began vibrating. Three missed calls and a bunch of e-mails flooded in.

"There must have been something blocking cell signals at León's place," said Fisk, checking the source of the calls. All three were from Dubin at Intel.

"Shit."

"What?" she said.

"That false alarm this morning. My boss is going to try to yank me off this."

Garza checked the time on her phone. "Vargas is scheduled to leave the consulate soon for the Independence Day celebration."

Fisk thought briefly about ignoring Dubin and continuing on with Garza. But he did not want to become a distraction. He wanted the Secret Service and Garza's EMP men focused on the job at hand—protecting Vargas, stopping Chuparosa—exclusively.

It would be an hour's ride back to midtown, but Fisk chose to drop her off at the consulate first. Then he would check in with Dubin by phone.

"One thing I think is clear," said Fisk, as they neared the consulate.

"What is that?" she said.

"Unless you can find Chuparosa beforehand, Andrés León is a likely no-show at his own restaurant tonight. He seemed more concerned about the assassin than your president."

"I think you are right."

"Hey," he said, grasping her arm as she tried to hop out at the curb at Thirty-ninth Street and Park Avenue. "Be careful."

Fisk called Nicole instead of Dubin.

"The *Post* already has pictures up online of you going after that photographer outside the Mexican consulate," she told him, her voice low. "It says, HERO TERROR COP ON MEX PRESIDENT DETAIL. You knew you weren't supposed to be there . . ."

"Dubin been by?"

"Back and forth from his office a dozen times, but he's not talking to me. You need to come in."

Fisk said, "This thing is still live." He was most worried now about getting inside the restaurant that night. The way things were going, Fisk himself would be on a No Fly, Detain On Sight list before then. "Tell him I got a flat tire," Fisk said.

Nicole said, "I am not telling him anything of the sort."

"Okay, then tell him he can fire me tomorrow at nine A.M., if he wants to. But not before."

"You have a sit-rep meeting scheduled with the United Nations security team regarding the General Assembly meeting."

Fisk heard a beep. He had another call coming in. Kiser from Rockaway.

"Nicole, I'll call you back."

"Wait, what am I really supposed to tell Dubin—"

Fisk switched over, picking up Kiser's call. "Nice job cracking down on the paparazzi," said Kiser.

"Thanks. What have you got?"

"Three more bodies identified. All you need to know from that is that one was a coyote who went by the name Raoul. A trafficker of women, real piece of fried shit. That's interesting because of the alert that went out under your name for that Mexican hooker."

Fisk nodded. "Silvia Volpi."

"Got a guy here saw her name in the news. You should talk to him."

The Celebración de El Grito de Independencia took place at a park in Woodside, Queens. The banner over the stage read ¡VIVA MEXICO! in the flag colors of green, white, and red. Women in traditional huipils, as well as dresses from Michoacán and Tabasco, the men in wide, red-rimmed sombreros and charro suits. Mariachi bands played throughout the crowd, and men threw down their hats and kicked up their heels in dance.

All very clichéd, and yet, Garza thought to herself, all very wonderful just the same.

EMP agents wearing less formal guayabera shirts filtered through the crowd undetected. Snipers were positioned on surrounding rooftops. Cameras at every entrance were capturing pictures of entrants and filtering them through facial recognition software.

Garza sipped a Diet Coke through a straw, feeling very anxious but ready. She looked out from the wings of the small stage again, seeing past the families and couples enjoying the day, looking for anything that didn't fit.

She heard the footsteps of a group behind her, and she knew the president was near. She turned to see him following two EMP agents around the corner, his eyes on his speech. This stop was another chance to refine the remarks he was preparing to deliver at the formal treaty signing that night.

When President Vargas looked up, he saw Garza and went to her. Garza relaxed, anticipating an apology for his being so short with her earlier.

He said, "This needs to go off like clockwork. I must return to the hotel in time to shower and change and prepare."

Garza waited a beat before answering. "Yes, señor," she said.

Vargas nodded, stepping back. He was apparently unaware of the offense he had caused her earlier.

Normally she would not have been so bold, so forward, as to speak out of place. But the new president's manner grated on her. The lack of respect she felt from him was an affront.

She said, "I do not believe Andrés León will be in attendance this evening."

The president looked at her with a very odd expression. It was as though he had not heard her correctly . . . and had heard every word she had said at the same time.

He stepped forward, keeping his detail back with an impertinent wave of his hand.

"What did you say?" he said.

"Andrés León," said Garza, unbowed. "Or whatever his name used to be."

Vargas squinted as though trying to guess at her intent in telling him this. "That information is extremely privileged. You should not know about him."

Now it was Garza's turn to parse his words. "Why not, Señor Presidente?"

He scowled at her use of the formal. "Because, Comandante, such knowledge is powerful and even dangerous. Who else knows? Tell me now."

Garza only told him because he would eventually find out anyway. "An NYPD Detective named Jeremy Fisk."

"The one you've been going around with these past few days."

Now she was not happy. " 'Going around with'?"

Vargas got closer, ensuring that their conversation remained private. "If it were to be made public that I am in any way affiliated with a man like León, it would weaken my hand."

"Why is that?" she said.

"That is none of your business, Comandante."

"Because he seems like a man eager to right his wrongs. You certainly have taken advantage of his largesse."

Vargas's eyes flared. "This is very much a game of perception. When the right things are done in the wrong way, people revolt."

"The wrong way?" said Garza.

The president made to end the conversation. "Some things are better left unstudied, Cecilia," he said. "Some stones are better left unturned."

The 101st Precinct police station was a brick and limestone box occupying the entire corner at 16-12 Mott Avenue. The arched doorway was accented on both sides by green hanging lanterns featuring the old-school, slanted, stylized NYPD font reading 101st.

Fisk quickly found Kiser, who led him to an interview room. A young Vietnamese man in short sleeves and a home haircut sat at the table waiting for them. Near him, setting down and neatly folding a Vietnamese newspaper, was a more Americanized Asian wearing a white shirt and a maroon necktie.

Kiser said, "Nam Thring is his name. This fellow is Jerry, a translator we use."

Jerry nodded.

Kiser said, "Mr. Thring, uh, evidently has had a *relationship* with this Silvia Volpi. At least twice. He says she was very beautiful, very innocent. Second time he saw her, it was business as usual, except that on his way out she slipped him a folded piece of paper. Pressed it into his hand, clamping her hand over his mouth to tell him don't say anything. She pushed his hand into his pocket to hide it there. Then watched him walk out of the room without a word.

"He says he didn't open the note until he got back to his home. It was a flyer for a car wash place, the kind people leave under doors and elasticized to door handles. There was writing in the margins, done in a small hand. It was all in Spanish. Mr. Thring does not speak Spanish, but knew a friend who did and brought the note to him. Mr. Thring thought it might be a mash note or something, I guess. Instead it was a plea for help.

"It gave her full name, the Mexican city she was kidnapped from, the names and addresses of her parents. In it, she said she was being held captive by force, in total silence, unable to leave the building she was in. She said she did not know where she was, what town or city. She feared she was going to be traded or sold again. She asked him to go to the police."

Fisk exhaled. "Which he did not."

"Too scared," said Kiser. "That's his excuse. He didn't do anything except throw away the note. He didn't come here on his own. His friend, the one who translated the note from Spanish, turned him in. Recognized the girl's name. Mr. Thring is also living in this country illegally."

Fisk looked at Jerry, the translator. He was a little too disgusted at Mr. Thring to look at him just yet. "How did he first meet her?"

Jerry asked Thring in rapid-fire Vietnamese. Thring answered him slowly, eyes downcast.

Jerry relayed, "An online advertisement for massages, on a Vietnamese site."

Kiser said, "Illegals advertising for illegals. That way nobody goes to the authorities."

Fisk said to Jerry, "I need an address. Right now. Where was she?"

Thring answered back that he did not know.

Fisk said, "A house? An apartment? You weren't blindfolded. Describe!"

Thring answered that it was in a part of the city he was unfamiliar with.

Fisk said, "Jesus, you went there twice. He have GPS on his phone? The address in there?"

Thring shook his head, unable to meet the eyes even of his translator.

Fisk dug out his own phone. He went to Google Maps Street View. "Give me his address."

Fisk entered it. A tall apartment building in Kew Gardens, Queens.

"Okay," said Fisk, taking Jerry's seat so Thring could see the display. "Turn right or left?"

It went like that, painstakingly, and with many wrong turns. Block by block. Fisk learned the Vietnamese words for right, left, and straight.

The display had him heading toward the Williamsburg end of Bushwick, just over the line from Queens into Brooklyn. A residential area gave way to a mostly industrial area on the other side of Flushing Avenue. Lightly traveled, no retail business. The neighborhood was still a decade away from loft conversions, coffee bars, and hipsters.

Fisk moved virtually through the side streets of this neighborhood, coming to a large garage door covered in peeling paint the color of dried blood. Opposite the garage was an unbroken wall of warehouse.

"This is it?"

Thring nodded, relieved that his eyes could find the floor again.

Fisk turned to Jerry. "I need the layout of the place inside."

Thring was not very helpful. Jerry translated, "You knock on the door. It is dark. They take money and bring you down basement, unlock door to room."

"Unlock door?" said Fisk.

"Many doors," Jerry translated.

Many girls, thought Fisk.

Fisk knew Garza would not be answering her phone, so he texted her and e-mailed her a link to the address in Bushwick. She probably wanted to stay put with the Mexican president, but it was her call.

Dubin was at lunch when Fisk reached him. He talked over Dubin's opening diatribe, laying out where he was headed and why.

"You want a SWAT team?" said Dubin.

Fisk had had about enough. He said, "Barry, this is me. Do it. Or don't. I'm not waiting."

And he hung up.

Dammit, Fisk thought. I'm going to have to do this alone.

Fisk parked two blocks away. He jumped out and popped his trunk, pulling the Remington 870 shotgun from the bracket inside. He checked to make sure it was fully loaded, then filled the elastic cartridge carrier on the stock with another ten rounds of buckshot.

He pulled on his ballistic vest, did the straps, then slipped on a blue Windbreaker over that. It read NYPD on the back in bold yellow letters. If and when the SWAT team arrived, he hoped that and the badge in his belt carrier would be enough.

He slammed the trunk shut. A woman walked by him, carrying a string grocery bag, looking at him nervously, speeding up as she hit the corner and turned away.

Fisk's heart was beating rapidly. He started down the sidewalk with the shotgun held out in front of him with both hands.

Cecilia Garza did not check her messages until President Vargas was safely away from the podium and back in the clutches of his security detail. Two persons had been intercepted in the crowd, one suspicious man with a backpack and another wearing a hoodie in the hot midday sun. Neither turned out to be any threat.

The text from Fisk was vague and contained misspellings. That alone spoke to its immediacy. Did he have a lead on the Mexican prostitute who had pointed out Virgilio to Chuparosa? She found the address. She tried to call Fisk, but it went right to voice mail.

Vargas was moving back to the hotel soon. She did not know what to do.

Fisk jogged down the sidewalk toward the red garage. He could see the camera mounted on the building above it, but he was not in range yet. Trying the garage door was a third option at best, and going in through the door Thring had entered was a suicidal second. So he looked for a better first option.

Cutting around the building before it led to a side door up a flight of four rusted stairs. It was locked, of course, but the door had a little give against his hip, so he brought the butt of the shotgun down on the handle. It broke, and he kicked in the door.

Abandoned. Or at least emptied, awaiting a new tenant. Concrete dust lay on the floor, a file cabinet on its side. Through that room and down a hall, he found another exit door. Through the window he could see his target building. There was a bulkhead secured with a chain and lock.

Fisk rushed back through the rooms looking for anything heavy he could use. He found a length of post pipe and picked it up. He only had one shot at this, two at the most.

He rushed back to the exit and unlocked the door, opening it to daylight. He hopped off the stairs quickly and crouch-ran to the bulkhead, looking up at the building for windows. There were none. He heard nothing from inside.

He set down his shotgun and slid the chain so that the lock was fully exposed. He could not hope to break the lock, but thought the force of the blow might pull off one or both of the bulkhead handles.

He reared back and swung. The *TRONGG* sound echoed, and he saw the handles bend.

He gave it another full swing without taking time to think about it—*TRONGG*—and the handles popped off, one bolt each.

He pulled off the chain, nervously checking both ways, waiting for someone to come upon him. A dog barked close by, as near as the next building over.

He grasped the half-removed handles and only then wondered what he would do if the doors were locked from inside. The padlock outside seemed to throw that into doubt, however, and when he pulled . . .

. . . the door opened with a sick groan.

Cement stairs coated with dust and dead bugs, leading to another door—its lock plate broken.

Fisk thumbed the flashlight button on the fore grip of his 870 and pushed the door open.

The man known as Chuparosa was upstairs watching a baseball game soundlessly on a laptop computer when he heard the twin clangs.

Watching baseball helped him to focus. He was dressed in his black pants and tuxedo shirt, his bow tie ends dangling from his winged collar. It was a recording of an interleague game from August. The Yankees were playing the Braves in Atlanta, so there was no designated hitter. The Mexican leagues had adopted the DH at more or less the same time as the American League, and Chuparosa did not understand the reason behind splitting Major League Baseball down the middle. The game was improved by the designated hitter rule—it was a fact!

Fortunately the Yankees were up 3–1 in the seventh. Chuparosa's uncle, the one who raised him, had always revered the Yankees organization as the greatest sports franchise in the world. Chuparosa hated his uncle unreservedly, but agreed with him in this thing only. His ball cap sat atop the table next to the computer, between it and a copy of *H Para Hombres* magazine with a picture of an almost naked Ninel Conde on the cover.

The noise was so startling and so loud, so obvious, he immediately dismissed it as the product of a nearby worker. But nothing could be left to chance.

Tomás Calibri came running into the room, buttoning up his trousers, the sound of the flushing toilet coming through the bathroom door.

"What is that, *patrón*?"

"Find out," said Chuparosa.

Calibri reached for the silenced MP5 submachine gun standing by the door.

Chuparosa said, "We are just a few hours away from glory. Do not take any chances."

The flashlight mounted on Fisk's Remington 870 was a recently purchased SureFire—incredibly powerful, but it gobbled batteries at an outrageous rate.

Inside the broken door to the basement, Fisk briefly swept the dark room, making certain no one was there to shoot him as he silhouetted himself in the doorway. Then he thumbed the flashlight off again. He did not want to go dark-blind. Nor did he want to tip off his location.

The noise of his entry had surely alerted anyone inside the warehouse.

He moved left, along a narrow walkway, cutting quickly through the blackness, ears straining.

Footsteps, above. He switched his light on again, directing it at the ceiling. Heart pine over massive old wooden beams. The creaks were farther away than that. A second floor above him.

He moved quickly down the hallway—too quickly, misjudging the end of the hall and bumping into the wall so abruptly he saw stars. He stopped, shaking it off. He turned right. He blinked the SureFire on and then off again.

Along the wide side of the room stood a series of unlabeled doors. As many as eight.

He aimed the light down, low to the ground, minimizing its illumination, and hurried across the gritty cement floor to the first door.

He put his hand on the knob but did not turn it. "Hello?" he whispered, remembering Thring's description of the room the hooker had been locked inside.

"Come in," said a female voice, barely audible, trembling.

Fisk tried the door, shotgun muzzle up. The knob turned. The door only locked from the inside, to keep its occupant from escaping. The flashlight blinded the young girl inside, who was no older than fifteen, sitting naked on a bare cot next to a chair with folded bedsheets stacked upon it.

With one thin arm, she blocked her eyes. With the other she attempted to cover her small breasts.

Fisk froze there for a moment. Then he grabbed the knob and pulled the door shut again.

Fisk backed away from the door. He looked down the wide room at the other doors.

Best to leave them locked in for now.

He quickly checked his silenced phone. No reception down here.

He put his phone away and thumbed off the light, picking his way across the room in darkness. The odor here was foul, the air uncirculated. He neared the end of the room and thought he could make out a flight of stairs headed up. He turned on his SureFire again . . . but the image he saw before him burned itself onto his retina, even after he shut off his flashlight again.

There, against the wall and on the floor, the amount of dried, brown blood was astonishing.

Slung against the paneled wall, splashed against the concrete floor.

Fisk held his breath in an attempt not to breathe in the fumes. He thumbed on the light again.

He saw the divots in the floor, amid all the smeared blood. He swung his light to the corner, where stood a tool resembling a post-hole digger, its blade crusted brown.

The scene was even grimmer the second time he looked at it. Grim and infinitely sad.

This was where the Rockaway thirteen had been decapitated and otherwise maimed.

Chuparosa checked the exterior surveillance cameras, front and back. There was nobody outside the building, no vehicles except those parked along the curb, nothing moving. No police cars, no vans.

If it was a cop, he had come alone. Which meant he was crazy or stupid.

If it was not a cop, who could it be? The unluckiest thief in the history of the world? Or another, unexpected threat?

Chuparosa buckled on his holster containing the Glock 21. He reached for the M4 carbine he had stolen from a drug dealer three weeks before.

He decided he wanted to keep eyes and ears on Calibri, and started down the stairs after him. Tomás Calibri had been shot twice fighting communist guerrillas during his stint in the Mexican military, where he was awarded the Condecoración al Valor Heroico and the Cruz de Guerra. Three years later he offered his mercenary services to the Zetas. He was a man of questionable intelligence, in Chuparosa's opinion, as well as being a little insane—but he was a good man in a fight.

Calibri was starting toward the door to the basement. As Chuparosa came off the bottom step, the elevator from the basement groaned to life, the thick cable starting to pull the car upward.

Chuparosa motioned to Calibri to take up a position opposite him by the elevator door. Calibri could cover the elevator while Chuparosa watched the basement door, and they could each shoot without concern for hitting each other.

The elevator hummed and whined and shuddered as it moved up toward them.

Whoever this strange visitor was, they had him.

Chuparosa, thought Fisk, quickly surveying the room by flashlight. He spotted a freight elevator gaping open, a rectangular slab of darkness in the wall. He thought to try the stairs first—quieter—but he had already announced his presence with the bulkhead chain.

The sound of the freight elevator would certainly put whoever was upstairs on alert, but it was time to take a chance. He was alone in an unfamiliar building. The advantage was theirs.

The Hummingbird might be up there.

The freight elevator was an ancient thing. It operated with a worn, old-fashioned brass handle that you pushed one direction or the other. Right was up, left was down. A spring forced it back to the off position as soon as you let go of it.

If it even worked.

There were no automatic doors, no safety features, just a telescoping grating that you pulled across the face of the elevator. Or not. It operated either way.

Back in the good old days before the Occupational Safety and Health Administration, before city inspectors and class action lawsuits, if you didn't pay attention and you hung your foot out of an elevator, it was severed at the ankle. And it was your own damn fault.

So Fisk did not have to close the grating or the door to get the elevator to move. Instead he simply pushed the brass handle to the right. The elevator sighed deeply, then jerked to life, rising slowly.

He knew he would only have a moment to find out whether he could pull off the trick he was considering. He risked a flash with his SureFire as the base of the elevator rose, and he crouched and surveyed the undercarriage to see if there was anything there he could grip and hold on to. As it moved upward, he saw that the base consisted of a network of iron struts. The bottom cable was straightening slowly. Fisk switched off his flashlight and moved quickly.

He grasped one of the struts with his left hand and dangled there, the shotgun in his right. He turned so that he was facing in the direction of the door as the car rose.

He realized he would again only have a few moments to evaluate his situation once he reached the first floor. If he was spotted, he would have to let go and fall back into the darkness—and probably break both ankles. The pit in which the elevator rested contained some kind of base or spring assembly to cushion the elevator, so there was an excellent chance he would fall on something very hard—maybe slicing his flesh or even impaling himself.

So dropping free of the elevator was the least attractive option.

His hand started to burn. The strut was hardedged and thin, cutting into the base of all four fingers. The elevator shook, thumped, paused, then continued onward. Each movement threatened to break his grip. Fisk was concerned that if he had to hang there too long, the sharp edges would cut right through.

The top of the elevator was rising into view on the first floor.

A voice, whispered, Spanish: "Empty. A diversion."

"The stairs then." The second voice was softer, dubious.

Fisk hoisted the pistol grip of his shotgun up into firing position. It was a pump gun, which meant he needed both hands to cycle it. Since he was hanging with one hand, Fisk had only one shot. Then it was either fall back into the dark uncertainty, leap onto the first floor and take the fight to the voices, or hang on and ride up to the top floor.

As the base of the elevator cleared the lip of the first floor, Fisk could see again. Two pairs of feet, shiny black shoes, one near, one farther down the hallway. Toes facing away from him.

Time crawled as the gap beneath the elevator and the floor grew larger and larger. Fisk only had one shot. He had to be sure.

Just then the near set of feet jogged down to join the other at the end of the hall. A bolt was thrown and they started through a door.

Before they disappeared, he saw a submachine gun in the second one's hands.

Fisk heard, under the groaning of the elevator mechanism, footsteps echoing on the metal stairs.

They were going down just as he was coming up.

Slowly the first floor scrolled fully into Fisk's vision. His waist passed the floor, then his thighs, then his knees.

Enough finally to swing out and jump. He hit the ground with a thump—no way to land softly—and paused to shake the fire out of his left hand and forearm. Another second or two and his grip would have failed. It had been that close.

He was one man with a shotgun against two men with submachine guns. The smart play was to retreat, to get out of the building and wait for support.

Then he remembered the girls trapped down in the basement.

And the bulkhead door, open to freedom.

As he was starting down the hall to the open door, a figure suddenly appeared in it. Dressed in white and black like a waiter, he also had a large paunch. He raised the muzzle of an MP5 and unleashed a short, disciplined burst of submachine gun fire.

Fisk felt as though he'd been hit in the chest with a brick.

Instinctively he pulled back on the trigger of the 870 as the impact shoved him backward. The roar was deafening in the enclosed space.

But the gunman was already gone. Fisk's ears were ringing too loudly to hear his own footsteps on the metal stairs going down.

It was only then that Fisk realized he'd been shot. He looked down. All three rounds had struck his vest, which, because of the gunman's apparent military training and skill as a shooter, had saved Fisk's life.

A worse shot might have hit him in the face or the neck or the groin or the arm.

This guy had put three rounds dead center, destroying nothing but Kevlar.

A man that good would not make the same mistake twice. Center mass was standard military training, but once you knew your enemy was wearing body armor, you went for the head.

Fisk pumped the shotgun and charged down the hallway. For the first time in his life, he felt an odd fatalistic sense that things just might not break his way. And to his surprise, it did not really bother him. Something about it seemed natural and right.

The whole series of thoughts just came and went like a small dark cloud passing over the sun on a summer day.

He rushed through the doorway to the stairs. If the men had been waiting, he would have been cut to shreds.

They were not. Fisk ran to the bottom, passing the bloody wall and floor, passing the horrified screams of the girls behind the locked doors. The open door above left enough light that Fisk did not have to use his SureFire. He did not want to risk moving his hand off the rifle pump anyway.

As Fisk turned into the narrow hallway, he fired a quick round just to keep them honest. It lit up the tight space, but Fisk saw no one. He racked the 870 again and continued his charge.

He popped up the bulkhead stairs into the light, aiming right and left down the narrow space between buildings. No one.

The door to the next building closed slowly, with a click.

Fisk had to follow. He was racing toward the door when he saw a figure enter the sidewalk space at the far end of the walkway.

Garza had come too late. The Emergency Service Unit heavy rescue truck was parked outside the warehouse Fisk had pointed her to, agents in full tactical gear fanning out. Garza held out her credentials, worried they would not be respected by this fast-moving rapid-entry unit. She was approaching them from the side when she passed the space between the warehouse and the building to its immediate left.

A man wielding a shotgun turned on her from twenty yards away, almost firing. He pulled off his aim . . . and it was Fisk.

There was a bright fire in his eyes. He took his hand off the pump of the shotgun just long enough to point her hard around the other side of the building next to the warehouse. Then Garza watched him run up the stairs, throw open a side door, and enter.

Garza spun away, pulled her Beretta, and started off at a sprint around the other side of the building, looking for a way in.

A sustained burst from the MP5 went barely wide as Fisk slapped the trigger of the 870.

Another deafening roar. Buckshot spraying the wall.

Yelling. Spanish. Fisk could not make it out.

His ears were screaming. His chest was aching. He was running.

His mind told him to keep moving, to count his shots.

He slid out into the open, seeing an iron spiral staircase in the middle of the building, leading up to the second floor. The ceiling in the old industrial building was twenty feet high, so the staircase twisted twice, making anybody who ascended it visible from all parts of the warehouse floor for several seconds. To clatter up the stairs in the presence of two well-armed shooters was to invite death. To retreat was to trap himself like a rat.

He ignored the tempting stairs, continuing room by room. He peeped around a corner, saw movement.

The shooter raised his MP5, firing already, rounds biting into the floor on their way toward Fisk.

Fisk pumped, aimed, and fired the shotgun.

The shooter's head erupted in an explosion of red.

The man crumpled on the spot.

Fisk did not slow down for a moment. He ran past the twitching body to the next doorway. He peeked around the corner. Looked clear.

He ducked back, plucking a couple of cartridges from the rack along the gunstock, loading them in. He was feeding in a third when a burst of gunfire sounded and a needle of fire went through his forearm.

He dropped the shotgun. His left hand opened spasmodically, and he gripped it with his right, getting blood on his palm.

He reached for the shotgun, pulling it to him. He pumped it one-handed and fumbled for the trigger, backing away from the holes in the wall where he had just been standing.

Yelling outside. Cop sounds. They were close.

More shouting. Thumping of feet. Directionless.

Suddenly everything went quiet.

Fisk had a premonition.

"Comandante?" he called out.

No answer. More footsteps.

"Stop, NYPD!" said Fisk, his left arm jerking, right hand aiming the shotgun.

Footsteps. Fisk fired at the doorway, a warning shot.

The buckshot tore into and through the wall to the left of the frame, going wide.

His hearing was gone again. Fisk set down the shotgun quickly in order to grasp the pump, trying to reload one-handed.

He jerked it, but the rack did not catch. The cartridge had misloaded.

He was jammed.

A man swung into view in the doorway. The lower left side of his white shirt was red with blood, but he held his weapon firmly.

Fisk recognized the face. The expression.

The Hummingbird looked at Fisk sitting on the floor with the shotgun. His lower lip curled into a sneer.

"You are not the comandante," he said.

Then suddenly he looked up, raising his aim.

Too slow. *Crack-crack-crack* from behind Fisk.

Chuparosa's head flew back. His torso twisted, his free hand going to his neck, out of which pulsed blood.

He fell to the side and began kicking, trying to crawl away.

Fisk turned. Garza stood in the doorway in a balanced shooter's stance. Her cheekbones were flushed and her black eyes were wide and intent, glazed with adrenaline. A goddess of wrath.

She walked past him, Beretta on Chuparosa. He was still kicking, trying to get away.

She came up behind him, ready to shoot. Wanting to shoot.

She never got the chance. The kicking stopped, and the assassin's body lay still. He was dead.

BOOK FOUR

Fisk heard about the aftermath from the emergency room at Beth Israel Medical Center in Brooklyn.

Eleven girls. Eleven young Mexican women, ages fifteen to twenty, had been locked in the basement of the warehouse.

Eleven young women had been saved.

The man Fisk had wounded and Garza had killed was all but confirmed to be Chuparosa. Learning his real name would take time. No matter what they might learn about the man, the killer known as the Hummingbird had been stopped forever.

The Teixeira Brothers truck was discovered in the garage. A remote control robot was sent in to open the cartons of oysters safely.

The disassembled gun parts were discovered packed inside.

Forged security passes were found near a laptop computer paused in the seventh inning of a three-week-old broadcast of a Yankees–Braves game. The issuing name was traced to an apartment in Bensonhurst, where a young caterer's assistant named Elian Martinez and his wife, Kelli, were found murdered.

FISK SUFFERED A LEFT ulna fracture. Damage to his ulnar nerve, the largest unprotected nerve in the human body—when bumped, it is often referred to as the funny bone—was negligible. He was fortunate in that the round had passed through a wall before striking him, lowering its velocity. The attending physician, knowing Fisk was a cop, informed him that he came just millimeters from retirement.

He was to remain in the hospital for observation for twenty-four hours, the standard window of time when "compartment syndrome" could occur. Restricted blood flow to muscles and nerves due to pressure from an injury could lead to loss of the limb.

Fisk's left forearm would be set in a hard cast in the morning. In sixteen weeks, the fracture would be repaired.

"Sixteen weeks of desk duty," said the attending physician with a smile, thinking he was being funny.

Cecilia Garza visited Fisk sometime before six o'clock.

Fisk said, "Don't you have the dinner soon?"

Garza shook her head. "Called off. Everything has changed."

"Of course," said Fisk.

"I tried to call you," said Garza.

"My phone . . . I must have lost it during the shootout. Maybe near that elevator."

Garza nodded absently. "They will find it."

"Sure."

He watched her. There was something odd about her manner.

He reached for her arm with his good hand. "Where are you?" he asked.

"Right here," she said.

"Adrenaline hangover," he said. "I've been there. They gave me some painkillers, so I think I'm missing out."

She looked at his arm again, wrapped in thick gauze. "You were lucky."

"I was. We were."

Garza smiled, but there was nothing behind it. She spoke before he could ask her what was wrong again. "The dinner is essentially canceled. I suggested we move it to our consulate, where proper security can be guaranteed and the treaty can be signed in relative seclusion."

"Obama isn't still going?" said Fisk.

"No. Vice President Biden will be on hand for the signing, but will not stay for dinner."

Fisk nodded. "Hey," he said, reaching for her hand. "You got him. The man you came here for."

Garza looked at his hand in hers, but her grip was slight. "That part does not seem real."

"Is Señor León going to attend the dinner? Now that the bad guy has been killed?"

Garza squeezed Fisk's hand once before letting go. "I made sure to extend President Vargas's personal invitation." She smoothed out a fold in the bedsheet near her side. "After the affair, we are returning home. Tonight. It's been arranged."

"Tonight?" said Fisk.

"President Vargas feels the need to get home. To be visible in the wake of this threat. And, I am sure, to be seen as victorious."

Fisk studied her face. There was no victory in it. "Letdown, right?" he said. "It's understandable. You've been searching for this guy for . . . how long?"

"Long time," she said.

"It never feels like you think it will," said Fisk. "Does it?"

"No."

Her eyes dampened, and Fisk grew concerned. This was not like the Ice Queen at all. She had won. She had protected her president and triumphed over this killer without a face, this agent of terror.

Garza turned away, aware that Fisk was watching her eyes.

"Hey," said Fisk. "Don't make me worry about you, now. Take some time to process this."

And then he realized what it must be. He was shocked he hadn't thought of it before.

"The girls," he said. "The kidnapped girls. You saw them?"

Garza nodded. "I saw them."

"I understand. You're thinking of your mother and your sister."

She was still turned away from him. Fisk watched her hands ball into fists . . . and then release.

When she turned to him, he expected to see tears—but there were none.

"What was it you were telling me last night?" she asked. "At the hotel lounge. About catching Magnus Jenssen?"

Fisk swallowed, not expecting to go there. "I think I said that it is never the victory you think it will be."

Garza nodded. "We have to be better than those we hunt. That's what you said. That this is what defines us. People like you and me."

Fisk nodded.

She went on. "You said that this cycle of murder and retribution, of terror and fighting terror . . . it sickens us all. Like radiation poisoning, just being near evil."

Fisk nodded again. The last thing he had expected was to hear his wine-soaked words read back to him. He had a very bad taste in his mouth, and it was not from the painkillers.

"Time," he said. "That is all you can hope for. That in time everything will be clear to you, and you can move on."

"I have given it time," she said. "So much time."

Fisk was about to correct her, in that it had only been a few hours. But in the next moment he had forgotten all about that, as Garza leaned down and kissed him on the lips, softly but lingeringly, her hand caressing the side of his face.

She pulled away, their faces parting. Fisk was smiling, but in her eyes was a less certain expression. He waited for her to speak, but she never did. Abruptly she turned and pushed through the bay curtain, walking away.

Intel chief Barry Dubin poked his bald head inside the curtain, eyes widening in relief. "Just walked in on some old woman by mistake."

Fisk said, "What's in the bag?"

Dubin was carrying a paper bag in the same hand that held his iPad. Dubin unfurled the top of the bag and reached inside. "Nicole said I should bring one of these for you."

It was a sandwich inside a clear plastic triangle from the vending machine in the Intel break room. "Chicken salad."

Fisk closed his eyes drowsily. "You're taking that with you when you leave."

Dubin dropped the gag sandwich back in the bag. "How's the wing?"

"I'm going to make a full recovery."

"Good. You want to sleep?"

"No." Fisk opened his eyes.

"Hey, I'm glad you're okay."

Fisk said, "That's not an apology."

Dubin smiled, his gray goatee smiling with him. "Let's see how all the evidence shakes out before we see who needs to apologize to whom."

Fisk remembered something. "My phone. Lost it at the scene. Can you get someone to get it?"

"Sure. How many painkillers did they give you?"

"Not nearly enough," said Fisk.

"I have some photos from the warehouse. From Chupa . . . the Hummingbird, however you pronounce it. His workshop apartment there. You want to see them, or wait?"

"Gimme."

Dubin flipped open his iPad cover and turned it over to Fisk. "There's a couple of short videos and high-resolution photos."

Fisk looked at the oysters taken from their cartons, the hidden gun pieces. "Oysters, huh?"

"And guess what?" said Dubin. "The Mexican president has a shellfish allergy."

Fisk looked at images of the two corpses, Chuparosa and the other man. Then the bloodied wall and floor, the site of the decapitations.

"I don't get it," said Fisk.

"What?" said Dubin.

"This plan was destined to fail. Assembling a gun inside the perimeter? Okay, points for that. Assuming he got it inside past the Secret Service's millimeter wave scanner. But those agents around the president—either president—would have seen a gunman coming from twenty feet away."

Dubin stroked his goatee. "You're not wrong."

Fisk shook his head, his mind a little muddled from the medication. "He was too smart for that. Unless there's something else we're missing."

Dubin's hand came away from his beard, his finger swiping the screen back to the thumbnails.

"The guy made a video. Like a suicide bomber, I guess. To be viewed after he died."

Fisk was surprised. "Really? Anything to it?"

"It's tough to watch. He recorded it during the beheadings."

Fisk hissed out a breath between his numb teeth. "Jesus. What's he say?"

Dubin said, "No idea. It's in Spanish."

Fisk looked at Dubin, a former spy. "No Spanish?"

Dubin shook his head. "Korean and Thai. A little German."

Fisk sniffed. This didn't seem the time to brag about his five languages. "At least you can order takeout well."

Dubin frowned. "I like you better sober."

Fisk looked at the video icon, debating. Some things you cannot un-see. That, in essence, was his job.

"Did Garza see this?"

"I'm sure she did."

Fisk nodded. "Fine," he said, and tapped the icon, and the video began.

The Mexican consulate was swept by security again just before seven thirty. Garza left the inspection halfway through, finding a ladies' room to throw up in.

She hit the handle and let the roar of the flush drown out her gasping. She went to the sink and splashed cold water on her face, wiped off her lips, then looked at herself in the mirror with one hand pressed against her forehead.

She was hyperventilating. She gripped the edge of the vanity, clamping her eyes shut and willing herself to relax.

"Everything all right, Comandante?" asked the second security officer as she rejoined the inspection.

"Please proceed," she said, ignoring the taste of vomit in her mouth.

SHE HAD EARLIER WALKED through each and every room of the building herself, checking doors and windows. None of it mattered much to her now, but she went through the motions. She listened to the head of consulate security, a tall, soft-spoken, competent man.

Which rooms were the safest, which doors were blast-proof, which hallways contained cameras and which ones did not. She had been through it all before . . . but she wanted to have the entire building in her head, clear as a bell.

They completed the final security tour of the consulate building just as the food arrived under guard from Ocampo. A skeleton crew of chefs and servers were put through a rigorous security check, including both pat-downs and a trip through the airport-style millimeter wave scanner. The entire security procedure would be thorough and slow. Garza felt her belly start to roil again and excused herself, retreating to a small room of video monitors on the fourth floor of the consulate.

She breathed slowly through her nose, watching as a viola player and a cellist were submitted to rigorous frisking, their instruments examined and reexamined. Nothing like a near miss to remind people of the importance of preventive security.

An EMP agent looked inside the control room, finding her there. "Señor Presidente is asking for you."

Garza nodded and followed him out of the room.

President Vargas was seated alone inside a meeting room, his chair turned to face a windowless wall. His elbows were on his thighs, palms rubbing together.

Garza entered, and Vargas looked up as though surprised. He stood, straightening his jacket, and went to her.

He said, "Is everything ready here?"

Garza nodded. "Yes, Señor Presidente."

Vargas nodded once, slowly. He had something on his mind.

"Kind of a bust now, but we'll make the most of it. I don't know about you, but I am quite anxious to return home."

Garza nodded.

The president rubbed his palms together again. "In any event . . . very well done today, Comandante. I am sorry if I was . . . short with you, or rude. It was not my intention."

"Fine, Señor Presidente," she said.

Vargas looked at her. He wanted more. "I know you are an outstanding *federale*, and exceptional at what you do . . . exceptional in every way."

Garza clasped her hands tightly behind her back, looking to the side. Waiting for this to be over.

President Vargas said, "Is there anything you'd like to get off your chest, Cecilia? I feel as though I am apologizing to a wall."

"I prefer 'Comandante,'" she said.

Vargas said, "Very well."

"May I go now?"

After a moment, he said, "Yes. Certainly."

Garza got as far as the door before pivoting hard and walking back to him.

"I will not work for you in Mexico City. I will never have dinner with you. Once we return to Mexico, I hope to never have to speak to you again."

Vargas looked away, puzzled, trying to understand the source of this outburst. "What is it, Comandante? Speak."

Garza tried to hold her tongue, feeling she had already said too much. "He was not here for you," she said.

"What do you mean?"

"I was mistaken. Chuparosa did not come to New York to try to assassinate you."

Vargas shook his head. "Of course he did. And you stopped him. Brilliantly."

Garza's smile came out warped with anger. "No," she said. "He was not here to kill the president of Mexico. He was here to kill someone measurably more influential."

Fisk pushed through the hospital exit doors with his good forearm, his left arm in a blue sling.

Dubin ran out just behind him. "Fisk! Stop! You're delirious."

Fisk stopped on the curb at the ambulance bay. "Where is it?" he said angrily.

"Where is what?"

"Your car," said Fisk. "Where is it?"

Dubin said, "Look, Jeremy. Listen to me. Are you having a reaction to the medication?"

"I'll get a goddamn taxi."

"Here," said Dubin, pointing.

Fisk went off toward the unmarked car with NYPD plates in the nearby handicapped spot. "Gimme your phone."

"No."

"I need a phone!" said Fisk.

An attendant came out the door after them. Dubin was torn between explaining their quick getaway and staying with Fisk.

"Here," he said, handing Fisk his phone and getting inside the car.

"Code," said Fisk.

"Uh . . ." Dubin had to do it in the air. "Five nine one four."

Fisk played with it while Dubin started the engine and backed out.

"No good," said Fisk. "I need my contact list."

He put the phone on top of his side of the dashboard. It promptly fell to the floorboard.

"Hey!" said Dubin, fishing with his hand, finding it near Fisk's shoe, then pulling on the man's seat belt. "Where the hell am I supposed to be taking you?"

"Mexican consulate. Thirty-ninth and Park."

"Mexican . . . ?" Dubin stopped, braking hard. Looking at him. "Fisk. It's over. You stopped it, remember? You're going to hurt yourself. They want you to stay for observation—"

Fisk said, "It's not over. It's not over. Drive, Barry. Go."

"Why?"

Fisk pointed straight ahead. "So we can stop a murder."

The reception hall was slowly filling with diplomats and their spouses. President Vargas was greeting the arrivals. Vice President Biden was due any minute, and the street closure was already in effect outside. Then the formalities would officially begin.

Cecilia Garza wiped a bead of sweat from the damp hair at her temple. She watched the monitor until she saw the man she was looking for, making conversation on his way through the final stage of security and entering the "tent," or secured area.

Garza choked down a swallow and walked downstairs to intercept him. Andrés León wore a black suit with silver accents on the lapels, pants with matching cuffs, and silver-toed cowboy boots. His braid was pulled back more neatly than it had been that morning.

"Comandante Garza!" he exuded when he saw her crossing the room toward him. "The woman of the hour, everyone!"

Applause from the rest of the attendees, which shocked her, making her stop when she would have thought no power in the world could have slowed her pace. She stood for a split second listening to their hollow clapping, then continued to the large expatriate, who insisted on making a scene.

"What bravery! What fortitude! And a woman! What a shining example of Mexican mettle!"

Garza reached León, trying to keep her expression calm as she gestured to the hallway. "Don Andrés, may I offer you a tour of the premises? I know you don't get out much."

"How can I resist any request from Comandante Garza on a great day such as this? A privilege! An honor! Lead on, Comandante!"

She did, past smiling onlookers, stepping out into the hallway leading to the portrait room.

"Will it be long, Comandante?" he asked. "I haven't yet had a cocktail."

"Not too long," she said, without turning around. She opened the door and stepped aside for him to enter.

He passed her, walking inside with his hands out in a gesture of appreciation. "All the greats."

Garza closed the door behind them. Portraits hung around the room's only bench, lit from lamps above each frame. Emiliano Zapata. First President Guadalupe Victoria. Hernán Cortés. Diego Rivera. And the most recent addition, the writer Octavio Paz.

"Magnificent," he said. "Oh, the lure of the homeland. So kind of you to show me this. So nice to be out of my cage."

Garza nodded, telling herself to stay focused. "What was your name, Don Andrés? Your former name. Your real name."

León reacted with surprise. "Strange question."

"I tried to look you up this afternoon, using both police and Department of State resources. I could not find any so-called financier fitting the profile you described to me this morning."

"Please, Comandante." He spread his hands in supplication. "I don't even like to think of it. On a night such as this? Tonight is about the future." He waved at the portraits. "The past is history."

"No," said Garza, shaking her head strenuously. "No, it's not. It's right here with you, right now. Which bank did you work for?"

León sighed, smiling and shaking his head. "So many."

"Name just one."

León crooked his head, looking at her with one eye nearly closed. He had noticed her growing more agitated. "I should return to the reception. I was promised a cocktail."

"Chuparosa did not come to New York for President Vargas," said Garza, getting the words out quickly.

"No?" He reacted with exaggerated surprise. "But how could that be?"

Garza took one step toward him, all she allowed herself. "He was here for you."

León pursed his lips, finding this very curious.

Garza said, "You realized that when we went to see you earlier today. You figured out that he had found out about you, your true identity, somehow. Someone like him is the reason why you live behind that wall, those guards, this foreign government."

León sighed heavily. "I am sorry, Comandante Garza—"

"León. Lion." Her next words reeked of the vomit still on her breath. "Ochoa. Wolf."

León's façade of innocence faltered. "Ochoa?"

"He would have succeeded in killing you here," she said. "Because safeguarding presidents is our first priority. The Hummingbird was exploiting that certainty to allow himself a shot at a much more elusive, yet much more worthy target. Someone who leaves his gilded cage but once each year. Yes, Chuparosa would have been killed in the act. But not before he killed you."

León looked at the nearest portraits before answering her. "And you warned me, Comandante Garza. And then you killed my assassin." León—Ochoa, the former cartel leader—bowed slightly at the waist, obscenely.

"You scrubbed your home in Mexico, your cars, everything. And had another man live in them for a time. Then had him killed in your place." She took another step toward the man. "Your plastic surgery did not result in a fatality. For you, it was a complete success. For the man living in your house—and for the doctors after they performed the surgery—it was indeed fatal. It was his DNA the American DEA matched."

She looked at his face, the one he had grown into in the years since it was rebuilt. So few photographs existed of Ochoa, and all of them grainy.

"Or perhaps," she said, "the DEA made sure it matched. Why did you flip? Why did you turn your back on your former self?"

León's contempt for her was showing. "Prison was coming. My time and my luck were both running out. The end comes for everyone. I did not want it to come for me. So I made a new beginning. I accepted it. I became a new man. A mansion in the United States instead of a shithole prison in Guadalajara. The choice was an easy one. Retirement in secret. And yes—interestingly, an opportunity to atone."

"To settle scores with your former rivals. But I thought the past was history."

"You are very dedicated and enterprising, Comandante. Now, if you don't mind—"

Garza stepped back and drew her Beretta. She settled into a balanced shooter's stance, the weapon trembling slightly in her hands.

She said, "I want to tell you a story about my mother and sister."

Fisk and Dubin were trying to badge their way through three rings of Secret Service security, still a block away from the consulate. Dubin was alternately trying to work his phone and stepping between Fisk and another agent, trying to talk them through another checkpoint.

"She's going to kill him," Fisk kept saying.

Fisk's arm was throbbing with pain. He could not get anyone to listen to him.

She was going to ruin herself for revenge. Fisk had to stop her.

Andrés León looked at the weapon trembling in Cecilia Garza's hand. If he was nervous, he did not show it.

"Comandante," he said. "Put down your weapon."

Garza smiled painfully. "Welcome home," she said.

León held a hand out toward her, trying to stop her from doing anything rash. "This is not Mexican soil. We are in a consulate in New York City, still subject to their laws. You can't shoot me here and expect to claim it rightful under Mexican law—"

Garza said, "I know full well there is no extra-territoriality here. This is not sovereign territory of Mexico. However, I know also that the host country may not enter the consulate if it acts as a refuge." Garza felt her shivering ease as she said these words. "You are surrendering to me, Mr. Ochoa. Surrendering to the daughter and sister of two women you kidnapped and forced into sexual slavery."

León swallowed and said, "I did no such thing—"

"You did! You and your people! No one crossed you! No one did anything that displeased you! You did it!"

"Comandante, listen to reason. You are upset.

Your emotions are running away with you. Please listen to me. This thing you are trying to achieve, it will never work. The United States needs me too much to let me go."

"You are in my custody now, a Mexican citizen in the custody of a *federale*. They dare not intercede in this matter. Because then the people of the United States and the world will know that they took you in. Knowing who you were. What you were. And that they hosted you, that their taxpayers funded the 'retirement' of a former Mexican drug cartel leader and trafficker in human lives."

"No," said León insistently. "President Vargas himself will not stand for this."

"He will!" said Garza. "He will have no choice. I give him no choice. Either he turns a blind eye to this . . . or else I tell everyone in the country just who was behind his rise to prominence. Who funded his miraculous political victory. And that the person he entrusted to help craft this antitrafficking treaty was a filthy trafficker himself."

Garza backed to the only door to the room, opening it.

"Whereas if he goes along, then it is simply another example of the former administration being corrupted by association with the criminal element."

Fisk never made it inside the consulate. In part because of his own dire warnings while trying to be let through the outer perimeter, the vice president's interior security ring closed ranks around the detail. No one was allowed in or out until the vice president and his eleven-car motorcade were many blocks away.

Dubin returned from a conversation with a Secret Service agent he knew and pulled Fisk aside on Park Avenue. "Nobody was killed. No shots fired. The dinner went off without a hitch."

FISK ARRIVED AT TETERBORO AIRPORT in New Jersey just in time. The presidential jet was idling on the tarmac, the big Boeing 737 having been cleared for the small airport by a rare special dispensation from the FAA. Bags were being loaded in.

Fisk's arm was screaming at him, his fingers and thumb completely numb. He used his Intel badge to get onto the tarmac. Though well outside the radius of the Boeing 737, he was close enough to see the heavyset man in the gray braid being led aboard the plane by EMP agents—in handcuffs.

Fisk felt all the tension go out of him then. It was

an incredible feeling, as though Garza's soul had been spared. León was alive. He held his bad arm, hoping to take some of the pressure off it, and was about to turn and leave when he saw Cecilia Garza leave the contingent boarding the aircraft, starting toward him.

It must have been the blue sling that caught her eye. Her raven-black hair whipped around from the night wind and the wash from the turbines.

She looked drained, exhausted. He must have looked like hell, too.

"You watched the video," he said.

She looked away and nodded.

"What happened?" he asked.

"I wanted to kill him," she said. "I wanted it so badly. To put him down right there inside the consulate . . . and suffer the consequences, whatever they might be."

She looked behind her to make sure she still had time. The last people were starting up the stairs. She only had a moment.

She turned back to Fisk. "I learned from you. I am bringing him to justice. As you did Magnus Jenssen. I am obeying the rule of law, not of vengeance. Blood vendettas are the old Mexico. This"—she pointed to the aircraft, its prisoner waiting on board—"is how we will bring about real change. By owning our past and looking to the future." She touched the shoulder of his bad arm gently. "You set the example. I thank you."

She kissed him again.

"I said it before," she said. "We are too much alike."

She gave his good arm a squeeze, then turned, black hair flying, jogging to the bottom step of the wheeled staircase and then up to the door of the plane, looking back at him one more time before entering.

Eight days later, Fisk was lying in his bed, sleeping fitfully with his arm in a cast, when his cell phone awoke him. He looked at the display, then sat up, pushing a pillow behind his head. The phone rang twice more while he was trying to decide whether or not to answer it.

"Fisk," he said groggily.

"You bastard."

It was Dave Link, his friend from the CIA. "Hi, Dave."

"You fucked me. If it gets out that I got you inside for that meeting, I will deny everything. Then I'll fucking drone-strike your house."

"Okay."

Silence on the other end.

"Okay?" said Link. "What the hell is wrong with you, man? How'd you do it? On TV, they're saying it was karma. I know better. I know it was Jeremy Fisk."

Fisk's mouth was painfully dry. "I gotta go, Dave."

"Lose this number. You and I are strangers from this moment forward. Understood?"

"Understood."

Click. Fisk lowered his phone. He felt very warm and a little shaky.

He sat there in bed for a while before turning on the television.

The news jumped out at him from CNN. Magnus Jenssen was dead, after serving only a few weeks in prison. The cause of death was apparently a previously undetected, fast-moving cancer.

The CNN graphic read: A FITTING END?

Fisk turned off the television, letting the dark reclaim the room. He stared into the nothingness, his left forearm itching as though the hard cast were infested with bugs.

He thought of his meeting with Jenssen, the terrorist taunting him about the weakness of America's overly tolerant system of justice. Fisk remembered the aftermath of the meeting, how he cleaned up the remains of the cupcake he had brought for him using the thick foil wrapper Fisk had baked it in . . . which was designed to shield the bearer from exposure to alpha radiation from the microgram of deadly polonium-210 contained therein. Polonium that Fisk had stolen from the evidence in the smoky-bomb case he had busted.

Fisk settled back into bed.

Jenssen was dead and gone.

Fisk tried to picture Krina Gersten in this moment of supposed victory, and the awful truth was . . . he could not. Not completely. Not anymore.

Gersten was fading away.

He could picture Cecilia Garza, however. Leaving him on that airplane with the criminal she had spared, thanks to his example.

Fisk rubbed his good hand over his chest. He wondered how much his exposure to radiation had shortened his life. How much his organs had been affected on a cellular level, and what health surprises lay ahead of him.

This retributive act had corrupted him—not only morally, but also physically.

Which, to him, seemed just. Time would tell.

ACKNOWLEDGMENTS

To Noelle, Olivia, Serena, Elliot, Zoe, and Rex for their patience, support, and understanding. To Chuck Hogan for his friendship and support. And to Richard Abate and David Highfill for making me look good. Thank you all.

If you enjoyed
The Execution,
don't miss the thrilling next book
in the series featuring
NYPD detective Jeremy Fisk
from *New York Times* bestselling author
Dick Wolf

Coming soon in hardcover
from William Morrow
An Imprint of HarperCollins Publishers

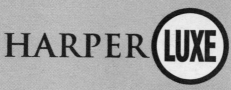